THE BLACK CAT SEES HIS SHADOW

KAY FINCH

BERKLEY PRIME CRIME
New York

BERKLEY PRIME CRIME
Published by Berkley
An imprint of Penguin Random House LLC
375 Hudson Street, New York, New York 10014

Copyright © 2017 by Kay Finch
Penguin Random House supports copyright. Copyright fuels creativity, encourages
diverse voices, promotes free speech, and creates a vibrant culture. Thank you for buying an
authorized edition of this book and for complying with copyright laws by not reproducing,
scanning, or distributing any part of it in any form without permission.
You are supporting writers and allowing Penguin Random House to continue to
publish books for every reader.

BERKLEY is a registered trademark and BERKLEY PRIME CRIME and the B colophon
are trademarks of Penguin Random House LLC.

ISBN: 9780425275269

First Edition: June 2017

Printed in the United States of America
3 5 7 9 10 8 6 4 2

Cover art by Brandon Dorman

For Tripp, our family's cool dude artist

ACKNOWLEDGMENTS

There are so many people who help to bring a book to life. My family—Benton, Derrell, Missy, London, Audrey, Tripp, Melinda, Jonathan, Alicia, and Hudson—makes my world special and helps shape my fiction. Thanks, Mom, for understanding why I sometimes need to put my phone on "do not disturb." My wonderful critique group tells me where I've gone wrong and what I've done right. Many thanks to Amy, Bob, Dean, Julie, Kay 2, Laura, and Susie for providing encouragement, suggestions, support, and laughs along the way. Bill Crider's famous VBK's—Keanu, Li'l Ginger Tom, and Gilligan—inspire my fictional felines. Thanks to the incredibly supportive cozy mystery community, especially to readers who've contacted me to report how much they love Hitchcock the cat. Thanks to my agent, Jessica Faust, for her help and commitment. My editor, Michelle Vega, and the folks at Penguin Random House have made this journey such a pleasant one. Thank you all!

1

THE CLERK SCANNED the packet of crunchy tuna treats and tossed it on the conveyor belt to her left. "These are the best, Miss Sabrina. My cat, Oreo, adores them. She eats three every single time, and if I try to stop at two, she won't give me a moment's peace until I hand over that third one."

"Cute." I already knew quite a lot about the personality of Libby's tuxedo kitty, and I learned a new tidbit every time I shopped for groceries. The sixtyish woman lived alone with the cat, and she spoke about the pet the way a mother speaks of a favorite child.

"That Hitchcock is one lucky fella, gettin' all these treats," she said, "even if he is the bad luck cat."

"He's—" I stopped and clamped my lips together. I knew from experience that repeating the words "not bad luck" for the hundredth time would do no good. It annoyed the heck out of me that the people in Lavender continued to judge

Hitchcock by some ancient legend and didn't give him credit for all his good deeds.

Libby continued scanning the groceries from my cart. "You stockin' your pantry or gettin' ready for the contest?"

My basket contained two pumpkins, several bags each of flour and sugar, and enough miscellaneous baking supplies to suggest I planned to take part in the annual Pumpkin Days Festival Bake-Off.

"Haven't decided," I said, "but I dreamt about pumpkin pie last night, and I won't sleep again until I have some."

Libby totaled my order and began sacking the groceries. "Did I ever tell you about the time Oreo dropped her catnip mouse in my cake batter when my back was turned?"

More than once.

I nodded and stuck my bank card into the reader to make my payment. "And your cousins freaked when the cake was cut."

"Did they ever. Wouldn't take one bite. I thought it was sweet, like one of those Mardi Gras cakes where you find the little baby inside."

She chuckled and shook her head like she couldn't believe her relatives refused to overlook a minor thing like a catnip mouse imbedded in their dessert.

I took my receipt, wished her a good night, and pushed my cart toward the door. Libby was already chatting about Oreo to the customer behind me as I vowed to keep a closer eye on Hitchcock whenever I baked.

I quickened my step, eager to get home and introduce my cat to the most yummy tuna treats ever. If my evening went according to plan, I'd be baking in Aunt Rowe's kitchen earlier than my usual middle-of-the-night stints. Things were hopping at her Around-the-World cottages. Every unit was rented for the week, most by vendors coming in for the festival. Judging by the forecast, the weather would cooperate with brilliant sunshine over the next week. Walking to my car, I enjoyed the slight nip in the air, which to us Texans meant the temperature had dropped to the seventies.

I was admiring the lovely pinks and yellows that colored the sky around the setting sun when a slamming truck door startled me. Beyond the spot where I'd parked my car, a man in jeans and a fringed suede vest over a white shirt left the pickup and headed for the store. I went back to enjoying the pretty evening sky until his hand shot out and clutched my shopping cart, stopping it short.

I spun to face him. "What the—"

The man stared at me in wide-eyed astonishment. "What in tarnation are you doing here?"

I raised my brows. "Excuse me?"

What does it look like I'm doing?

His ruddy complexion reddened, and he fixed me with a dark-eyed stare. His steely gray hair frizzed around his head like a scouring pad. "I told you to stay away. What part of that did you not understand?"

"I don't know—"

"I meant far away. This is my turf, and you know it."

I'd been walking around Lavender for nearly a year and now this guy wanted to know why *I'm* here? Why was *he* here?

"Do I know you?" I said.

"Your bein' here is only gonna cause trouble," he said.

"Look," I said, "I have no idea what you're talking about, Mr. . . . ?"

"Very funny." His voice reminded me of a snarling dog. "You need to slink back to that rock you crawled out from under."

He had made no move toward me besides latching on to my cart like a recalcitrant toddler, but his gruff words set off an adrenaline rush. I tucked a hand inside my purse and rested my fingers on the phone in the side pocket.

"Obviously, you have the wrong person," I said.

"Don't play little miss innocent with me," he said. "I guarantee it won't work this time."

He released my cart and took a step toward me, the small

movement raising the threat level several notches. I pulled out the phone, intent on calling Sheriff Jeb Crawford directly on his cell phone.

"Who're you callin'?" The stranger made a swipe toward my phone, but I twisted to keep it out of his reach.

"Whoever I want to," I said.

A man behind me hollered, "Hey!"

Heavy footsteps slapped across the blacktop, and the second man came into view. I recognized this one. Gabe Brenner, one of the festival vendors, had checked into Aunt Rowe's Melbourne cottage earlier in the day. How did he just so happen to be in my personal space—again?

When the stranger made another grab for my phone, Gabe pulled back and let a heavy fist fly. His punch connected with the stranger's chin and caused the older man to stagger back.

"You keep away from her," Gabe said.

"Says who?" the other man said.

"I do." Gabe turned to me. "You know this dude?"

"No," I said. "Never saw him before in my life."

The older man straightened, one hand held to his chin, and glared at me. "You haven't heard the last of this, sweetheart."

"Watch it, mister," Gabe said, "or you'll be sorry. She might even sic her bad luck cat on you."

Outraged, I looked at Gabe. "He is *not* bad luck." The guy had only met me—and the cat—for the first time less than eight hours ago. How had he already heard that stupid nickname?

"Are you kidding?" said the older man. "You brought the cat, too?"

I shook my head, trying to make sense of the conversation. I met the stranger's gaze. "I don't know what your deal is, but you've mistaken me for someone else, and I'll thank you both to leave my cat out of this."

All I wanted was to get away from these men and go home to bake a pumpkin pie. Was that too much to ask?

The stranger looked from me to Gabe, who stood by my side with fists clenched, then turned away. Instead of heading into the store, he stalked back to his truck and climbed in. Moments later, the truck roared out of the parking lot.

Gabe put a hand on my shoulder. "Are you okay? You want me to follow him? I will, you know, if you want me to."

"No, you don't need to follow him."

"Then let me help you with the groceries."

"No," I said firmly. "I'm fine, and I can handle this."

"Why was he harassing you?" Gabe persisted.

"Sounded like he mixed me up with someone else."

"How's that?" Gabe said, his voice softening. "There's only one like you, Sabrina."

I ignored the comment.

Now that the bigger problem was gone, I'd have to figure out what to do about Gabe. He'd taken an instant liking to me and Hitchcock when we met and had shadowed us around the cottages to the point that I'd left the premises to get away from him. The lovesick-puppy expression he wore when he looked at me made me nervous, but the stalkerlike vibe he threw off really gave me the heebie-jeebies.

2

I MANAGED TO CONVINCE Gabe that I was fine to drive home by myself. After I had my groceries in the car and got on the road, I heaved a sigh of relief. Since we were both headed to the same place, though, the guy was tailing me in his food truck. Gabe was going to sell battered and deep-fried bacon, of all things, at the festival, which explained the greasy odor that seemed to hover around him. Seeing him in my rearview mirror made my skin prickle. I hoped to high heaven he'd back off when I got to Aunt Rowe's house.

I tried to relax and enjoy the festival decorations as we headed through town on our way back to the cottages. Strands of orange lights glittered from trees and storefronts. Yellow and scarlet mums filled flower barrels and window boxes. Jack-o'-lantern flags hung from light poles, and banners advertising Lavender's Pumpkin Days hung high over the streets. The festival officially began at noon the next day.

Booths were already set up around the town square and along the sidewalks. Food trucks would line up along the mowed field on the edge of town.

I had visited Aunt Rowe during Pumpkin Days as a kid, but I never realized what a huge undertaking it was to put on an event of this size. With the arrival of so many vendors, Lavender's peaceful atmosphere had already changed. I couldn't even imagine how many tourists would flood our small town over the next week. I expected to have my fill of the crowd in the first day or two. After that, I would take advantage of some quiet time at home to work on my novel in progress while everyone else was off at the festival.

Fifteen minutes later, Gabe pulled into the Around-the-World Cottages driveway right behind me. I blew out a breath of relief when he veered off toward the Melbourne cottage. Then my thoughts turned to baking. If all went according to plan, I'd be eating fresh pumpkin pie in a couple of hours.

That thought fled when Aunt Rowe's house came into view. Things were usually quiet on the home front by eight, but not tonight. In the twilight, I could see dozens of people clustered on the lawn, drinks in hand, talking and laughing. I caught a glimpse of Thomas, my aunt's grounds manager, scanning the back lawn like a nightclub bouncer.

My cat was watching over the festivities, too. I smiled at the sight of Hitchcock's outline in the window over the kitchen sink. He gravitated toward action, so it was no surprise that he was hanging at Aunt Rowe's instead of waiting for me in the Monte Carlo cottage, where we lived.

I looped grocery sacks over my arms and grabbed one of the pumpkins, then went in through the back door and walked through the utility room toward the kitchen. Country music—the Oak Ridge Boys, if I had to guess—came from the living room. The house smelled of coffee and cinnamon.

"Hi, Hitchcock," I said, then stopped short when I realized there wasn't one square inch of open counter space to deposit my purchases. "What's all this?"

The cat jumped from the sill to the edge of the sink, then to the floor. He came over to rub against my legs. "Mrreow."

Jumbo packages of paper products, chips, and baked goods, along with trays of fruits, veggies, cheeses, and cold cuts filled every available space. Stacks of canned soft drink cases sat on the floor. The breakfast table held desserts, including stacks of boxed store-bought pies.

Aunt Rowe had mentioned something about a hospitality suite for the vendors. I must have missed the fact that she planned to play hostess herself. Glenda, Aunt Rowe's housekeeper and cook, was nowhere in sight, and I didn't blame her. The ordinarily neat-as-a-pin kitchen had a claustrophobic feel. I elbowed a stack of potato chip cartons over a few inches so I could deposit my sacks on the counter.

I left the pumpkin in the sink, then knelt beside Hitchcock and ran a hand down his back. "Obviously, I won't be baking here tonight. Maybe not for a while."

He trilled a response.

"I'll be lucky to find room to store anything in the pantry. Might have to lug my stuff back to our place." I had prepared a few no-bake desserts at my cottage, but the small kitchenette didn't have an oven to support my serious baking habit. I checked the pies, counted three pumpkins, and wondered how fresh they were.

A chorus of female voices and laughter came from the living room, piquing my curiosity. I stood. "What does Aunt Rowe have going on in there?"

"Mrrreooow," Hitchcock said, and the sound came out like a warning as I headed toward the laughter.

I checked the living room, surprised to see four card tables set up in the center. Each held a pedestal mirror and a basin of water along with various sizes of tubes and bottles. The scent of eucalyptus filled the air. Three women sat, one

per table, with hair held back by fuzzy mint green headbands that matched the goop smeared on their faces. Their attention was on a woman who stood in front of them like a teacher at the head of a class.

"The clarification-processing phase takes six minutes," she said, "then we'll move on to the freshening phase. Sit back, close your eyes, and let the rejuvenation begin."

As the green-faced women closed their eyes, the leader pulled a compact from the pocket of her royal blue dress and checked the mirror. She had big hair, blond and curly, in a style Dolly Parton might admire. She took a swig from a can of Diet Coke and cleared her throat.

"Feel the transformation, ladies," she said. "After your treatment, you'll look five years younger. That's the Pure Velvet promise."

Hitchcock, who had joined me at the doorway, looked up with a can-you-believe-this-baloney expression. "Mrreow."

The group leader turned at hearing the cat's voice and saw me.

"Hi there." She approached me with a hand out, and we shook. "I'm Britt Cramer, with Pure Velvet Facial Transformation Systems. Care to join us?"

"No thanks." I introduced myself. "Is my aunt here?"

"In her office," said one of the green-faced women. "With Herr Schmidt."

The others giggled.

"Herr Schmidt?" I said.

"Henry Schmidt," she said. "The festival chair. Used to teach high school German. Likes when people call him Herr instead of Mister."

"I may have heard about him," I said.

The woman laughed. "If you're related to Rowe, I'll bet you have. I'm Maybelle."

"Nice to meet you," I said. "I guess all of you are here for the festival."

"That's right," Maybelle said. "I sell soy candles."

The other women chimed in to tell me their names and what they would be selling at their festival booths.

I made appreciative noises as I headed for Aunt Rowe's office. "Good luck with the rejuvenation."

"We'll have before and after pictures on display at my booth," Britt called after me. "You'll want to try Pure Velvet for yourself after you see them."

Did I look like I needed to take five years off my appearance? I didn't think so, and I continued down the hall without responding. I heard Aunt Rowe loud and clear before I reached the office.

"We don't need typed rules for the pumpkin toss, Henry," she said. "It begins Saturday at eleven. People walk up, pay the fee, throw three pumpkins. A very simple concept."

I reached the doorway and looked in. Like the women in the living room, Aunt Rowe wore a mint green headband to match the product smeared on her face.

She spotted me. "Sabrina, please come in here and tell Herr Schmidt that no one in their right mind will give a flip about rules on how to throw a pumpkin."

I didn't want to get in the middle of their discussion, but both Aunt Rowe and the slender man across the desk from her were looking to me for an answer.

"I doubt many people would stop to read rules even if you had them," I said.

Aunt Rowe folded her arms over her chest. "Exactly."

The man harrumphed. "We cannot take chances when people are paying good money."

Aunt Rowe gave me a see-what-craziness-I-have-to-put-up-with look.

"This isn't rocket science," she said. "People come to the festival to have fun, Henry. F. U. N. Maybe you're not familiar with the term."

I couldn't see this straitlaced guy in dress slacks, white shirt, and polka-dot bow tie setting much stock in fun.

He pushed his dark-framed glasses up on his nose. "A game without rules is a game for fools."

"Spare me," Aunt Rowe said.

"Arguments can begin over things as simple as foot placement," Herr Schmidt said.

"Fine. You can be the foot placement judge. Meanwhile, I'll be busy with the pumpkin cannon."

"The what?" Schmidt said.

"The cannon," Aunt Rowe said. "We're setting it up south of the town square, in that clearing by the feed store. We'll load the pumpkins there and shoot them toward the field. It'll be a hoot."

Schmidt stood and scissored his hands in front of him. "Out of the question."

"Every fall festival worth its salt has a cannon," Aunt Rowe said. "Lavender needs to keep up with the times. It'll be the talk of the town."

"A cannon sounds dangerous, Aunt Rowe," I said.

Herr Schmidt said, "The town cannot accept liability—"

"Don't worry," Aunt Rowe said. "You put me in charge of the pumpkin activities, and our plans are final. The cannon arrives tomorrow morning. Now, speaking of rules, it's time for me to rinse this gunk off my face and go to the next fountain-of-youth step. If you don't recognize me tomorrow, I'll be the young lady behind the cannon." She stood and lifted her chin as she left the room.

Herr Schmidt looked at me. "Can you talk some sense into her?"

"That usually doesn't work," I said, "but I can try. Give me a minute, and I'll be back."

"Fine," he said.

I left the room with Hitchcock trailing behind me. Though Aunt Rowe had said she was going to rinse her face, she wasn't sitting in the living room with the other women who were now busy applying something white and frothy to their skin.

I headed toward the bedroom wing of the house, but I didn't make it as far as Aunt Rowe's room before the front doorbell rang.

"Now what?" I muttered and retraced my steps to answer the bell.

Hitchcock beat me to the foyer, and he stared out the side window at the front porch. It was nearly full dark by now, so I flipped on the porch light as I flung the door open.

Hitchcock let out a low howl, and for a moment I thought he was trying to warn me about something on the other side. The little boy with the black cat and the woman standing on the porch didn't seem to present any danger.

The woman had her eye on the boy for a moment, but then she raised her head, and our eyes held and locked. Her hair was shorter than mine, her face a bit thinner. Otherwise, seeing her gave me the eerie sensation that I was looking in a mirror.

Beside me, Hitchcock arched his back and hissed at the other cat.

"Hello," the woman said. "I'm Tia Hartwell, and I'm looking for Herr Schmidt. Is he here?"

3

TIA HARTWELL AND I stared at each other for a few seconds. I wanted to ask her questions. *Where do you live? How old are you? Who are your parents?* I corralled my thoughts and answered her initial question. "Yes, Herr Schmidt is here. Come on in."

The woman, along with the little boy and the cat, stepped into the foyer, and I closed the front door. The boy had his eye on me. I could imagine the wheels turning inside his little head as he glanced from me to the woman I assumed was his mother.

"We look a lot alike, don't we?" I said.

The boy nodded solemnly. "Merlin thinks so, too," he said, indicating the cat in his arms.

The cat's large dark eyes were focused on me until Hitchcock arched his back, hissed again, and took off like a shot down the hall. Merlin squirmed in the boy's arms.

"I'm sorry Hitchcock isn't being very friendly, but curiosity will get the better of him. He'll come around."

Tia smiled timidly. "Cats will be cats."

I beckoned for them to follow me. Much as I'd love to pause and quiz this woman about her background, I also wanted to know why she was here. We found Herr Schmidt seated in the dining room. Cecil and Winnie Moser, a cute senior couple who'd checked into the Florence cottage the day before, had pies lined up on the table. Winnie was cutting slices and filling paper dessert plates. Cecil placed the plates on a large serving tray. A banquet-sized coffeepot sat on the buffet next to a stack of Styrofoam cups and containers of cream.

"What's your preference, Herr Schmidt?" Winnie said. "Pecan, pumpkin, or apple?"

"Pumpkin, of course," Schmidt said. "In honor of Pumpkin Days."

"Right-o." Cecil, a short man with a fringe of gray hair around a bald spot, slid a piece of pumpkin pie across the table to Schmidt, then turned and spotted us. "What have we here?" He looked from me to Tia, then at the boy and cat.

"This is Tia Hartwell," I said. "She came to talk to Herr Schmidt."

Schmidt paused with a forkful of pie halfway to his mouth. "About what?"

"I have an issue with my booth assignment for the festival," Tia said.

Schmidt checked the watch on his left wrist. "You can see me tomorrow morning. Festival business is handled between eight a.m. and eight p.m."

I frowned. "You were talking festival business with Aunt Rowe not ten minutes ago."

"If she had cooperated, we would have finished prior to eight," he said. "Which reminds me, have you discussed that problematic topic with her?"

"Not yet. I don't even know where she is at the moment."

Winnie pushed gray curls back from her temple, careful

to keep her sticky fingers away from the hair. She laughed, a coarse, throaty sound. "Rowe's outside, bragging about the pumpkin cannon and handing out pie to everyone within shouting distance."

"There will be no cannon," Herr Schmidt said.

I ignored him and said, "I hope she washed that green stuff off her face before she went outside."

"She did," Cecil said. "They asked my honey-bun to have one of them facials, but I told her she's pretty as a picture just as she is."

"Oh, you." Winnie hit him playfully on the arm, then turned toward Tia and me and leaned forward to squint at each of us in turn. "Well, Tia, aren't you the spittin' image of Sabrina? Are you sisters? Cousins?"

"To the best of my knowledge, neither," I said.

Winnie addressed the little boy. "And what's your name, sweetie?"

He looked up shyly. "Damon."

"And how old are you? About six?"

"Seven," he said.

"Have a seat, darlin'," Winnie said. "Let's get y'all some pie."

"We don't want to be a bother," Tia said, but Damon had his eye on the dessert and looked hungry.

"No bother at all." Winnie pulled a chair out for the boy, who sat eagerly with the cat on his lap.

Tia sat beside Damon and accepted a cup of coffee from Cecil.

"I'd like to hear why Tia came," I said, "and since you're right here enjoying your pie, Herr Schmidt, you may as well listen up."

"Right-o," Cecil said.

Schmidt didn't look happy, but he turned to Tia and waited.

She pulled a sheet of paper from a pocket, unfolded it, and held the page for him to see.

"I need to have my booth moved to a different location."

Schmidt scanned the piece of paper. "You're the artist."

"I am," she said.

"You're in booth twenty-seven on Promenade Street. A prime location. What's the problem?"

"The location itself is very nice," she said, "but I can't be anywhere near the man in twenty-two. I need a different spot."

"Booth assignments are final." Schmidt pointed at the bottom of her paper. "It says so right here. No changes will be made, especially not at this late hour."

I looked at Tia. "Is the man in twenty-two by chance fortyish with wiry gray hair?"

She nodded. "His name is Calvin Fisher. Do you know him?"

I related the story of the man who'd stopped me in the grocery store parking lot. "No doubt he thought he was talking to you, Tia, but you must not know each other all that well or he'd have realized his mistake. We may look like sisters, but I'm sure you're younger than me, not to mention thinner."

"We ran into Fisher a few months ago at a bazaar in San Angelo," she said, "and he treated us very badly there."

"Badly how?" Winnie said.

"For one thing, he doesn't care for children. He had an issue with my son staying in the booth with me."

"That's none of his business," Cecil said, "unless the boy was raising a ruckus."

Tia looked fondly at Damon, who was shoveling apple pie into his mouth at a high rate of speed. "He's quiet and spends most of his time drawing."

Damon swallowed a bite of pie and said, "That man was mean to Merlin."

"True," Tia said. "He didn't want Damon or what he called 'the evil black cat' anywhere near him."

Maybelle, her face freshly scrubbed, entered the dining room. The living room skin rejuvenation session had apparently come to an end. "No one who believes black cats are

bad luck should even be allowed at the festival," she said. "Anybody gives you a hard time about your little boy or your cat, tell 'em to come talk to me."

"I second that." I turned to Herr Schmidt. "Under the circumstances, you should make sure Tia is far away from this character."

The skin rejuvenation woman, Britt, entered the room behind Maybelle. "Calvin Fisher is the scourge of the earth," she said. "He comes to all of these events wearing his I'll-make-you-a-great-deal smarmy salesman face. Behind your back, he's nothin' but trouble. I ever get the chance to give that man a facial, it's gonna be laced with cyanide."

Whoa. That was harsh.

"I don't want to cause trouble," Tia said again, "but I'm asking you to make an exception in this case and move me to a different spot. Otherwise, I'll have to leave, and I can't afford to miss this opportunity."

Schmidt eyed her with a slight shake of his head, and I knew he was going to turn her down. "Changing of rules leads to trouble and confusion," he said.

Why was this guy such a curmudgeon, and who the heck put him in charge of an event that was supposed to be fun?

Winnie wiped her hands on a napkin and stepped forward. "What if Cecil and I trade places with Tia?" she said. "That will save the boy and the cat, not to mention this nice young lady, from having to deal with a bully."

"That's a fine idea, Winnie," Cecil said. "If the man is a nuisance, I'll tell him how the cow ate the cabbage."

"How about it, Herr Schmidt?" I said. "Wouldn't you rather stop the conflict before it starts? Have the festival begin on a happy note?"

Everyone watched Schmidt as he scanned the room. "Looks like I'm outnumbered." His gaze rested on the Mosers. "If you will sign an agreement stating the terms of this trade and absolve the festival of any responsibility, then I'll allow the switch."

I clapped my hands, glad for a solution to the conflict. "Good."

Schmidt turned to me. "And you still need to speak with Rowe about that other matter."

"Yes, sir." *As if talking to Aunt Rowe about the cannon would make a difference.*

The Mosers and Tia wrote out and signed an agreement to keep Herr Schmidt happy, then we all had pie. The pumpkin pie wasn't quite as satisfying as the one I planned to bake myself, but I was happy to have it. By the time I showed Tia and her son to the door, Hitchcock and Merlin were chasing each other in circles. Damon tried to capture Merlin each time the cats raced by.

"If Fisher gives you any trouble," I said to Tia, "you can go to Sheriff Crawford for help. He's a friend."

"I appreciate the sisterly advice," Tia said, "even though we're not related."

I raised my brows. "Maybe we are somehow and we just don't know it. Where are you from?"

"I was born in Texas," Tia said, "but I didn't spend all that long here. My father was in the army. I'm glad to be back, though."

Damon had managed to get his hands on Merlin, and he picked the cat up.

"Time to go, buddy," Tia said. "We have a big day tomorrow."

I opened the door, and they stepped out onto the porch. People milled around in the front yard, and I spotted Gabe Brenner talking with another man.

I ducked into the shadow of the porch column. "Here's another piece of advice: While you're steering clear of Fisher, you might watch out for that guy, too." I peeked around the column to assure myself that Gabe wasn't looking in our direction.

Tia followed my gaze. "Which one?"

"The big broad-shouldered guy with dark hair. He's paying me too much attention, and I'm doing my best to discourage him. Since you and I look so much alike, I wouldn't be one bit surprised if he tried to latch on to you."

"Seems like dealing with difficult men is my lot in life," Tia said. "Don't worry. I'll watch my back."

4

THE STREETS OF Lavender were hopping the next morning when my friend Tyanne and I began setting up her festival booth on the sidewalk near her bookstore, Knead to Read. I planned to spend a few hours with her, then visit Cecil and Winnie Moser. They were eager to show off their vast salt-and-pepper-shaker collection, especially the black cat shakers they had described to me in detail. I figured Hitchcock and I would spend a little time checking out the festival and be back home by mid-afternoon so I could get in some writing time.

The day was sunny with a light breeze—perfect fall weather. Tyanne had a pop-up tent covering her booth area and book racks set up along the perimeter. A long folding table covered by a floor-length black tablecloth served as the sales counter.

"Wait till you see Tia Hartwell," I told Tyanne. "She looks so much like me it's eerie. She even has a black cat."

Hitchcock sat on top of stacked book cartons, overseeing our work. "Mrreow."

"Yes, you had lots of fun chasing Merlin. I hope you behave better here, or I'll put your harness on. I brought it with me."

Hitchcock jumped off the boxes and slipped under the tablecloth.

Tyanne laughed and turned back to the box she was unpacking. "I ran into a woman years ago in Boston who looked like me. They say everybody has a twin out there somewhere."

I placed a handful of paperbacks on a shelf and sat back on my heels. "They do?"

Ty shrugged. "Maybe this woman shares your DNA. She could be a second, third, fourth cousin. Have you discussed this with your aunt?"

"Not yet. She was too busy bragging about the pumpkin cannon she's renting."

"I heard about the cannon," Ty said. "Cool."

"Herr Schmidt doesn't think so."

"Herr Schmidt is a jerk," said a familiar male voice.

I turned to see Gabe Brenner standing on the other side of the table.

"Good morning," Ty said, then paused as she noticed the way Gabe was staring at me.

I stood. "Schmidt is a stickler for the rules. Maybe that's because he was a teacher."

"Could be." Ty walked to the table, putting herself between Gabe and me, and addressed him. "We'll open at eleven, the official festival start time. Is there a particular book you're interested in?"

Gabe hadn't even glanced at the books. I made introductions to fill the awkward silence. "Tyanne Clark, this is Gabe Brenner. He's staying at Around-the-World Cottages, and he's one of the food vendors."

"Oh," Ty said. "Good to meet you, Gabe."

Gabe kept his focus on me. "You doin' okay, Sabrina? Has that troublemaker bothered you anymore?"

I shook my head. "No. I haven't seen him."

"'Cause I can take care of him for you," he said. "I don't mind. Just say the word."

Tyanne looked at me, her brows raised with the unspoken question: *What troublemaker?*

I didn't want to get into it. I just wanted Gabe to leave. I wondered if he'd caught sight of Tia yet and whether he'd be attracted to her, too, or if it was some unknown factor that had the guy stuck on me.

"I don't expect any more trouble," I said. "You can go off and deep-fry to your heart's content with no worries."

"What kind of food do you make?" Ty asked.

Gabe rattled off his limited menu. "My mama says the deep-fried bacon is to die for. Come on over later and I'll give you both a free taste."

I liked bacon, but the thought of it battered and fried made me want to gag.

"We'll see," Ty said in her usual friendly tone. "Now we have to finish setting up. I'll bet you have a lot of prep work to do, too."

Gabe checked his watch. "Yeah. It takes a while to get all that oil heated up." He looked back at me. "Take care, Sabrina. Holler if you need me."

He turned and walked away. When he was out of earshot, Tyanne said, "He's a little creepy."

"Tell me about it," I said. "The guy started dogging me as soon as he checked in."

"Who's the troublemaker he mentioned?"

I told her about the scene at the grocery store and explained Tia's past history with Calvin Fisher.

"Maybe you should tell Sheriff Crawford," she said.

"Good idea."

We continued with the book setup, and Tyanne's teenage

employee, Ethan Brady, reported for work at half past ten. Hitchcock crawled out from under the table when he heard Ethan's voice, and the boy scratched the cat's head.

"We'd love to stay and visit," I said, "but I promised to stop by the Mosers' booth. They're staying at the cottages, too. I might walk around the festival a bit, but then I'm off to write."

"How's your manuscript coming along?" Tyanne said.

"Fast and furious," I said.

She rolled her eyes. "Uh-huh."

"Believe it or not, I wrote this morning before coming over here," I said in my best self-righteous tone. She didn't need to know I'd only gained two new pages.

Hitchcock allowed me to attach his harness without too much protest, and we took off. People hustled down the street carrying boxes and wheeling handcarts in the countdown to festival start time. It seemed every possible category of product could be found here, from hot sauce to leg warmers.

I cut across the town square, headed for the Mosers' booth on Promenade Street. Turning a corner, I heard a loud female voice and stopped in my tracks.

"Leave me alone," she said. "I traded places so I wouldn't have to see you."

Tia had a protective arm around her little boy. They stood near the cement-block building that housed the restrooms. Calvin Fisher addressed her in a low voice I couldn't hear. If the man's waving arms were any indication, his words were hostile. Why did he have it in for this poor woman? Concern washed over me.

I spied Deputy Patricia Rosales across the square. She appeared to be supervising as a band set up their instruments in the large center gazebo. It might be better for Fisher to get an official reprimand from the deputy than if I tried to intercede. Except that Rosales and I never saw eye to eye, especially now that I was dating the local game warden,

Luke Griffin, a man whom Rosales had her eye on. She wasn't likely to listen to me, and she might even have an unfair prejudice against Tia since we looked so much alike.

Hitchcock glanced at Fisher and turned to me. "Mrreow."

"I agree. That man deserves a swat upside the head. I'm going to talk to him."

I started in that direction, but then Fisher did an about-face and walked away. Tia spun and went in the other direction with Damon. That's when I noticed Herr Schmidt approaching with a clipboard clutched to his chest.

I guessed neither Fisher nor Tia wanted to talk with the man, and I didn't, either. I hadn't discussed the pumpkin cannon with Aunt Rowe. No doubt that would be the first question out of his mouth if he saw me. I already knew she wouldn't change her mind, so what was the point? I took a few steps backward, intent on slipping away without Schmidt noticing me, and almost stepped on Winnie Moser.

"Hi there, Sabrina. Isn't this a grand day?"

I turned and took in the woman's bright smile. "Sure is."

Winnie wore a bright yellow shirt appliqued with orange pumpkins and a scarecrow with a matching tote slung over her shoulder. The scent of cigarette smoke mingled with her floral perfume.

"Lovely things for sale here," Winnie said. "Just lovely. I did some nosing around as people were setting up, but I must make some time for serious shopping. At the moment, though, Cecil needs me." She looked down at my cat. "Are you two coming to see our shakers?"

"We are," I said.

"Did we tell you we have over two hundred sets in our collection?"

"You sure did." I hoped she didn't plan to show me every single set. I did want to see the black cat shakers, but now I had an ulterior motive for going with her. I wanted to make sure Fisher was where he was supposed to be and not harassing Tia. I picked Hitchcock up. "Let's go."

As we hurried across the square toward Promenade Street, the band started playing the oompah-pah style of music I remembered from past festivals. Homage to the Germans who'd first settled in the area. The sidewalks began to fill with tourists.

Cecil looked up with an obvious expression of relief as we approached him. "Thank goodness you're back, Winnie. I worry when you disappear like that."

"I was browsing, dear." She flapped her hand casually. "You know how I get when I shop. Now let me see if I can remember where I put those black cats to show Sabrina." They seemed to have salt-and-pepper shakers of every size and description displayed on their tables, but Winnie knelt to shuffle through a cardboard box.

Catty-corner across the aisle, Calvin Fisher stood under a tent that covered tables filled with jewelry. The man wore a wide smile as potential shoppers approached.

"That's one smarmy fella," Cecil said in a low voice.

"He was very charming when he showed me his jewelry," Winnie said.

Cecil turned to look at his wife. "You should stay away from that man. He's trouble."

"But he has some beautiful pieces," she said, "no matter what Tia said about him. I admit the guy working with him seems kind of shady."

"I don't see another guy." I pretended to study the Mosers' display tables as I surreptitiously watched Fisher.

"There's another dude over there," Cecil said. "Showed up and started hollerin' at Fisher. Seemed like something was lost, 'cause they were turnin' everything upside down in a search. There he is."

A man with unnaturally black hair and wearing a black T-shirt with a skull on the front came around a curtain at the back of their tent.

"The shady one's name is Axle," Winnie said. "I heard them talking when I was over there browsing."

"They don't look like jewelry salesmen," I said.

"I'm sure they'll sell plenty," Cecil said. "Fisher's been schmoozing with the women since I got here."

"Except for when he was across the square harassing Tia," I said.

"Wonder what the real story is," Cecil said. "There's probably more to it than what she told us."

Winnie said, "Well, he's probably not as bad as the man who's selling good luck charms to protect against the bad luck cat."

My eyes widened, and I spun to look at her. "What are you talking about?"

"Look across the way," she said. "There's a tent with '*The Bad Luck Cat*' big as you please on a sign above the door. Man running it says he's selling good luck charms. There's another sign, too. Says '*Protect Yourself from the Bad Luck Cat*.'"

5

"NATURALLY, I HURRIED straight over there to see this good luck charm place as soon as Winnie mentioned it," I told Glenda the next morning.

"Of course you did." She had her hands full with the morning-after mess in Aunt Rowe's kitchen. The cottage guests had partied until well past midnight and hadn't picked up after themselves. Now, barely six hours later, I yawned and watched in astonishment as Glenda packed a record amount of dirty dishes into Aunt Rowe's dishwasher.

I gulped my coffee, then said, "I had to see the place for myself, but as soon as I got there, Hitchcock started raising a ruckus, and I realized he was right. I couldn't go in there with a black cat by my side."

"Especially not the bad luck cat," Glenda said.

Hitchcock sat on the floor near her feet. "Mrreow."

I glared at Glenda, though I knew she was goading me.

She bent and patted the cat's head. "Sweet boy. You know I didn't mean that."

"The tent is black as midnight and all closed in," I said, "with this curtain over the front door. Looks more like an eerie setting for a séance than a festival."

"Doesn't sound that unusual to me, being Halloween's just around the corner," Glenda said.

"I don't care if someone wants to take advantage of the Halloween season to make some money. I only want them to keep Hitchcock out of it. There's a photo of a cat on a poster outside the tent, and I swear it looks just like him."

"Do you think it *is* him?"

"I don't know yet. I'm just so dang disappointed. After we had that black cat adoption weekend in August and placed so many black kitties in their forever homes, I felt really good, like I'd helped to give this town a big attitude adjustment. Now this."

"You mean a cattitude adjustment?" Glenda said.

I had to grin. "Believe you me, I'm going to have a cattitude when I go over there this morning to check the place out." I lifted the plastic cover on a tray of kolaches and snatched one with peach filling. "Could have gone back after I brought Hitchcock home yesterday afternoon."

Glenda wiped around the things crowding the counter with a wet cloth. "I'm shocked you didn't."

"For one thing, Calvin Fisher was there, and I didn't want another run-in with him." I had already filled Glenda in on what I knew about Fisher and told her all about Tia, Damon, and their black cat.

"The man from the grocery store?" Glenda said.

"Yup. Curious that he would leave his booth when he was so busy with jewelry customers." I took a big bite of the pastry.

"Maybe he felt the urgent need to buy a good luck charm," Glenda said.

"Possibly." I shrugged. "Tia said he has a thing against black cats. Another reason I decided to come home and stay

home. Turned out to be a good decision, because I wrote a new chapter."

"Congratulations." Glenda picked up two trays of pastries. "Give me a hand with the fruit? Rowe wants the continental breakfast set up by seven."

"That's kind of early, considering the late partying everyone did last night." As I spoke the words, I looked out the window and spotted some of the guests in the distance outside their cabins. "Spoke too soon. People are milling around."

I went to the refrigerator and removed a fruit tray. "I'll help you, then I'm going to catch up with that man before he opens for business. Maybe I can talk him into removing the picture that looks like my cat."

"Good luck," Glenda said. "Hitchcock can stay here and keep me company."

"Mrreow," he said.

T HE good-luck-charm place—I refused to think of it as the bad-luck-cat booth—sat at the edge of what was usually an empty field near the elementary school. Half the field contained booths. The other half was used for overflow parking after the school lot filled. A row of RVs and trucks with trailers occupied a section cordoned off for vendor parking. I was early enough to snag a parking space on the street near the school and within sight of the black tent. I watched people hurry to and fro and sipped from my travel coffee mug. After a few minutes with no activity near the tent, I got out of the car to take a closer look.

As I stood several yards away from the tent and looked at the poster that strongly resembled Hitchcock, I felt my aggravation building again. Why on earth would someone think this was a good idea? Didn't he know cat lovers would refuse to step foot near such a place?

The curtain panels that served as a door were pulled together, so I couldn't tell if anyone was in there or not. Obviously, the person who set this up depended on the annoying signs to lure shoppers inside. I supposed that *"Ward Off Evil"* and *"Protect Yourself"* would stir the curiosity of certain personality types.

I moved closer and heard what sounded like boxes being shuffled around. On the street, dozens of people were out and about. I noticed a sheriff's department cruiser traveling slowly in my direction. I wouldn't mind running into Sheriff Crawford, but I didn't care to see either of his unlikeable deputies. The nearing of the car urged me into action. I walked up to the tent and pushed the curtain aside.

Rectangular tables lined the sides of the tent. In the dim lighting I could make out baskets of small polished stones and rabbits' feet on keychains. A man stood over a stack of boxes humming something that sounded like "The Battle Hymn of the Republic." I cleared my throat, and he turned around and gave me a once-over.

"I'm not open yet," he said, "but if you want some good luck, darlin', I could make an exception."

I opened my mouth, but words didn't come. Eddie Baxter, Twila Baxter's son. The son I thought of as the bad twin ever since he had tried to pick me up at the bar called The Wild Pony Saloon several months ago.

"No, thank you," I finally managed. "I'm here to complain."

He clucked his tongue. "The complaint department definitely ain't open this early." He turned back to his boxes.

"I don't approve of your signage," I said.

He scowled at me. "Say what?"

"You're perpetuating the silly legend that there's a black cat in town that causes bad luck."

His brows drew together. "Look, if you don't like what I'm doin', you can leave. I'm just makin' a buck. God knows

my mother and my brother aren't the only ones allowed to make a livin' in this town."

Now I'd stirred him up, and I wasn't sure that was such a good idea. I could imagine why he didn't fit in at the antiques store run by Twila and Ernie.

Before I could respond, a shaft of light crossed the tent's interior. I looked over my shoulder and sagged when I saw Detective Rosales framed in the doorway.

"Baxter," she said, "have you seen your pal Calvin Fisher this morning?"

I slowly turned toward Eddie so Rosales couldn't see my face.

"No, ma'am, Deputy," Eddie said.

"How about you, miss?" Rosales said.

How do I manage to have the bad luck of running into this woman while standing in the midst of these purported good luck charms?

"Haven't seen him." I answered without looking at her, but Rosales came closer until she stood beside me and checked my face.

"What are *you* doing here?" she said.

"Protesting this man's notion that cats can bring bad luck," I said. "Why are you looking for Calvin Fisher?"

"He's been reported missing."

Eddie said, "Probably sleepin' it off somewhere. Cal drank a coupla six-packs last night."

"Seems early to investigate a missing person," I said, "since people knew exactly where he was until last night. It's not even eight in the morning."

"Henry Schmidt is worried," Rosales said. "He and Fisher planned an early meeting, but Fisher didn't show."

"I ain't seen neither one of 'em," Eddie said.

Rosales looked like she wanted to say more to me, thought better of it, and left.

I hoped Calvin wasn't off somewhere harassing Tia. I didn't

know where the young woman was staying, so I couldn't check this out on my own. I was considering going after Rosales when a streak of something moving fast across the tent floor caught my eye.

"It's the dang bad luck cat!" Eddie shouted. "Stop that varmint."

The back wall rustled, and I had a clear view of a black tail slipping out beneath the tent.

Was that Hitchcock? No way.

Just in case, I bolted out of the tent and ran around to the back side. Sure enough, I spotted a black cat darting across the school parking lot and into the field.

"Hitchcock," I called, and it seemed like the cat hesitated for a split second before racing away.

Was that my imagination?

I ran toward the cat, realizing that if he didn't want to be caught I would never catch up. I'd left Hitchcock at home. This couldn't be him. Unless he'd hitched a ride into town from the cottages with one of the vendors without their knowledge. A trick that Hitchcock had perfected.

I kept running and reached the row of parked RVs and trucks. I stooped to look under the vehicles and caught a glimpse of four black feet trotting along.

If this *was* Hitchcock, what the heck was he doing all the way out here? He usually liked to stay around people. I scanned the vehicles. There were likely people still asleep in their RVs.

The cat might belong to one of them.

Maybe it wasn't Hitchcock after all—it could be Merlin. I didn't know if Tia had an RV. Even if she didn't, she could be staying in one with someone else.

Breathing hard from my run across the field, I slowed down to look for the cat between vehicles. Most of them were parked nose in. One side door stood open, and a man lounged against the RV smoking a cigarette.

"Mornin'," he said.

"Good morning. Have you seen a cat in the past few minutes?"

He nodded and pointed. "He went thataway."

I thanked him, walked faster, and spotted the cat sitting by the last truck in the row. He didn't attempt to run as I approached, and when I got closer I recognized Hitchcock's long lanky body.

I stopped walking and stared the cat down, fists propped on my hips. "Why on earth are you here, and what the heck are you up to?"

"Mrreow." He looked at me, then at the driver's-side door of the pickup.

I walked over and scooped the cat up. "You're going to give me a heart attack one of these days."

I straightened and scanned the enclosed trailer attached to the pickup hitch. I glanced into the front seat of the tall Ford four-by-four. Overhanging oak trees shaded the vehicle, but I caught a glimpse of a person inside. The front seat was reclined.

"We don't want to wake people up if they're not ready to wake up," I whispered as I tiptoed away from the truck.

"Mrrreeeoooowww," Hitchcock said, as loud as I'd ever heard him.

What's he trying to tell me?

I stopped walking and looked into the cat's eyes. His attention returned to the pickup, so I backed up, went to the door, and stood on tiptoe to look inside.

The man reclining in the driver's seat was Calvin Fisher, but Fisher wasn't asleep. At least not unless he slept with his eyes wide open.

6

MY HEART RACED as I looked at the body through the truck window. I thought about rapping on the glass to see if Fisher reacted. Maybe he only seemed dead. People meditated. Daydreamed. Prayed.

Calvin Fisher praying? Not likely, unless he sent up a last-ditch-effort message as he felt his life drain away. In any event, I shouldn't disturb the man. The scene. Whatever.

Besides, knocking on the window would leave a mark behind, one the authorities might trace to me. I wanted no connection to this truck or to the possibly dead man inside. And I sure didn't want the superstitious crazies to blame my cat for whatever had happened here. I could simply walk away, leaving no evidence of myself or Hitchcock behind.

Don't be a wuss, Sabrina. Call for help.

As I juggled Hitchcock from one arm to the other so I could pull out my phone, the man with the cigarette ambled toward me.

Oh, great. A witness.

"See you caught up with your cat," he said.

I forced a smile. "Yes, thank goodness." I held my phone up and saw no bars in the corner of the screen.

No service. Just my luck.

I held the phone higher and moved a few feet ahead.

"Whatcha doin'?" the man said.

"I have to make a call." I moved to my left.

There. One bar.

I used my thumb to punch in 911. The phone screen said *"Calling"* for a moment before signaling that the call had failed.

The man watched me closely. "What's wrong? You look like your heart's gonna jump clear outta your chest."

Good grief, the guy was staring at my chest. I dialed 911 again and turned away from the man. Why couldn't he just leave? I didn't need him placing Hitchcock and me at the scene of—what exactly? A fatal heart attack? A stroke? I didn't care if people talked about me, but the fear that they might lay blame on Hitchcock bothered me. I could just hear them making up some story about my cat causing Fisher the bad luck that killed him.

The man came up behind me and stood so close I could practically feel him breathing on my neck. I turned to look at him. "Could you *please* give me some space?"

His eyes, shaded by bushy gray brows, narrowed. "What are you really doin' over here?"

I sighed and decided I might as well give in and tell him what was going on. "I came after the cat. That's it, but now—"

"You a friend of Fisher's?"

"No, but—"

"Saw another gal out here, looked kinda like you but not—" He leaned toward me and studied my face.

"Not as old. I've met her. We have a problem, Mr. . . . ?"

"George. Look, I don't mean no disrespect. Fisher told me to watch out for people around his truck. Sounded kind of paranoid, you ask me, but I don't mind helpin' a guy out. That's all I'm doin'."

I moved the phone from my ear to check the screen. Another failed call.

"When did he tell you that?"

"Last night," he said. "Granted, he was more'n three sheets to the wind at the time."

Hitchcock fidgeted in my arms. I didn't have his harness, but I had a feeling he'd stick around to watch the drama unfold. I let him jump to the ground and said, "Do you have a phone I could try?"

George frowned. "For what?"

"Calling nine-one-one. I'm not having any luck with mine." I punched in the numbers a third time.

"Don't have to call the cops," George said. "You want me to shut up, just say so."

"I'm not calling because of you," I said. "I'm calling because of Fisher."

"Huh? Why?"

I tipped my head toward the pickup. "Because he's in there, and he doesn't look so good."

"Guy drank a boatload last night." George went to the side window and looked into the truck. "Ah, jeez, he's more'n hungover. He looks dead."

"I know. That's why I'm calling."

"Save yourself the trouble. Deputy's right here."

My heart fell to my stomach. I turned and spotted Rosales halfway down the row of vehicles, walking our way.

George waved his arms and yelled, "Hey, over here!"

Hitchcock looked toward Rosales and a low growl rumbled in his throat.

I stooped to pat his head. "I know, boy. Sorry, but there's no way around her."

George ran to meet the deputy. They exchanged a few words, then Rosales jogged in our direction. She ignored me and Hitchcock and went straight to the driver's door, pulling on gloves. George stood inches behind the deputy and looked over her shoulder as she opened the door and

leaned in toward the body. I had no desire for a close-up. After a few seconds, Rosales thumbed on her radio and spouted commands.

"Roll without sirens," she said. "We're right in the thick of the festival."

I knew without asking that she'd have a fit if I tried to leave, so I walked over to stand under the shade of a live oak to wait. Hitchcock stayed with me and sat at the base of the tree. The cat had what seemed like a nervous purr going, or maybe it was excitement, like a kid with a ringside seat at the circus. Soon he'd have more action to watch. No doubt the routine cadre of backup deputies, paramedics, and firefighters would report to the scene.

Across the field, the street filled with cars as festivalgoers arrived. They'd have something extra to gawk at today. Rosales and George talked near Fisher's pickup. From her inactivity, I assumed Rosales had unofficially pronounced Fisher dead. After a couple of minutes, the deputy approached me.

"What are you doing here?" she said.

"My cat ran into the field, and I followed him."

"The cat ran to a truck that happened to contain a dead man?"

Yup, but I don't want to admit that to you.

"He's dead?" I said. "For sure?"

"Yes," Rosales said. "You didn't answer my question."

"My cat ran into the field," I repeated, "and I caught up to him near the truck. Then I noticed the man inside."

"Did you touch anything?"

"No."

"Did you recognize this as Fisher's truck?"

"No." Given more time, I might have realized this was the truck I saw Fisher in at the grocery store, but that was nowhere near my first thought.

"Did you see anyone else?"

I motioned toward George. "Only that guy."

He came our way, possibly taking my gesture as an invitation to interrupt us. "I thought Fisher was sleeping in that big blue RV," he said. "Belongs to his buddy. He asked me to watch the pickup, but no way I expected to see him in there. What d'ya think happened? Heart attack?"

Rosales regarded him with a stern expression. "It's too soon to know the cause of death, sir. Do not start needless rumors."

My stomach felt queasy as I thought about the events that would lead up to an official report.

"Are we free to leave?" I asked as Hitchcock rubbed against my legs. "You know where to find me if you have any more questions."

Rosales looked me up and down as if she were trying to gauge my dress size. Then she surprised me by saying, "Let me know if you remember seeing anyone else in the vicinity. Otherwise, you can go."

"I remember someone," George said.

I cringed as he began to describe Tia to Rosales. Reports of the young woman's argument with the dead man were sure to follow. People loved to spread stories, and they wouldn't care if the gossip ended up causing trouble for an innocent woman. For all anyone knew, Tia had walked across this parking area on her way to set up her booth this morning. Could be as simple as that. I picked up Hitchcock and walked away.

"Maybe we should find Tia before she hears about this from someone else," I said.

I MADE a quick stop at my car to grab my tote, and I deposited Hitchcock inside the bag. Without the harness to keep him in line, this was the next best option. My arms already ached from carrying him, but I didn't want the cat drawing attention to or endangering himself by wandering loose around the festival.

A polka started up as I passed the square on my way to Tia's booth. Questions ran through my head.

Was Fisher's death accidental?

What had Tia been doing near his truck?

Why had Fisher been with Eddie Baxter the day before he died? Earlier, Rosales had called them pals.

What was the topic of Schmidt's planned meeting with Fisher this morning?

If Fisher died of a stroke or a heart attack or alcohol poisoning, none of the answers mattered. But if his death was caused by foul play, they would matter in a big way. The writer in me couldn't let go of the notion that someone had done him in. Fisher was exactly the sort of guy to cross the wrong person—one who wanted him gone for good.

But who was that person? And how had they killed him? *Stop it, Sabrina. We don't know he was murdered.*

Hitchcock popped his head out of the tote and meowed just as I noticed Merlin lounging on the corner of a table up ahead. Tia sat nearby sketching on a pad sitting on an easel. I couldn't yet see her model. Hitchcock rustled around in the tote, eager to get loose.

"Okay, okay, but you better behave yourself." I knelt to release him and, as expected, he ran straight to Merlin. The cats hissed at each other, but their hearts weren't in it, and they batted at each other playfully.

Tia looked over her shoulder at me and smiled, then went back to her work. She wore her wavy dark hair pulled back and tied with a colorful scarf that complemented her plum sweater. Delicate hoop earrings nearly reached her shoulders.

Browsers congregated around the artist's booth. Tia displayed charcoal portraits and floral watercolors. She sketched quickly, and the closer I got the more I realized her work in progress reminded me of Luke Griffin. I edged around a big woman who blocked my line of sight and saw it was, in fact, the game warden. He glanced my way, as if he'd felt my presence, and grinned.

Luke wore his warden uniform. He normally worked on Fridays. What had brought him here to have his picture sketched by a beautiful young woman on a Friday morning? I recognized the flush of jealousy even as I told myself to tamp it down.

A dusty green CR-V was backed up to the booth, the hatch open. Damon sat over the bumper, his little legs dangling. Totes and rolled sleeping bags filled the space behind him. The boy held a sketch pad and, like his mother, his hand moved quickly as he drew.

Luke stood and walked over to Tia, who had already finished her work. A few potential customers had formed a line. I walked to them as Luke handed some bills to Tia.

"Hey," he said, "you want your picture made you'd better get in line."

I shook my head. "I came with news for Tia."

Tia stood and turned to me. "About what?"

"Calvin Fisher."

She frowned. "I don't care to hear anything about that man."

"A deputy will probably come to talk to you," I said quietly. "Fisher is dead."

Luke said, "Who's Fisher?"

"One of the vendors," I said. "He was found in his truck a few minutes ago."

Tia's expression showed little emotion—perhaps a touch of curiosity. She backed up a step. "How did he die?"

I shrugged. "No one knows yet, but a bystander mentioned your name to Deputy Rosales."

Her frown deepened. "Thanks for the heads-up. I need to get back to work."

Luke took his sketch, and we moved away from Tia's booth. Merlin and Hitchcock rolled around under the table that held Tia's supplies, and I didn't have the heart to break up their fun just yet.

"What does she have to do with this Fisher dude?" Luke said.

I told him the little I knew about Tia's connection to the dead man.

"Rosales won't go easy on Tia," he said. "She looks too much like you."

"Is that why you're here? Attracted to the younger model?"

He took my arm and pulled me close. "No way. I like this version much better."

I leaned into him and smiled. "Good to know. So, I was surprised to see you here. You're not working today?"

"I am, but I saw Tia and her little boy last night and made it a point to come here this morning to give her some business."

"Hmmm, sounds like you *were* attracted to her."

"Only because they appeared to be living in their car," he said. "Spotted them last night in the lot behind the library."

"Oh." The car didn't look big enough to live in. "That sounds uncomfortable."

"At the coffee shop this morning Max told me she painted portraits. Figured she can use all the business she can get."

"She mentioned—"

A loud boom interrupted my sentence, and a pumpkin sailed over our heads. I had forgotten all about the problem of Aunt Rowe's cannon.

7

LUKE KEPT PACE with me as I crossed the town square. We headed for the field next to Albert's Feed Store where a crowd surrounded a large orange cannon mounted atop a flatbed trailer. I patted the tote hanging from my shoulder with Hitchcock inside and heard a reassuring trill. The cat seemed content even though I'd interrupted his play session with Merlin.

"What's the rush?" Luke said. "The cannon isn't going anywhere."

"I have to see for myself that Aunt Rowe isn't endangering herself or anyone else with this wacko idea of shooting heavy artillery at a festival. Why couldn't she center her attention on something simple, say, the pumpkin carving contest?"

"You mean the activity that requires the use of a very sharp knife?" he said.

I rolled my eyes. "You know what I mean."

"I do, but I don't think you have anything to worry about. Pumpkin cannons have been around a long time."

"I hoped she would take up safer hobbies now that she's approaching her seventies."

"I don't see your aunt becoming a woman who sits in her rocker knitting a scarf."

Hitchcock poked his head out of the tote. "Mrreow."

I laughed. "That's an understatement."

We edged through the crowd for a better view of the action. Pumpkins lined the perimeter of the trailer. Aunt Rowe, in black leggings and an orange tunic, strutted Vanna White–like around the cannon. A muscular guy in skin-tight jeans and a shirt that fit him like Spanx chose a pumpkin from the pile and presented it to my aunt. She held the pumpkin high and made another lap around the trailer to whoops and hollers from the crowd.

Luke chuckled and leaned close to my ear. "She's in good shape. That's a hefty pumpkin."

He had a point. "I can't help worrying about what she'll do next. Fall off the trailer and break her neck? Try to ride a pumpkin across the sky?"

I was only partially joking. I didn't like the looks of the propane tank connected to the cannon. Couldn't things like that blow up?

The man with Aunt Rowe picked up a microphone. "Ladies and gentlemen, I hope you're enjoying our little preview. If you'd like to operate the pumpkin cannon yourself, come back tonight, six to eight. In the meantime, see the posted schedule for the other games and competitions." He pointed toward a billboard next to the feed store. "We want y'all to have a great festival experience. Now, put your hands together for the lady who made all of this possible"—he raised his voice to a shout—"Miss. Rowena. Flowers!"

He set the mike down and clapped vigorously as he approached Aunt Rowe. He took the pumpkin from her and

placed it into the cannon. Then, in a surprising move, he swept Aunt Rowe off her feet, tossed her to adjust his hand-hold, and bench-pressed my aunt like a hundred-pound barbell. The crowd went wild while he held Aunt Rowe in a supine position over his head and made a lap around the cannon.

When the heck did she learn this stunt?

A range of emotions flitted through me. Shock. Awe. Fear. My eyeballs felt like they might pop out of my head. I turned to Luke. "Seriously? He couldn't find a twenty-year-old for this trick?"

"She may have volunteered," Luke said. "Who's the guy?"

"I don't know, but I need to find out."

I watched in amazement as the man lowered Aunt Rowe to the trailer platform. When he turned to pull a lever on the cannon, I spotted the ad on the back of his shirt: *"Train with Thorn."*

"Her personal trainer," I said. "I should have guessed. Never met the guy, but she's always spouting 'Thorn says this' and 'Thorn recommends that.' I didn't know he was so—" I stopped short of describing the guy as *"ripped"* or *"hot."*

Luke looked at me. "What?"

"Strong," I said.

"Yeah." Luke grinned. "I need to get to work. Will you be okay here?"

"Of course," I said. "Hitchcock and I are going to give Aunt Rowe a talking-to about unnecessary risk."

"Good luck with that," he said and gave me a quick kiss on the lips.

Heat flooded my cheeks. This time my racing heart wasn't caused by fear that Aunt Rowe would hurt herself. I watched Luke walk away and realized that he was the kind of *"hot"* that I found way more interesting than that guy up on the trailer. Thorn, or whoever the heck he was.

The cannon blasted again. As most spectators followed

the path of the flying pumpkin, I noticed Aunt Rowe descending the steps from the trailer and hurried in her direction.

"Hi there, Sabrina." Aunt Rowe's face was flushed. Ball-shaped pumpkin earrings dangled from her lobes. "And Hitchcock." She patted my cat-shaped tote and Hitchcock poked his head up to meow at her. "Did y'all catch my act? What do you think?"

"I *think* a daredevil is inhabiting my aunt's body," I said. "What in heaven's name made you try something so risky?"

"Thorn's helping me build my strength," she said. "You have any idea how many muscles are affected by holding myself straight as a board?"

"No, I don't, but I'm betting you'll be aching in places you didn't even know you had by tomorrow."

She shook her head. "Nah. We've practiced over and over and, look, I'm still standing."

"Uh-huh."

"This was a hoot," Aunt Rowe said. "Did you know there's an annual Punkin' Chunkin' competition every year up in Delaware?"

"No. How would I know that?"

"Thorn was tellin' me about it," she said, "and I'm thinkin' about entering and—" She stopped talking and stared at a spot over my shoulder. "Oh Lord, here comes trouble."

I turned to see what she was talking about and saw Herr Schmidt marching in our direction. His arms pumped at his sides and I could see the angry bluster in his expression as he drew closer. He walked straight up to Aunt Rowe and got in her face.

"I told you *no cannon*," he said. "We can't assume this liability."

"Don't be ridiculous, Henry," Aunt Rowe said. "Did you see how far that pumpkin flew? People love it."

"The cannon goes," he said. "Take it back."

"I didn't personally bring the cannon, Henry," she said sweetly. "Sorry, I can't help you."

His complexion reddened. "No one who registered for this festival requested permission to bring a cannon onto the premises. Was it him? I don't recall seeing that young man's name on any registration form."

He watched Thorn, still on the trailer. Several young ladies stood on the ground and stared adoringly at him like groupies at a concert.

Aunt Rowe held her arms out and looked around. "We're in a field, Henry. This isn't a big deal."

"Have you forgotten the organizational meetings we held to prepare for this event?" he said.

"Hardly." Aunt Rowe shook her head. "You went on and on with your rules and regulations."

"Exactly, because they are important. We can review the typed copies if you like."

If the man got any more worked up, I feared he might hyperventilate.

Aunt Rowe waved a hand at him. "No thanks."

"I thought everyone understood at the time," he said. "Rules are made to be followed, and this . . . this . . ." Schmidt gasped for air.

Aunt Rowe stepped toward the man and put a hand on his arm. "Henry, calm down. Why don't you tell me what's really going on with you?"

His brows rose. "There's nothing going on except for you people who think you can ignore the rules and do whatever you please."

"Your distress is obvious," she said, "and overblown. What's up?"

He crossed him arms over his chest. "Okay, fine, I'll tell you. Your spectacle with this cannon took me away from searching for a missing friend."

Aunt Rowe's forehead creased. "What friend?"

I, of course, knew where he was headed. Schmidt had obviously not yet heard about Fisher's death. I couldn't for the life of me imagine the two men as friends. *Were* they,

or did Schmidt want to portray their relationship in this light for some reason? In any case, he was already so agitated that this seemed like a really bad time to tell him what had happened.

I cleared my throat. "Detective Rosales was looking for Calvin Fisher earlier. I guess you haven't gotten any word from her yet."

"I have not," Schmidt said.

Aunt Rowe said, "Then by all means go look for the man. He must be around here somewhere."

"He's not operating his booth," Schmidt said, "and the rules state that all booths are to open no later than nine a.m."

Good Lord.

"Is that the only reason you're looking for him?" I said. "To enforce your rules?"

A shadow crossed Schmidt's face. "What other reason would there be?"

"You called him a friend, so I thought you cared about his well-being." I shrugged.

A siren whooped, and we turned our heads in unison. An ambulance moved slowly down the main road, coming from the direction of Fisher's truck. They might have had his body onboard.

Schmidt said, "What's an ambulance doing here? What is it now? Did a flying pumpkin crash into someone's head?" He looked at Aunt Rowe and shook an index finger at her. "I told you that cannon would be trouble."

I couldn't take any more of his whining and stepped between him and Aunt Rowe.

"Would you please leave my aunt alone?" I said. "You have worse things to worry about, and they don't have anything to do with any pumpkin."

He stared at me. "Worse things? Explain yourself."

Now you've stepped in it.

Aunt Rowe could read my face better than Schmidt could. "What's wrong, Sabrina?" she said.

I addressed her. "I heard from more than one source that Herr Schmidt's friend drank quite a lot of alcohol last night. Whether or not that has anything to do with his current condition, I don't know."

Aunt Rowe frowned. "What's his condition?"

I sighed. "Calvin Fisher was found dead in his pickup truck this morning."

Beside me, Schmidt nearly shouted. "Dead? He can't be dead."

I turned to him. Those left behind often go into a state of denial, except this wasn't the usual weepy, oh-no-what-horrible-news reaction. He seemed angry.

"I'm afraid it's true, Herr Schmidt." I stopped short of mentioning I'd seen the body myself.

"Fisher couldn't have picked a worse time to drop dead," Schmidt said, his complexion reddening. "I need to see about this."

He spun on his heel and marched toward the town square.

"What a weird reaction," I said to Aunt Rowe as I watched Schmidt stalk across the grass. "He sure didn't sound like a friend."

"He sounded like Henry Schmidt," she said. "The person with a rule for everything, including when a man's allowed to die."

8

"**W**HAT DO YOU think Schmidt's going to do?" I said.

"Not our problem," Aunt Rowe said. "I'm sorry to hear a man died, but so long as Schmidt quits harping about the pumpkin cannon, I'm good."

"I don't think he'll quit," I said.

"Neither will I." She looked at her watch. "I have to get back to the house. What're your plans?"

"I seriously need caffeine, so I'm going to Hot Stuff."

"Getting back to your writing," she said. "That's good."

Aunt Rowe knew I liked to write at the coffee shop, but today I hadn't given writing a thought. My laptop was at home, but Aunt Rowe didn't need to know that. Half of writing was letting thoughts mull around in the subconscious. Maybe I could jot down some ideas while I enjoyed a cup or two of Lavender's Sunrise, my favorite blend.

"I can take Hitchcock home with me if you like," Aunt Rowe said. "Isn't he about due for his afternoon nap?"

"Great idea." I didn't want the cat with me when I went back to continue giving Eddie Baxter a piece of my mind about his good luck charms. "So long as you promise me you won't take him anywhere near that cannon."

"Give me some credit," Aunt Rowe said. "I'm a better pet-sitter than that."

Hitchcock meowed and popped his head out of the tote to rub against Aunt Rowe's arm after we made the transfer, and they headed for home.

I negotiated my way through the shoppers browsing at booths along the sidewalk and made it to Hot Stuff a few minutes later. "You Should Be Dancing" blared through the sound system. I welcomed the upbeat tune even though it brought to mind the fact that Calvin Fisher wouldn't be dancing ever again. Assuming he ever had.

Due to the festival and added tourism, the coffee shop had a steady stream of business that would rival the busiest Starbucks in Houston. I enjoyed people watching for several minutes until a booth opened up, and I grabbed the seat. Looked like Max Dieter, the shop owner, had hired extra help to deal with the added business. Before long, he came over himself with a mug in hand.

"Here you go, madam." He placed the mug on my table with a flourish. "Your usual."

"Thanks, Max." I looked up at him. "You look spiffy today." He and all of his employees wore white shirts and pumpkin-print bow ties with the customary Hot Stuff aprons.

He beamed. "I like to make a good first impression. Add a little something extra to attract the newbies in town for the festival."

"Looks like it's working."

"Speaking of newbies, how about that woman who looks like you?"

"What about her?"

"Who is she?" he said. "I mean, I didn't think you had a sister."

"I don't." I frowned as I realized Aunt Rowe hadn't said one word about Tia. I hadn't thought to tell her about the other woman, and for once she'd missed the latest Lavender gossip. Probably because she was so tied up with that silly cannon.

"Tyanne says everyone has a twin out there somewhere," I said.

"That may be true." Max snapped his fingers. "Say, what are you entering in the bake-off?"

I shook my head. "I haven't decided if I'm going to enter."

"What?" He put a hand to his chest. "The best baker in Lavender? You have to enter. You're a shoo-in."

I shrugged. "There's too much going on for me to think about baking. I'd have to do practice runs and taste tests. Maybe next year."

"Aww, c'mon. The pumpkin crunch you made a few weeks back is a sure winner."

"Sorry. Aunt Rowe's kitchen is jam-packed now, and I don't see a baking session happening there anytime soon."

"Shucks, Sabrina, that's disappointing. But you still have a couple of days to change your mind. Meanwhile, enjoy the coffee."

He bopped away before I could continue to protest. He hadn't brought up Calvin Fisher, which meant he hadn't heard about the death. No way would Max keep news like that quiet. Just because I didn't broach the topic myself didn't mean I'd put Fisher out of my mind. Until someone verified that the man died of natural causes, my imagination would continue to run wild. In my mystery writer's brain, the sudden death of an unlikeable guy like Fisher equaled a strong possibility of murder.

And what was up with Herr Schmidt's odd reaction to learning of his supposed friend's death? What if Schmidt knew all along Fisher was dead, and he pretended ignorance? Could he be a killer who asked Rosales to look for Fisher as a ploy to throw the authorities off his scent?

Knock it off, Sabrina. Herr Schmidt's strange behavior doesn't make him a killer.

I sipped my coffee and leaned back against the booth. Closed my eyes for a second as I enjoyed the flavor and imagined the caffeine seeping into my bloodstream. Tried to remember what was happening in my chapter in progress.

"Hoped to find you here," said a gravelly female voice.

My eyes popped open as Rita Colletti plopped into the chair across from me. Talk about ways to ruin a good cup of coffee. I had done a darn good job of avoiding the woman since she announced her intention to open a law office in Lavender. Now here she was, invading my safe haven. I wondered what had possessed the lawyer to think it was okay to interrupt me so rudely.

It's Rita Colletti. What did you expect?

Rita wore a chocolate brown business suit with a fuchsia blouse that clashed with her brassy red hair. She leaned forward and placed her elbows on the table. Through dark-framed glasses, she studied me like I was a butterfly pinned to a poster in a science fair exhibit.

I didn't feel like playing nice. "What do you want, Rita?"

Back when I'd worked for her at the Houston law firm, I called her Ms. Colletti, but there was no need for that now.

Rita reached into her jacket pocket and pulled out a business card. She slid the card across the table toward me.

"I opened my new law practice," she said.

I put my mug down and looked at the contact information for Rita's office to take note of the address, more so I could avoid the place than anything else. Below her firm name, the card noted "Criminal Law—Family Law—Estate Planning." I knew she was double board-certified in criminal and family law, though she had only handled family-law cases when we'd worked together. Estate planning was a new venture for her.

"The office is all set up. You should stop in."

"Why?" She had to know I didn't want anything to do with her. At one point, she'd asked me to do some clerical work, a request I'd declined in no uncertain terms.

"I'm hearing some gossip about you," she said.

"Gossip's a common pastime in small towns."

"About you and the dead man," she went on. "There's a witness. Maybe more than one."

My annoyance meter shot up, but I pretended nonchalance. "A witness to what?"

She glanced around and lowered her voice to a pitch I could hardly hear over the jukebox music. "You had an altercation with the dead man."

It wouldn't surprise me if Libby, the grocery store clerk, had taken in every detail of my interaction with Fisher and already told everyone she knew what she'd seen.

"He talked to me once," I said. "So what? There's no real connection between us."

"You found the body," she said.

How could she know all this so soon after the fact? *That man, George, must be talking about me.*

I took a deep breath. Her accusing tone had caused my pulse to race.

"Why are you here, Rita?"

"Chances are you're going to need some help."

"Wait just a minute." My tone rose, and I forced myself to lower my volume. "You must have forgotten all about the rules of professional responsibility, Rita. You hang out in hospitals these days, too, to drum up business?"

She straightened. "Of course not."

"So why do you think I'd need help from an attorney? I take it that's what you're saying. I need *your* help."

"Exactly." She pointed to her business card. "You'll see I'm spreading my wings and handle all sorts of cases, far more than family law."

Heaven help me.

I looked up at the ceiling and shook my head. "I don't need an attorney, and you'd better hope no one reports you to the bar for solicitation."

Her brow creased. "I came to you as a favor, out of an allegiance to my former employee."

Good one. Coming from the woman who'd once insisted I could work on Christmas morning since I didn't have any children.

I studied her face and what seemed like a sincere expression. Should I feel bad for dwelling on the lawyer's past sins? Nah.

"Thanks for thinking of me, Rita, but I'm sure I don't need a lawyer. Seriously. Thank you, but no."

"You shouldn't be so hasty," Rita said, "and you should think about your sister, too."

I rolled my eyes. "I don't have a sister."

Rita reached across the table and put her hand on my arm.

I looked down at her perfect pink nails. After a few seconds, I gathered myself and met her eyes.

"What are you doing?" I said.

"I'd be happy to help you and your sister," she said. "Anything either of you said to me would be privileged."

"Read my lips," I said. "I *do not* have a sister. I don't get why you're here bothering me."

"This could become a very serious matter," Rita said. "You and Tia Hartwell are both persons of interest in the death of Calvin Fisher."

"I know the man died, but how can anyone be a person of interest at this point? No one knows what happened to the guy."

Rita sat back. "They've ruled this a murder. The deputies are looking for a killer."

Why would she be here making these things up unless she had actual facts? "Based on what?"

"Evidence found in the truck, by the body."

"What did they find?"

"I don't have all the details. They'll do an autopsy, of course. Toxicology testing. Guy might have been poisoned. You probably know the drill, being a mystery writer and all."

"Yeah, I know the drill. He could have overdosed all by himself, too. Or took meds that didn't mix with all the alcohol he drank. I don't appreciate your accusations."

"The authorities made the call, not me," Rita said. "I'm sure they have good reason. Oh, and you didn't hear any of this from me, all right?"

I tamped back my annoyance to ask another question. "How did you find out about the foul play?"

"You know me. I keep an ear to the ground."

I knew her all right, which is why I wanted her to leave.

"I don't need a criminal attorney. Even if I did—"

"You should know the news is out there about your argument with the dead man in the grocery store parking lot," she said, "not to mention the fact you were standing beside his truck this morning when he was laid out inside"—she lowered her voice and leaned in again—"dead as a doornail, pardon the cliché. With this set of circumstances, it's highly possible the family could come after you—or your, uh, Tia— for any number of reasons."

I rested my forehead in my hands, then realized Rita might interpret my posture as some admission of wrongdoing. I sat up straight and met her serious gaze.

"Your imagination is running wild, which is a good thing for a writer," I said, "but a very bad thing for a lawyer trying to drum up business. So if you'll excuse—" I paused and allowed her words to soak in a bit deeper. "Wait, you said family. What family?"

"The man had a wife and four children, three of them under the age of ten," she said. "From all reports, they are understandably devastated."

I swallowed hard, sad to learn Fisher had left a family behind. So if the guy had kids, then why was he so bothered

by the presence of little Damon at prior festivals? Assuming Tia's story was true.

"Fisher's family will arrive in Lavender by early evening," Rita said. "They asked to speak with the person who found him, among others. As your attorney, I would advise you—"

I wanted to put my fingers in my ears and sing, "La-la-la-la" to block out Rita's words. Instead, I sipped my coffee and focused on the lyrics coming through the jukebox.

I've always liked this seventies tune. I was born, born, born, born to be alive.

Thankfully, I *was* alive. Fisher wasn't so lucky. His family wanted to talk to me. Why did they think that would help? I had no answer for the question, but I knew I wouldn't be able to live with myself unless I honored their request.

9

I LEFT RITA COLLETTI sitting at Hot Stuff after telling her I had a pressing appointment. Not exactly a lie, since I felt an urgent need to meet with Sheriff Crawford. I hoped to high heaven I'd find him in his office. I wanted to know how Rita had found out so much information so quickly. Was Deputy Rosales speaking out of turn? Trying her best to drop me in the grease? That wasn't going to work out for her, since I had nothing to do with Fisher's demise.

The whole situation was preposterous. All I did was chase Hitchcock across a field and happen across a body in a truck. Not a run-of-the-mill morning, but still. End of story. Except it wasn't the end of the story. Fisher's family wanted to talk to me, for crying out loud. I had to get Sheriff Crawford's take on all this before things got totally out of hand.

Normally, I would hop in my car and drive to the building the sheriff's department shares with the Lavender Bible Church. But with the added tourist traffic and booths set up

on what seemed like every square inch of real estate, walking was more efficient.

I cut across streets and between buildings to come out behind the booths set up along the parking lot. A quick scan told me the church ladies were selling handmade quilts, homemade jams and jellies, themed decorated picture frames, and Christmas wreaths and stockings. Quite an assortment, and they had plenty of chattering potential buyers.

Aunt Rowe's friend Helen waved to me from the Christmas booth. I lifted a hand in response but didn't tarry and headed straight through the sheriff's department entrance, located toward the back half of the building. One cruiser sat outside, and I sure hoped it belonged to Sheriff Jebediah Crawford himself.

Inside, the atmosphere was considerably quieter and dimmer than the outdoors. Laurelle, the dispatcher, caught sight of me and brightened up the space with her smile.

"Hi there, Sabrina. How are y'all doing today?"

Y'all?

I looked behind me to confirm I was alone. "I'm good. Is the sheriff in?"

"You don't have to pretend with me, girl," she said. "I know you've seen better days. What a bad run of luck, finding that body."

I didn't like bad luck references, so I shrugged and looked down the corridor to the offices. "Is he in?"

"He sure is. I just brought him some lunch, but he'll be glad for you to go right on in."

I came here often enough to quiz Sheriff Crawford about crime-scene questions related to my fiction, and he seemed to enjoy his role as author advisor. I enjoyed spending time with him because of his easygoing manner, which reminded me of my late father. Aunt Rowe and the sheriff were close friends, too—more than friends, if he had his way.

Laurelle leaned forward and stretched to look over her desk to the floor. "Where's Hitchcock?"

"At home with Aunt Rowe," I said.

She frowned. "I could've sworn I just saw him not five minutes ago on my way back from the food trucks."

"I'm sure you're wrong," I said, not feeling sure at all. I hoped the slippery cat hadn't already escaped from my aunt. To ease the worry, I pulled out my phone and texted Aunt Rowe. "Is Hitchcock with you?"

She responded quickly. "Yes, sleeping on fresh laundry."

"He's at home," I told Laurelle. "Maybe you saw Hitchcock's new friend, Merlin."

"I don't know any Merlin."

"He's here for the festival," I said. "Belongs to one of the vendors."

I walked down the corridor and entered the sheriff's open doorway as he took a big bite from a barbeque sandwich. Next to the sandwich wrapping sat an assortment of other foods. Looked like take-out for five. The sheriff motioned to me and grabbed a napkin with his free hand.

"Pleasant surprise, Sabrina. C'mon in and help me out with the grub. Don't know where Laurelle thought I would put all this food. Have you eaten?"

"As a matter of fact, no," I said. "What's on the menu?"

He put his sandwich down and smoothed his Tom Selleck mustache with the napkin before unwrapping the other foods.

"Sausage on a stick, corn on the cob, sweet potato fries, and"—he paused as he picked up a piece of the last item for inspection—"I'm not sure what this is." He held up the battered curly object and sniffed. "Smells like bacon. Try a piece?"

I shook my head. "No thanks. The guy cooking that stuff is another one of my problems these days. Not the biggest one." I grabbed a fry and popped it in my mouth.

The sheriff picked up his sandwich. "Want to tell me about the highest-ranking issue and work your way down?"

"Well, you know about Calvin Fisher and that I'm the one who discovered his body."

He nodded. "Heard all about that."

In between fries and a sampling of the sausage I reported my conversation with Rita Colletti. "Who are these supposed witnesses who think that I have something to do with his death? I don't understand what they could possibly have seen me do."

The sheriff frowned. "I'm more interested in how the lawyer found out about them." He must have seen my next thought on my face. "Don't go blaming Deputy Pat for having a big mouth."

"Does she?" I said.

"Not when it comes to official business."

"How do you know this is a case that needs investigating rather than a death from natural causes?"

He kept his eyes on me as he picked up his bottle of water and took a long swallow, then took his time putting the bottle back on the desk. "You know I can't discuss a case with you, Sabrina."

"I hope Rita is completely off the mark when she's acting like I need representation."

He raised his eyebrows.

"Okay, you can't talk about the case. I get that, but I can't just leave it alone. I can't shut up and go away."

He reached for the fries, paused, and sighed. "Why does Colletti say you need a lawyer?"

"She says Fisher was murdered. Possibly poisoned."

"And I say she sounds like the one with the big mouth."

"But where did her information come from?"

"Leave it alone, Sabrina."

"But why—"

The sheriff wore his stern-father-figure expression. "Leave. It. Alone."

I picked up a french fry and swirled it in the flecks of salt in the paper tray. "New topic. Kind of."

"About?" he said.

"Fisher's family. Rita said they're coming to town."

He picked up his sandwich and took another bite.

"She says they want to talk with the person who found him, and that's me, but why?"

He swallowed before responding. "I don't have an answer, and I don't recommend you talking with them. You don't have to do it."

"Rita said they might come after me."

He nearly threw his sandwich down. "Oh, for the love of—"

"They're coming here to Lavender, like today." Panic rose in my chest. "How do they even know about me? Can you answer that? Did these witnesses—whoever they are—know Fisher's family somehow? Call them up and say, 'Guess what, Calvin's dead. You need to get right over here to Lavender. And by the way, we think we know whose fault it is'?"

"Calm down, Sabrina. We'll get to the bottom of this. I'll have a talk with Miss Colletti, for one thing."

A new thought occurred to me. What if the witnesses had seen Tia and mistaken her for me the same way Fisher had at the grocery store?

That made sense. George said Tia had been over by Fisher's truck. What had she been doing there?

I didn't like being blamed, but I didn't want to sic anyone— not the sheriff, or the family, or especially Rita Colletti—on Tia. If she was truly alone in the world supporting a son and a cat and living in her car, the poor thing had more than enough on her shoulders. I didn't want to do anything to add to her trouble. I would talk to her myself and get a read on whether she had any involvement in what happened.

I sliced off another piece of the sausage and popped it into my mouth, then made a show of checking my watch and stood.

"Oh my, I really must run."

The sheriff eyed me suspiciously. "Don't you want to tell me about your problem with the bacon-frying dude?"

"We can talk about him later," I said, "or maybe not. He makes me jumpy is all, but maybe the festival will end and

he'll go back to wherever he came from and everything will be fine. See you."

I turned and headed for the door.

"Remember one thing, Sabrina," the sheriff said.

I looked over my shoulder at him. "What is it?"

He fixed me with the all-serious father stare again. "You *do* have the right to remain silent."

10

LEFT THE SHERIFF'S office and considered going straight to my car and driving home. I could lock myself up in the Monte Carlo cottage with Hitchcock and get busy writing. Without a doubt, a good, safe option. If Fisher's family arrived in Lavender and insisted on talking with me, they'd have to jump through some hoops to find me.

If they wanted Tia, well, she was a big girl and could take care of herself. She apparently traveled to and from festivals on her own on a regular basis. From all appearances, she'd survived just fine without my help up until now.

So why was I going to Tia's booth to question her? Where had this weird feeling of responsibility—of connection—come from? I wanted to help her or at least know that I'd tried. Must be that darn impression that I was standing in front of a mirror when I looked at the woman. Growing up, I often wondered what it would be like to have a sister. Now people were assuming Tia and I *were* sisters and that felt odd and nice at the same time.

I picked up my pace, eager to have a conversation if she wasn't too busy with customers. I was usually a pretty good judge of character, but I could possibly learn Tia wasn't the quiet and innocent type she appeared to be, which sure would be a shame for little Damon's sake.

I passed the small stage, where the band was playing a polka I couldn't put a name to. I slowed my pace as I approached the artist's booth. No crowd of customers at the moment, a perfect time for the two of us to talk. But as I peered around the corner of a display wall, I noticed the closed back hatch of the green car. Tia, Damon, and Merlin were nowhere in sight.

"They went to grab a bite of lunch," said a stout, fortyish woman at the next booth. "I'm watchin' her stuff, so if you see somethin' you wanna buy, I can help. You want your picture painted, you'll have to wait for her to get back."

"Thanks," I said with a smile.

The woman stood behind a table of colorful fabric place mats and other table accessories. Her hair was a mass of tight reddish curls and she wore large-framed turquoise glasses. I walked in her direction and noticed her eyes widening.

"My, my, you sure do look a lot like Tia. You must be a relation."

I shrugged. "Not that I know of, but maybe a distant cousin. How long ago did they leave?"

"Twenty minutes, maybe. I offered to pick lunch up for them since I was over there a good hour ago—'cause for me it doesn't matter what else is goin' on, when it's time to eat, I have to eat—but she said no, that they would go and check out the food themselves. Sure waited a long time, though, and with that little one of hers so quiet and patient, even though I knew he had to be hungry as a lion. But they finally went, with that kitty of theirs trailing after like a little shadow the way he does." She glanced at her watch, then offered a

hand. "Hi, I'm Lorene Pilsner. Like the beer, though I don't drink the stuff. Never acquired the taste."

I felt like I needed to gasp for breath after listening to her. "Good to meet you, Lorene. I'm Sabrina Tate."

Her smile broadened when I introduced myself. "Are you Sabrina Tate, the author?"

"Well, I do write. I—"

"Ohmigod, it's so excitin' to meet you. When is your book comin' out? I *love* to read, and I'm really lookin' forward to it, even though I spend most of my time sewin' things like this." She swooshed her arm toward the table. "Readin' is my next-to-favorite pastime, especially when it's one of those books that keeps me up till the wee hours. Is your book one of them?"

"I think it's a page-turner, but I'm still waiting on an offer from a publisher."

Her brows lifted nearly to her hairline. "Oh, you'll get one. The bookstore lady, Tyanne, told me all about your book. I visit her first thing every time I come to Lavender. She fills me in on the latest and greatest books, and I stock up enough of 'em to last me the next half year or so. She says you're a wonderful writer. And if she says so, then I believe it wholeheartedly, and you should, too."

"Thanks. I'm keeping my fingers crossed." I looked around but didn't see any sign of Tia, and I turned back to Lorene. As talkative as this woman was, she might be able to tell me more about Tia.

"Say, do you go to a lot of these festivals?" I said.

"Sure." Lorene smiled. "All the way from Amarillo to Brownwood, El Paso to Corpus Christi. The Hill Country's my favorite, though, and of course I can't go to *all* of them every year. Texas is *way* too big, so I have to alternate."

"Sounds like you cover quite a distance. I'm surprised you have time to sew or read at all."

"I do a lot of the hand stitchin' right here." She indicated

her chair and an upside-down box that served as a counter for her supplies, then she noticed a woman who appeared to be checking for a price. "Eight dollars apiece," she said, "four for twenty-eight."

The customer smiled and kept browsing. Lorene turned her attention back to me.

"I guess you know Tia from other festivals?" I said.

"Oh, sure, ever since this past spring." She pushed her turquoise glasses higher on her nose and studied me like a mother who suddenly realized she should be more protective of her child. "Why do you ask?"

I was glad to know Tia had someone looking out for her. "Guess it's the mystery writer in me. Naturally curious, especially when there's someone who looks so much like me."

She paused for a moment and seemed to accept my reasoning. "I try and watch out for them best I can. They're all alone in this world, bein' as Damon's daddy skedaddled the minute he learned Damon was comin'. That's just so wrong."

"I totally agree." My heart went out to the little boy, living without a father and moving from festival to festival. Did Tia ever stay put long enough for Damon to make a friend?

"She makes a livin' best she can," Lorene said, "but I've told Tia more'n once that her talent could take her places bigger'n any ol' festival. Granted, she'd probably have to settle in a big city to find the right spot, and I don't blame her if she doesn't want to raise Damon in such a place."

I wondered about relatives and family trees and whether any of Tia's branches could possibly be connected to mine.

"Where are they from?" I said.

"Lampasas, she told me. Lil' ol' place with not much more'n six thousand souls. Don't blame her for not stayin' there, though they *do* have a fair every year from what I hear. Haven't checked that one out yet."

"Where do they live now?"

"I'm not sure as she wants anybody to know," Lorene

said. "I think they move around a lot, and she homeschools her boy. It's more'n I could tackle, believe you me, but she says it's easier than you'd think. Tia keeps to herself mostly, but even so sometimes the nasties come out and try to cause her trouble."

"You mean men like Calvin Fisher?"

Lorene nodded fervently. "*Exactly* like him, though I understand she won't need to worry herself about that man anymore. Nastiness probably caused him a big ol' heart attack. Can't say I'm gonna miss seein' him around."

"Why do you think he was so nasty to Tia?"

"Oh Lord, that man had a temper just wouldn't quit. Every time little Damon went anywhere near his place he threw a complete fit, but you know how little boys love to run and play and hide. And maybe, just maybe, the man coulda put up with that, but he wasn't gonna stand Merlin bein' anywhere near him for a second."

"He didn't like cats?"

"It was more'n that. He was *afraid* of that cat, but Merlin didn't care one bit. He'd jump up on that jewelry display just as soon as he'd jump up here to check out my place mats. I do believe he was on my table today when I wasn't lookin'. I swear I got every stray hair off first thing this mornin' but there's more." She leaned over to pick a piece of hair off the tablecloth.

"Sounds like Fisher was a superstitious guy."

"Maybe, but it don't make one lick of sense that he's afraid of a cat and not that man he was always hangin' with."

"You mean Axle?"

"Yes," she said. "Scares me just to look at him."

"What's the guy's last name?"

She thought for a moment. "Can't say as I ever heard a last name."

"Did Axle also give Tia a hard time?"

She shrugged. "Never saw him as much as talk to her. That Calvin, though, he was always yellin'. '*Keep your kid*

away from me.' 'Lock your cat up or I'll take care of him myself.'"

"Jeez, he sounds awful, like the kind of man who should never have kids of his own."

Lorene shrugged. "Heard he had kin over in Austin. Never saw 'em."

With Austin less than two hundred miles away, Fisher's family would arrive before dinner, a fact that gave me a deadline for heading home.

"Calvin tried to tell Tia where she was allowed to go and where she was not," Lorene said. "Like he could make her stay away from every festival he planned on attendin'. Like he had dibs on 'em."

"Like someone died and made him boss," I said.

"Exactly." Lorene gave a curt nod. "And now look who died."

Lorene's customer approached with a selection of products, ready to make her purchases. The woman had given me so much information, I felt almost dizzy. "Nice chatting with you," I said. "I'm going to see if I can catch up with Tia."

I strolled the food truck aisles, careful to dodge the deep-fried bacon truck run by Gabe Brenner, but I didn't see Tia, Damon, or their cat anywhere. We could have crossed paths and they might already be headed back to their home base. I thought about what Lorene told me and figured Luke could be right about the little family living in their car. I couldn't help but wonder what circumstances would lead a person to make that kind of decision—or to settle for that kind of life.

I rounded a corner, my mind off on fictional tangents about Tia's life, and noticed Cecil Moser in front of the salt-and-pepper-shaker booth waving his arms.

"Sabrina," he called. "Over here."

I'd forgotten the black-cat shakers Winnie wanted to show me, though I meant to return and buy them. Is that what he was worked up about? I hurried over to the man.

"Have you seen my wife?" he said, worry lines creasing his forehead.

"No, but I was looking for Tia and Damon, not Winnie. What's going on?"

"I saw Tia and the boy heading for the food a while back," he said. "Winnie was already gone then. She likes to slip away for a smoke. Thinks I don't know what she's up to, but of course I do. And she won't quit, no matter what I say. I just wish she wouldn't be so long about it."

"She's probably chatting with someone and the time got away from her," I said, then followed his gaze across the aisle.

Henry Schmidt stood talking with Axle at the jewelry booth. Women browsed and held pieces up to the light for inspection. One of them handed an item to Axle with some cash, and he bagged her purchase.

"I'm surprised to see the jewelry booth open," I said to Cecil. "I assume you heard about Calvin Fisher."

He nodded gravely. "I did, and that kind of news makes me worry more about my Winnie."

"I'm sure she's fine." I patted his arm. "If I see her, I'll send her back here pronto."

"Bless you," he said before turning his attention to browsers at his table.

I passed the jewelry booth and eyed Schmidt and Axle, who seemed oblivious to my presence. The fact that Axle had the place open for business made me think he and Fisher must not have been very close. I was equally surprised that Schmidt didn't have some rule against Axle running a place that had initially belonged to Fisher. Or maybe he did have a rule, and that's what the men were discussing. I couldn't help but wonder what Schmidt and Fisher would have discussed if their early morning meeting had happened as planned. Maybe Axle was covering that ground with Schmidt.

Leave it, Sabrina. Not your problem.

I was still trying to turn my focus away from the men

when I spotted Tia and Damon wending their way down the aisle toward me. Then a streak of black hurtled ahead of them. The cat dodged people, flew by me, and leapt up on the jewelry display.

Dear Lord, don't let it be Hitchcock.

It wasn't Hitchcock, but I didn't feel any better about the fact that Merlin was now being swatted at by both Axle and Schmidt. Tia and Damon were running full tilt toward the scene, but I couldn't bear to watch another second and ran to intervene.

"Stop that right now." I jumped up to the table and stuck an arm between the men and cat. "You should be ashamed of yourselves."

Merlin batted at a row of bracelets and stared at Axle with a ha-ha-you-can't-get-me expression.

"I'm not Cal, and I'm not scared of any blasted black cat," Axle growled. "I know how to get rid of 'em."

I met his dark gaze. "Don't you dare touch this cat." I put a hand out for Merlin. "Come on, boy. Let's get you out of here."

Merlin ignored me and jumped to the ground. Tia and Damon reached us, and the boy scooped Merlin up.

"The rules state very clearly," Herr Schmidt said, "only service animals are allowed in the rented spaces."

"I don't give a flip what your rules say," I said and turned to Tia. "We don't need to listen to this."

"Who's gonna fix this mess?" Axle said.

I smiled at him. "I think you are." I put a hand on Tia's arm. "Let's get out of here."

She walked with me and Damon kept pace, holding Merlin tight. "He won't get my cat, will he?" the little boy said.

"No, honey," Tia said. "We'll put him in his carrier, and he'll be fine."

Damon glanced over his shoulder. "That man was awful mad."

"Not quite as mad as his friend used to be," Tia said under her breath.

I looked at her. "Fisher?"

She nodded.

"I need to talk to you about him."

She stopped walking. "Why?"

"I've heard some things. You and I may both be questioned about his death."

Her eyes flicked to her son, who had stopped a few yards ahead when he realized we weren't with him.

"I don't know anything about that," she said.

"A man told me he saw you near Fisher's truck this morning."

"I don't even know his truck, so how would I know if I was near it?"

"You wouldn't, but you *were* there according to a witness, over in the field where people are parking." I paused to look her in the eye. "Were you over in the field?"

"I went looking for Damon, not for that man."

"This morning?"

"Yes. Damon was playing with this little kite he made. He felt a good breeze, and he went over to the field. Except I didn't know where he went, so I was frantic."

Damon had walked over to us and heard his mother's last statement.

"I'm sorry, Mama," he said.

"It's okay now." She put her hand on his head and ruffled his hair.

The gesture struck me as achingly familiar. Dad had done the same to me countless times when I was a kid, then teased me when my curls got so tangled together we could barely drag a brush through them.

"I need to go to work," Tia said.

"Can we talk? Later?"

"After the festival maybe," she said.

People walked by, some slowly to look at us with curiosity, and I wondered how many assumed we were related. I studied Tia's hair, her brow, the shape of her face.

And knew why I felt so connected to this stranger.

She reminded me of my father. People had always told me I favored him, and Tia favored me.

We both favored Dad.

Was it possible we were both related to him?

"What is it?" Tia said.

I shook myself to stop my runaway imagination. Too much was happening for me to focus on this personal emotional issue right now. I had to save it for later.

"Fisher's family is headed to town," I told Tia. "People saw each of us arguing with him. His family will ask questions. Do you happen to know any of them?"

"I don't," she said. "I never saw him with anyone but that one." She threw a hand toward the jewelry booth and Axle.

"What's Axle's last name?"

"Never heard one," she said.

"The sheriff will get to the bottom of whatever happened. I don't want either one of us falsely accused of anything."

"Neither do I," she said.

I looked at her and tried not to imagine Dad in her features. "We have enough food for an army over at the cottages. You could come to my place."

"And see Hitchcock?" Damon said.

I smiled. "Merlin and Hitchcock can have a playdate. If you like, I could take Merlin home with me now. Don't know about you, but I'd feel better with him far away from Axle."

Tia eyed me thoughtfully, and I expected her to turn me down. She looked at Damon and the cat for a moment.

"Yes, that's a good plan," she said. "Damon, honey, Miss Sabrina will keep Merlin for us until tonight."

Damon smiled at his mother and handed over the cat. "Thank you."

11

M Y NATURAL CURIOSITY might have kept me at the festival, where I could ask more questions of more people, but little Damon had entrusted me with his precious cat. Taking care of Merlin took priority. Twenty minutes after leaving the festival with him, I pulled into the Around-the-World Cottages driveway. The cat, in his carrier on the passenger seat, had settled down within the first few minutes of the drive and was a well-behaved companion. Interesting that I had sent Aunt Rowe home with my black cat, and now I was headed home with a second black cat. I could see myself becoming a crazy cat lady someday. If Merlin ever needed a home, I'd probably volunteer to give him one. Spend my hours playing with cats instead of doing the work I needed to do.

While I left the festival behind, my questions came home with me. Who were Tia's parents? I wondered. I didn't seriously think the woman was related to me, even though her

resemblance to Dad was what drew me to her. That's all it was, really, a resemblance.

"Your mama looks a bit like me," I said to the cat, "that's all. No sense making a big deal out of a coincidence." I kept my left hand on the steering wheel as I coasted along the drive and poked the fingers of my right hand through the carrier's wire door to scratch the cat's head. Felt him rub against them. "We'll go to my place and see if Hitchcock's hanging around. He'll be excited to see you."

In a good way, I hoped.

I made the bend approaching Aunt Rowe's house. With most of the people staying here this week at the festival, the grounds were quiet. A strange SUV sat in the driveway parked next to Aunt Rowe's car. It was after three, a common time for new guests to check in, but I didn't think we had any vacancies. Could be one of Aunt Rowe's friends got a new car. It looked expensive. Shiny. Slick.

I drove to my place and took Merlin's carrier inside. Placed it on the living room floor. Since no curious cat came running to greet us, I figured Hitchcock was out roaming. He might have still been asleep on Aunt Rowe's laundry.

"Hitchcock, you home?" I checked the bedroom and the back deck and didn't find the cat. I set up a makeshift litter box for Merlin and put it, along with food and water bowls, in my bedroom, then took him into the room and closed the door.

"We'll keep you in a safe spot until Tia and Damon come over later." I hoped to high heaven we wouldn't hear anything from Fisher's relatives. Best-case scenario, the family would get every speck of information they wanted from the sheriff or his deputies.

I knelt on the floor to open the crate and Merlin tentatively poked his head out. He lifted his nose and sniffed the air.

"Hitchcock lives here, but he's not home right now," I said. "You remember Hitchcock."

Merlin walked to me and rubbed against my thigh. "Mrr."
I stroked his back. "Good boy. You can make yourself comfy here."

He went to a basket in the corner and batted at Hitchcock's catnip mouse, but I'd bet he would go to sleep if I left him alone for a while. I slipped out and closed the bedroom door behind me. The laptop seemed to call to me from the kitchen table that served as my desk.

You should be writing.

If I went to find Hitchcock, I'd get sidetracked. I knew myself too well. Since it wasn't time for dinner yet, I couldn't use eating as an excuse for not writing. I sure did miss baking, though, and since most everyone was at the festival, maybe I could make enough room in Aunt Rowe's kitchen to bake something before they got back.

Write first.

I sat at the computer and pulled up my work in progress. Read the last page I'd written. For some reason the scene reminded me that I had meant to go back to Eddie Baxter's tent and finish giving him a piece of my mind about his good luck charms, even though it wouldn't change anything. What did I expect him to do? Close down his grand money-making scheme just because I didn't like it? That would never happen, so I might as well swallow the aggravation and dwell on the fact that the festival would end in a few days and the tent would disappear. I'd have to figure out what to do, just in case Eddie planned to rent a booth again next year.

I was having a harder time getting over Rita's insistence that I needed a lawyer. Where the heck did she get her information? The sheriff didn't think Rosales had gossiped about me, but he could be wrong. Or maybe Rita personally knew that man—George—who saw me by Fisher's truck. She might have run into him, heard the news, linked me to the murder, and poof—Sabrina needs a lawyer and I'm her woman.

Yeah, right.

I pushed aside the reality of the day and delved into my fictional world. Over the next hour I managed to write three new pages. Better than nothing, but now I felt concerned about Hitchcock and eager to try out a new recipe I'd found. Maybe I could get Tia to tell me more about herself and her family tonight over a nice plate of pumpkin brownies and a pot of fresh coffee.

I reread the new pages, deemed them acceptable, and saved the document. I got up and checked my refrigerator to make sure I had milk on hand to offer Damon, then headed to Aunt Rowe's house on foot.

The sun was still high in the sky though the gorgeous fall day would soon begin to wind down. The grounds around the cottages were quiet but for birds chirping in the trees and the rushing Glidden River. The shiny car was gone from Aunt Rowe's driveway. Hers was there, but no doubt she'd be on her way back to the festival soon for the pumpkin cannon event.

I went in through the back door and into the kitchen. The place was less cluttered than the last time I was there, so I thought I should be able to clear the space to bake brownies. I'd use canned pumpkin for a shortcut. Aunt Rowe would probably be happy to take my fresh pumpkins to shoot out of the cannon.

Glenda came into the kitchen from the living room and her brows rose.

"Sabrina. Didn't expect you."

"Hey, Glenda. Is Hitchcock over here?"

"With Rowe in her office." She made a beeline for the laundry room.

"You mind if I bake some brownies?" I called after her.

"Suit yourself," she said.

Glenda was putting up with a lot due to all the extra people around, and I didn't want to add to her aggravation. I followed her and found her folding towels from the dryer.

"If you'd rather that I not make an extra mess in the kitchen, I can survive without baking."

"No, you're fine," she said without looking at me.

I stepped in closer to see her troubled expression. "What's the matter?"

"Just go on and bake," she said.

"C'mon. What's bothering you?"

"Heard about the dead man," Glenda said.

"And?"

"I'm just saying, your day got off to a bad start."

"Yeah, and the day didn't get any better." I told her about Rita Colletti visiting with me at the coffee shop.

Glenda shook her head. "Bless your heart." She picked up the pile of towels and headed for the bedrooms. "Go on and bake. You'll feel better."

I watched her go and wondered why she was acting so on edge. Had to be the festival hoopla. I shrugged and went back to the kitchen. Cleared a three-foot length of counter, got out a mixing bowl, and noticed Hitchcock strolling into the room.

"Hi, buddy." I bent to cup his head in my hands. Normally, he would respond to that with a meow, but he shifted out of my grasp and prowled around the kitchen table.

"What's wrong, boy?" Maybe he'd gone to our cottage and smelled the other cat inside, but Glenda said he'd been in Aunt Rowe's office. I gave him a scratch on the head and straightened.

"After I whip up a quick batch of brownies, we'll go home. Tia and Damon are coming over tonight."

"Who are Tia and Damon?"

I swung my head around and couldn't disguise my shock at the sight of the woman standing in the doorway with one elegantly manicured hand poised on the door frame. Now I understood what was going on with Glenda.

After two seconds, I closed my gaping mouth, then managed, "Mom. What on earth are you doing here?"

12

"I CAN'T COME TO visit my daughter every once in a blue moon?" Mom said. "Otherwise, I'd never see you."

Brenda Flowers Harrison hated the quaint little town of Lavender, Texas, and always had. Looking back to my childhood, I clearly remembered Mom's snippy discussions with Dad about visits to see his family in the Hill Country. I believed she would want to see me, but not so much that she'd make a trip to what she considered the boondocks to do so.

"I visited you on Mother's Day," I said.

"It's October," she said.

I wondered how many countries she had traveled to in the intervening months.

"Are you on your way home from a trip?" I took out the flour canister and removed the lid. "Where was the latest? Hong Kong? Caracas?"

She sighed. "Hong Kong was months ago. Why can't you believe we just came here to visit with you?"

For one thing, you're standing in Aunt Rowe's house. For you, that's way beyond the pale and—wait, did you say "we"?

"Dave's with you?" I said.

My stepfather was managing partner of the law firm where I had worked in Houston. I hoped to high heaven he wasn't going to give me the come-back-to-the-firm-we-need-you speech. Again.

"He is." She moved into the room, and I met her halfway. We exchanged our usual light hug, pat on the back, kiss on the cheek. Not the most heartfelt greeting, but Mom didn't like her hair mussed or her clothes wrinkled. Today she wore what looked like a lime green silk tunic with dark gray slacks and expensive-looking silver sandals. Her dark bob was slightly flipped on the ends, and silver earrings dangled below her hairline.

Hitchcock peered cautiously at my mother from beneath a kitchen chair. Reacting to Mom's anti-pet vibes.

I went back to the counter and pulled up the recipe app on my phone. Checked the directions for mixing the brownies. I thought about the slick car I'd seen in the driveway earlier. Ostentatious, just like Mom and Dave. I wondered where the car was now and whether they intended to stay longer than a few hours. Surely not.

"So where *is* Dave?" I said.

Aunt Rowe hurried into the kitchen and went straight to the refrigerator. "Visiting with your favorite person," she said.

I put my phone down. "And that would be who?"

"The lawyer," Aunt Rowe said.

Mom said, "I still can't believe Rita is willing to live out here in the middle of nowhere."

"She saw the light." Aunt Rowe took a single-serving bottle of peach tea out and unscrewed the lid. "People do if they give it a chance. Sabrina did."

I smiled. "I always knew I'd love it here. Finally got up my nerve to make the move."

"Nerve for what?" Mom said. "To escape from me?"

"I didn't say that."

"Give it a rest, Brenda." Aunt Rowe took a swig of the tea. "Sabrina's happy here, and you shouldn't try to ruin that."

"And you shouldn't lord it over me that you finally got your way and convinced her to move," Mom said. "There are wonderful places in the city she would love as well, if she'd give them a chance. She could work on her little hobby there just as well as here."

I felt my blood pressure shoot up at the condescending statement.

"Mrrreeooow," Hitchcock howled.

Mom looked down at the cat. "What is *wrong* with that animal?"

Aunt Rowe smirked. "He didn't like what you said."

"He's a cat," Mom said.

I went over to Hitchcock and bent to pat him on the head. "He's my cat, and he understands more than you think he does."

More than you do.

Mom waved a dismissive hand.

"I'll have you know Sabrina is well on her way to being published," Aunt Rowe said, "so you'd better get used to her success and just hope she doesn't put you in a book." She looked at me. "She'd make a danged good character, don't you think?"

I suppressed a grin.

"I guess you think you know my daughter better than I do," Mom said.

Aunt Rowe bypassed the chance to comment and scanned the baking ingredients I'd assembled. "What's cooking?"

"Pumpkin brownies," I said.

"Good grief," Mom said. "That doesn't even sound good."

I shrugged. "Matter of opinion."

Aunt Rowe said, "Testing recipes for the contest?"

I shook my head. "Not necessarily." I didn't feel like getting into a big discussion about whether or not I'd enter the baking contest. I wanted to know what Mom was up to.

"Is someone going to tell me why you're really here?" I looked from Mom to Aunt Rowe and back.

"I need to run," Aunt Rowe said. "Pumpkin cannon starts at six. You coming to watch, Sabrina?"

"Um, no. I have other plans."

"Dinner with me and Dave," Mom said. "That would be wonderful, darling."

I looked at her. "No. I have *other* plans. I couldn't have planned for dinner with you since I didn't even know you were coming. And I don't believe you came all the way to Lavender for one little dinner. What's going on?"

"I'll leave you two to chat," Aunt Rowe said, picking up her purse.

When the back door closed behind her I looked at Mom. "Spill."

"Why don't you join me and Dave for dinner this evening?" Mom said. "We can have a nice civil discussion."

"About what?" I said, not cutting her any slack. "Spit it out, Mom, or I'll leave right now."

Mom huffed. "You seem to have lost your manners, Sabrina."

I rolled my eyes. "Please tell me what you and Dave would like to discuss," I said. "I'm a busy woman, and I need to plan my schedule accordingly."

Mom said, "You remind me of your father."

"And I'll consider that a compliment."

Hitchcock came out from under the chair and leapt to the wide windowsill by the table. Mom waved a hand frantically to ward off cat hair that floated in the air like dust motes. Hitchcock sat and stared at Mom.

She moved to the farthest side of the table and pulled out a kitchen chair. She sat and kicked off her shoes.

"These heels are killing me."

I waited.

"It would be really great if you could come to Houston for another visit," she said. "We have some special events coming up, and there's a wonderful man I'd love for you to meet."

Is this what all the secrecy was about? She wanted to set me up?

"His name is Marshall Cortland," she went on, "and you will adore him."

I shook my head. "I'm involved with someone, Mom. I'm not interested."

"Oh." She studied my face as if trying to gauge whether I was telling the truth or not. "Who is he?"

"It's early in our relationship. He's a special friend, but I'd rather not get into details with you."

"That sounds like you're not serious about this gentleman."

"No—I mean, yes, I am serious. I'd rather not have him held up to family scrutiny just yet, that's all."

Mom lifted her chin. "Does Rowe know this man?"

I sighed and flicked my gaze heavenward. "Yes, but only because she lives here."

"He's a *local*?" Mom's voice dripped with disdain.

"Cut the snooty attitude," I said. "That's exactly why I don't want to discuss him."

"Can you tell me his name?"

"I'd rather not." I felt sure Luke could handle the likes of Brenda Harrison, but I wasn't ready to go there.

"Oh, for heaven's sake," Mom said.

I was beginning to think meeting with Calvin Fisher's family would be preferable to enduring this talk with my own mother.

After a few seconds of silence, she seemed to accept that I wasn't going to budge. She checked her Rolex watch. "Dave is coming by shortly, and we truly do have something to discuss with you. Something else."

"Go ahead and tell me. Save us all some time."

"Sabrina, please. You're using that tone I thought you outgrew at eighteen."

I blew out a breath. "Okay. I'm sorry." My desire to bake brownies had disintegrated, so I pulled out a chair across from her and sat.

"Dave has decided to run for a judgeship."

The change of topic came as a surprise, but I didn't see what it had to do with me. "Okay."

"He's working with a campaign manager, and they're discussing details. Marketing, polling, and whatnot."

"Why are you telling me this?"

"One of the things they want to do—soon—is family portraits."

I raised my palms. "I'm not Dave's family."

Mom pursed her lips. "Yes, you are."

"Whatever, but that would be nearly impossible to accomplish unless he's going to Photoshop us all into one picture. His kids still live in Michigan?"

"To the best of my knowledge, yes."

"Have you talked with Nick about this?"

My brother and his wife and kids lived in Houston, in closer proximity to Mom and Dave than he'd like.

"Not yet."

"Is this what you were discussing with Aunt Rowe?"

Mom shook her head. "I'm certainly not inviting Rowe to be in our picture."

I had never known Mom and Aunt Rowe to spend more than five minutes together in a room, and even then they were surrounded by others, not alone. "What were you and Aunt Rowe talking about then?"

"Old times," Mom said.

"Uh-huh."

Before I could say more, there was a knock at the back door.

Hitchcock jumped down from his perch and trotted in that direction. I stood.

"Hold on, buddy." I followed the cat. "Don't go trying to slip out on me."

I lowered my voice as I scooped up Hitchcock. "You need to stick around here for moral support."

"Mrreow," he said as I opened the door.

Gabe Brenner stood there in a pair of greasy jeans with a sweat-stained red T-shirt. The scent of bacon clung to him. He held a bouquet of pink roses out to me. "For you, Sabrina. Figured you'd be celebratin' tonight."

I frowned. What the heck was he talking about?

"Celebrating what?" Mom said, behind me.

Gabe chuckled. "Sabrina didn't share the news? She's rid of one big headache. The troublemaker's dead. That's good news, right?"

He said it proudly, almost as if he was bragging. A chill ran up my back as I stared at him.

Mom put a hand on her chest. "Sabrina, what's this, this man talking about?"

"There was an incident," I said.

"Man was after her," Gabe said. "Now he ain't."

Mom looked at me, aghast. "Sabrina, please, in the name of all that's holy, please tell me this man isn't your"—she lowered her voice to a whisper—"special friend."

13

I DIDN'T WANT TO say anything that would upset Gabe, especially if he'd disposed of Fisher. Is that what he meant? I wasn't sure what the heck to make of the man's statement, and I couldn't respond to Mom's insinuation about my relationship with Gabe by saying what I thought—*Are you out of your ever-loving mind?* Instead, I made a simple introduction.

"Brenda, this is Gabe. Gabe, Brenda."

Better if the man didn't know that she and I were related.

I turned to Mom. "I met Gabe Wednesday when he checked into the Melbourne cottage. He runs one of the food trucks."

"Oh," Mom said.

"I deep-fry bacon," Gabe said. "Wanna try some?"

Mom managed a pained smile. "No, thank you. I have—rather, *we* have—a dinner engagement. My husband will arrive to pick us up any second now, but thank you so much for the lovely flowers."

She took the roses from Gabe. "Good-bye now."

She shut the door. Impressive how she had smoothly cut off his conversation. I'd have to remember this the next time I wanted to get rid of someone.

She turned to me. "What trouble was he referring to?"

Telling her the whole story would only restart the you-need-to-move-back-to-Houston conversation. Hitchcock sat on the floor near my feet, and he looked to me as if waiting for the answer, even though he had been right there with me when I found Fisher's body.

Traitor.

"It's a long story," I told Mom. "You should forget you ever saw that man."

"I certainly wish I could," she said, "but you can't unring that bell. I'll go put these in water. Then you can explain."

She walked into the kitchen, and I considered escaping before she returned. I had no intention of going to dinner with her and Dave and hoped she said that only to get Gabe to back off and leave me alone.

I looked down at Hitchcock. "What do you make of this whole mess?"

"Mrreow," he said.

"Yeah, me, too." I walked into the kitchen. Mom had arranged the roses in a Mason jar that sat on the crowded counter by the sink. Hitchcock fidgeted on the floor nearby. I could tell he wanted to jump up there and get after the flowers, if only he could find a spare inch to land on.

"I'm guessing you don't care to take the roses to your place," Mom said.

"Absolutely not."

Something so pretty delivered with such a disturbing message. *Man was after her. Now he ain't.* Words spoken with a note of what? Pride? Victory?

You're reading too much into this.

Mom's phone buzzed, and she pulled it from her pocket and checked the screen. "Dave is two minutes away," she

said. "We're having dinner in Emerald Springs with a colleague of his."

So she wasn't going to pressure me into going with them. Good. I was only mildly curious about what colleague Dave had up here in the Hill Country.

"Heading home after dinner?" I said.

"No, we'll stay the night at the Hyatt. Now, you were going to explain."

I gave her the really short version of Fisher's death. A man died of unknown causes and was found in his truck. Gabe hadn't liked the dead man and called him a troublemaker.

She gasped. "Do you think he killed him?"

"All I know for sure is he punched the guy in the face yesterday when he thought the man was bothering me." I shrugged. "I have no idea if he did anything more. That's up to the sheriff to figure out."

"If anyone can solve a case, I'm sure Jebediah Crawford can," she said. "You should come with us, though, and stay out of this Gabe character's way. Just to be safe."

"I'm safe here, Mom. Don't worry."

A horn honked, and she looked toward the drive. "That Dave. I've told him time and again, it's impolite to honk the horn when picking up a lady." She checked her watch. "I'm sure he's worried about being late for dinner." She gave me a quick hug. "Unless you'll come with us, I'll check back to make sure you're all right."

She wouldn't take me to dinner with a colleague of Dave's unless I had a total makeover in the next two minutes. "I'm staying here, Mom."

After a dramatic sigh, she swept out the door. Though I felt relieved at her departure, I wished I'd asked her more questions. For instance, had she really come all the way to Lavender simply to say hello and ask me to pose in a family campaign photo? Or to tell me about Marshall Cortland?

She could have done either one by phone. The itch between my shoulder blades told me she had another motive for the visit.

I looked back into the kitchen and saw Hitchcock perched on the narrow windowsill above the sink with his nose in the flowers.

I clapped my hands, and he looked at me.

"Let's go find Thomas. I'll feel better with another set of eyes watching out for Gabe."

"Mrreow," Hitchcock said.

"Yes, the man who smells like bacon."

We left the house and walked across the grounds to the maintenance building. Thomas used half of the structure for his grounds-keeping equipment, while Glenda kept a stock-room for cottage supplies in the other half. Hitchcock ran in ahead of me and darted toward the big commercial riding mower. He loved to sit in the driver's seat. I didn't see Thomas, and I entered the stockroom to look for him. Floor-to-ceiling cupboards lined one wall and held soaps, towels, paper products, and coffee setups. Thomas stood in front of the refrigerator, from which he pulled out a bottled water.

He saw me as he twisted the top on the bottle. "Is the coast clear?"

"If you mean is my mother off the premises, then yes. Dave picked her up and they're headed to Emerald Springs for dinner."

"Sorry, Miss Sabrina. Don't take it personal. You know I have some history with that woman." Thomas ran a hand through his dark hair.

He'd grown up in the area and worked for Aunt Rowe practically his whole life. I knew Mom treated him like a second-class citizen.

"No offense taken," I said. "Yes, Mom's gone, but Hitchcock is here."

"Sitting on the mower again?"

I grinned. "Yup. How'd you guess?"

"Darned cat tries to freak me out, poppin' up where I least expect him, but I'm gettin' used to him."

I smiled, happy to hear Thomas talk about Hitchcock without mentioning the bad luck cat legend. A few months ago that never would have happened. "Can't help but like the little fella, huh?"

"I'm workin' on it," Thomas said. "What brings you out here?"

"I have an issue with one of the guests." I told him about Gabe's disturbing words. "He brought me flowers, and he's really giving me the willies. I'd appreciate it if you could keep an eye on him when you're here."

"Gladly," he said. "I'll add him to the mile-long problem list."

"What else is on the list?"

"The festival used to be laid-back. Peaceful. Fun. Not anymore."

"What's different?"

"Different times," he said. "We have Rowena and the cannon for one thing. I don't like her standin' so close when the thing goes off. She's asking for trouble."

"I agree. Can you make her listen to reason?"

"What do you think?" He raised his brows. "Schmidt tellin' her to get rid of the cannon only makes her more determined to keep it."

I nodded, letting him blow off steam.

"Now there's a dead man and evidence of foul play, and one of our guests might have killed him. It's too much."

"Wait, wait," I said. "What evidence?"

Thomas shrugged. "Heard talk about evidence found in the truck. Like something that didn't belong to Fisher."

"The killer left it behind?"

"Maybe." He took a long drink of water and wiped his mouth with the back of his hand.

"Any rumors about his cause of death?"

"Haven't heard any."

"How about someone who wanted him dead? Besides, apparently, Gabe Brenner."

"There's the woman."

My heart jumped. I didn't want to hear gossip about Tia. Too much gossip in the wrong ears might put her at the top of the suspect list.

"What woman?" I said.

"One in Barcelona. Lady with the face stuff."

I paused to steady my breathing. I remembered Britt. She'd commented about giving Fisher a facial containing cyanide. "I knew she didn't like him, but that's a far cry from actually killing a man."

"People do crazy things," Thomas said. "I'll keep an eye on Brenner."

"I appreciate that." I checked my watch. "I'm expecting company anytime now. Tia Hartwell and her little boy, Damon."

"The woman who favors you?" he said.

"Yes."

"I saw them yesterday." Thomas seemed less than enthusiastic. "They have a black cat, too."

"Now don't you worry about Merlin," I said. "He's in the Monte Carlo cottage as we speak. Already been here for a few hours, and we haven't had a stroke of bad luck, right?"

Thomas raised his eyebrows. "You already forget your mama's visit?"

"Ha-ha."

A round of laughter and whistling sounded outside, followed by the pop of firecrackers.

"I'd better get out there," Thomas said, "and try to keep the peace. One troublemaker may be gone, but we have plenty of others ready to take his place."

14

T HE EXPECTED KNOCK at my door came a little after seven. I'd asked Glenda to point Tia in the right direction when she arrived. I peered out a front window to make sure it was her and not Gabe before opening the door.

We exchanged hellos. Damon spotted Merlin playing with Hitchcock and darted into the cottage to see the cats.

I smiled at Tia. "C'mon in. Make yourself at home."

"Thanks." She came in and looked around. "Your place is adorable." She walked to the fireplace and ran her hand across the mantel, then looked at me. "I could sure make myself at home here."

"I know, right? It'd be a bit small for the two of you, though."

Damon looked up from the floor where he had already entranced the two cats. "Three of us."

I laughed. "Three. How could I forget Merlin?"

"I don't want to take up your time." Tia's expression turned serious. "You wanted to discuss something."

"Yes, but first, are y'all hungry? I have a load of food here. As much as this little fridge could hold." I'd brought food from Aunt Rowe's to prepare for their visit.

Tia looked hesitant, but Damon got up from the floor.

"My aunt bought a lot to feed festival vendors and you're one of them. As usual, she overdid herself. I'll show you what I have."

I took out sandwich fixings, potato salad, coleslaw, and a loaf of jalapeño cheese bread, then urged them to make themselves at home. While I filled glasses with sweet tea, they took turns using the bathroom to wash up. We fixed our plates, squished together around the small table—I'd moved my laptop and papers to the bedroom—and began to eat. I didn't want to talk about death with the boy sitting right there listening, so I went in a different direction.

"This is nice," I said, "all of us creative types together."

"Do you draw?" Damon said.

"I write books. Mysteries."

"Cool," the boy said.

"Did you study art?" I asked Tia.

She shook her head. "It comes naturally. I didn't have the means to get special training."

"You're lucky to have such a talent."

"Damon has it, too, but I mean to see that he *does* have the opportunities I missed out on. I'll have to work harder than hard to make ends meet."

"You have any help with that?" I stole a glance at the boy, but his attention was on the cats, who sat at the foot of his chair waiting for crumbs to fall.

"No help." Tia shook her head. "I made a choice, the wrong choice according to my parents, when I married. You might say they were right, but if that hadn't happened then—" She smiled lovingly at Damon and I got her drift.

"You're divorced?"

Tia nodded. "He's self-employed. Had the company before

we married and juggled the books to make it look like he earns next to nothing."

"So his support payment is very low. I've seen that so many times. I worked at a law office for a while."

"I'd be glad for the payment, if he ever made one."

"He doesn't pay anything?"

"Nope."

"You ever see him?"

She shook her head.

What kind of father doesn't care about seeing his son? I didn't ask the question aloud. Sadness for the boy washed over me. I checked Damon, who had wolfed down his sandwich and was trailing his napkin back and forth on the side of his chair to tempt the cats.

"May I be excused to play?" he said.

Tia gave him the go-ahead.

"Come back for dessert when you're ready," I said, then looked at his mother. She probably wouldn't want to hear me suggest filing a lawsuit against the deadbeat dad. Everyone knew lawyers cost a bundle.

"I spoke with a friend of yours today," I said. "Lorene."

Tia smiled. "She's a sweetheart."

"Said she met you at a festival, same as Calvin Fisher and I suppose several of the others."

"We're kind of like gypsies," Tia said. "Moving from one place to the next."

"I never thought of gypsies as people like Fisher and his buddy."

"They're the bad gypsies," she said. "I try to steer clear of them."

"Smart move, but now Fisher's dead, and we both argued with him in public. People saw us."

Tia put her partially eaten sandwich down. "You think I killed him?"

"Heavens no, and I didn't do it, either. I hope no one

thinks we're involved, but we should be prepared to fend off accusations. The real killer needs to be identified."

"You and I can't possibly do that."

"We can assemble clues," I said.

She sat back in her chair and appeared to digest that idea. "Why were *you* arguing with him?" she said.

"He mistook me for you," I said. "Apparently, he wanted you to stay away from the festival, but you came anyway. He was ticked."

She pursed her lips. "I knew he didn't want me here, but it's a good opportunity. I need the money, and he can't order me around. I thought switching places with the Mosers, keeping my distance, would fix that."

"It should have. What we're dealing with is a bad set of circumstances, and we can assemble facts for our side. So I'll go first. Fisher fought with me because he thought I was you. That's all I got. What can you list?"

Tia put her elbows on the table. "He didn't like cats."

"I heard he was afraid of Merlin."

"He was. He acted like the cat could put a spell on him. He didn't even like our names. He said Tia and Damon were witch names."

"Good thing he didn't know my name's Sabrina. He might have accused us of starting a coven." I sobered. "Or maybe he *did* know my name."

"He took an instant dislike to us," Tia said, "and it seemed like he blamed us for everything that didn't go his way."

"Good grief." I looked across to the living room. Damon sat on the fireplace hearth with his sketch pad on his lap and his pencil moving fast across the page.

"Maybe I should have listened and stayed away," Tia said, "but it wasn't right for him to claim every place where I could make a good bit of money."

"No. You registered for this festival same as him, I'm assuming. Say, had you met Herr Schmidt before you arrived in Lavender? He and Fisher seemed to know each other."

"I never saw Schmidt before," Tia said. "The man's quirky. I'd have remembered."

"What about Axle? Were he and Fisher always together?"

"No. Calvin was usually alone, and I could see why. Who'd want to spend time with him?"

"What about other people? Aside from the customers who bought jewelry, did you ever see anyone with him? People who annoyed him? Possible enemies?"

"I kept my distance," she said. "He's the one who made himself an enemy. Accusing Damon of snooping."

"Snooping how?"

She glanced at the boy. "He's curious, and he gets bored sitting and watching me all the time."

I nodded with what I hoped was an understanding expression.

"So one day Damon wanted to play hide-and-seek with one of the other children, and he hid under the table."

"Fisher's table?"

"Uh-huh. So the other child—a little girl named Sally—was counting. I was sketching her mother at the time, and I heard the girl say, 'Ready or not, here I come.' Next thing I hear is Calvin screaming."

"What did he do?"

"He stormed into my stall and threatened to turn me in to child protective services if I didn't get a handle on my boy. Damon was playing a game. He didn't care about the boxes under that table."

Boxes? Fisher could have been nothing more than a cranky, obstinate man, or the boxes might have held something of significance he didn't want the boy to uncover.

Tia snapped her fingers. "There is one other person who gave Calvin trouble. That woman giving the facials."

"Britt?"

"Yes. She goes to a lot of the festivals, too, and she *really* didn't like Calvin. Seemed like she went out of her way to give him a hard time."

"Was the feeling mutual?" I said.

Tia shrugged. "He wasn't nice to her, or to anyone else, except the people who bought his jewelry. He'd turn on the charm for them."

No telling how many enemies the nasty, two-faced man might have made. This was a bigger puzzle than we could solve in one night, and my sweet tooth was talking to me.

"How about brownies?" I'd gone back to bake after talking with Thomas.

Damon jumped up, but before he had brownies he wanted to show me the sketch he'd made while his mother and I were talking.

He had drawn us sitting at the table. I grinned when I saw that Tia and I didn't look very much alike in the boy's picture.

"This is very good," I told him. "You may become a famous artist one day."

My phone rang as I assembled brownies on a plate for my guests. I checked the screen and saw the call was coming from Sheriff Crawford. "There's milk in the fridge if you want some. Excuse me a second."

I picked up the phone and went into the bedroom to answer the call.

"The Fisher family is here in Lavender," he said. "They're asking to speak with you."

"Because . . ."

"You're the person who found his body," he said, "but like I told you before, you don't have to agree."

"I don't mind." So long as the question asking went both ways. "How many family members are there?"

"Fisher's wife, Coco, and—"

"Coco? Are you serious?"

"As a heart attack," the sheriff said, "and she has two children with her. A fourteen-year-old daughter and a toddler. Says the other two stayed at the hotel with her sister."

My chest felt tight at the thought of four fatherless children,

but my curiosity overruled sadness. I thought about the gossip Thomas had reported. "Did you talk with them about the evidence found in the truck?"

The sheriff paused. "I interviewed them and answered questions best I could. I told them what you reported, but they want to hear from you directly."

"Okay. I'll come over."

"They're in my conference room. I can tell them it's too late, if you like, and ask them to come back in the morning."

I glanced toward the other room. "Tia Hartwell and her son are here now. Do they want to speak with her as well?"

"Not at this time," he said. "Just you, but I can put this off."

"No need. I'll see you in about thirty minutes."

15

DROVE THROUGH TOWN on my way to the sheriff's office watching orange lights twinkle in shop windows as dusk fell. Festival stragglers wandered down sidewalks, seemingly without a care in the world.

Must be nice.

The tension between my shoulder blades would ease, I told myself, after my meeting with Calvin Fisher's family. Even more after I knew exactly what had happened to him and who was responsible. When I could rest easy that no one was accusing *me*. Or Tia. When Rita Colletti stopped bugging me.

Okay, maybe the tension would last a while.

The sheriff's call had cut my conversation with Tia short. When she heard I was off to a meeting at his office, she gathered Damon and Merlin. Said they had a big day ahead and needed to get to bed early. I wasn't finished quizzing her and wished I could offer her a place to spend the night.

No one should have to sleep in a car, but I felt sure that bringing up the subject would cause her embarrassment, so we went our separate ways.

I tried not to think about the fact that Tia had handed me her perfect motive for wanting Fisher out of the way. He'd threatened to turn her in to child protective services. That could ruffle the feathers of any mother hen and cause all sorts of problems. I sure hoped Tia had ignored his words and walked in the opposite direction.

When I pulled into the sheriff's department lot, I spotted Sheriff Crawford standing outside by himself. I climbed out of my car and approached him.

He looked behind me. "No Hitchcock?"

"Not this time," I said. "Why? You need pet therapy?"

"Wouldn't hurt," he said.

"Hitchcock wore himself out playing with Tia Hartwell's cat. Have the Fishers left?"

He shook his head. "Lord, no. They're in the conference room waiting on you. I needed a break."

"They're that upset?" Maybe I should have taken him up on his offer to postpone this meeting until tomorrow.

"Upset, yes, and unusual. I'm eager to see why the wife's so fired up to talk with you. Not sure what to make of these folks."

"What do you mean?"

"You'll see. Let's go inside." He turned and held the door for me, and we walked straight to the conference room.

"Mrs. Fisher," he said and introduced me.

I took in the room in one sweeping glance as he spoke. A mound of soggy, used tissues sat next to a box on the conference room table. A woman—blond, on the short side, and noticeably muscular—stood beside the table with a child on her hip. She wore bling-covered jeans like a second skin and a sequined scoop-neck shirt that barely contained her. The towheaded child—a boy if I had to guess—wore a

diaper and a shirt that said "*Mommy's Little Devil.*" A teenage girl dressed all in black stood with her back to the wall, thumbs working her phone screen.

I crossed the room to address the mother. "I'm very sorry for your loss," I said.

Her cheeks, already blotchy, reddened and her eyes filled. She reached for the tissue box and plucked a fresh one out to dab at her tears. "Please, call me Coco, and thank you. Thank you so much for coming."

"Of course," I said. "I'm glad to help if I can."

"I don't know how we'll go on without Cal," Coco said. "He took such good care of me and the kiddos. Amber here is a big help with little Wallie and the twins, Deke and Sis. They're just about to turn three, so I decided it best to leave them behind at the hotel with my sister. Boy howdy, they are a handful."

A glimmer of a smile showed through her tears, and I smiled in return. "They usually are at that age."

The girl in black lowered her phone and looked at me, her dark eyes glaring. "What were you doin' with my daddy?"

I blinked and glanced at the sheriff. "Not a thing. I didn't even know him."

All trace of Coco's tears vanished as she said, "Then why were you meetin' with him?"

"I wasn't." My words came out sounding defensive, but I couldn't help myself. What was up with these two?

Sheriff Crawford said, "Let's keep things civil. Why don't we all sit down and relax?"

"That's a dang sight easier to say than do when I got all this grief stirred up." Coco reverted to her wobbly, teary-sounding voice. She pulled out a chair and sat, then looked at the girl. "Sit, Amber."

The sheriff and I took our seats, then the girl and her mother had a three-second stare-down. Amber lost and slumped into a chair. I imagined her picture next to the

definition of "sullen" in an online dictionary. Wallie turned a pouty expression toward me and began to whimper.

Except for the baby, I had the distinct impression these people were putting on an act for us.

"Me and the kiddos will be lost without Cal, like a ship without a sail," Coco said. "We depended on him for, for everything." She turned on the tears again and reached for another tissue.

I couldn't picture Calvin Fisher with this woman, not to mention the four kids. "I'm sure you've had a hard time taking care of the family with your husband away at festivals so much of the time," I said.

Coco sniffed. "I can manage when I have to."

I looked at the sheriff to see if he was going to chime in with some pertinent questions for Coco. Maybe he'd already covered that ground, but I wanted information.

I turned to the woman. "When did you last speak with your husband?"

"I don't see where that's any of your business," she said. "What I wanna know is what you and he had goin' on."

"As I said before, nothing." I could practically feel my blood pressure surge. "Any contact I had with him was completely accidental. Circumstantial. You know."

Coco frowned. "No, I don't know. Witnesses saw you with him."

"I'm not denying people saw me *near* him. I was *not* meeting with him." I relayed my account of Hitchcock running into the field and stopping near Fisher's truck.

"So you're the one with the black cat," Coco said. "He talked about that cat always getting in his way."

"A lot of people have black cats," I said, determined not to bring up Tia's name unless someone else did. "I'm quite sure he never saw *my* cat. Not even when we were standing there right by his truck because, well, he couldn't see us at the point when I spotted his body inside the vehicle."

"How'd you know it was Cal if you supposedly didn't know him?" Coco said.

"I saw him yesterday—from a distance—when he was setting up the jewelry booth. Another vendor mentioned his name."

"Did Cal give you something to hold on to?"

I frowned, confused. "Give me something? No. Why would you ask that?"

"The sheriff here showed me Cal's personal effects."

"And you think something is missing?" I guessed.

"There should have been more," she said. "Did you see anyone take anything out of his truck?"

"No." I shook my head. "Maybe some things are at his booth. With Axle."

"How do you know Axle?" Coco said. "Are you in cahoots with him?"

"Cahoots? Absolutely not. I'm nowhere near cahoots with another living soul. I noticed—again, *from a distance*—that Axle appears to be in charge."

"He's *not* in charge." Her snippy tone caused the baby to start crying. "Now look what you've done."

"Sabrina didn't do anything," the sheriff said.

"Now you're siding with her," Coco said. "You small-town sheriffs are so unfair."

I wondered how much experience she had with small-town law enforcement.

"Mrs. Fisher," the sheriff said, "I understand you're upset. I assure you this case will be handled with all fairness. We will catch the killer and bring him or her to justice."

"I'm out of the loop," I said. "Just exactly how do we know Mr. Fisher was killed as opposed to, say, suffering a heart attack?"

"Cal was healthy as a horse," Coco said. "Someone murdered him." She let her tears flow, but somehow the grieving-widow act didn't ring true.

"We identified signs of foul play." The sheriff fidgeted in his chair. "Enough said."

Coco swiped under her wet eyes and came away with an index finger smeared with mascara. "Maybe *she* knows what happened to him. She might have been the one who cuffed him to the steering wheel."

What? I hadn't seen anyone cuffed to anything and wondered where she got that information. Or was she making it up as she went along?

I looked at the sheriff, but his expression remained blank. Coco railed on.

"She probably caused those bruises on my Cal's wrists, Sheriff, and just because she's your friend doesn't mean you should cut her any slack."

What on God's green earth was the woman talking about?

"I did not cause any bruises," I said.

"Make her tell us what Cal gave to her," Coco said.

I opened my mouth to speak, but Sheriff Crawford beat me to it. "That's enough, Mrs. Fisher. I don't hold with you making groundless accusations. Maybe it would help if you told us just what it is you're looking for."

Coco stood to hand the baby to Amber before turning to the sheriff. "Cal said we'd be able to catch up on our bills when he came home from Lavender," she said, not answering the sheriff's question.

"He promised we would go find me a car," Amber said.

Maybe Fisher had experienced particularly good sales at the Pumpkin Days Festival in the past, but how much money could a person make selling costume jewelry? Then again, I didn't know anything about the Fishers' financial situation.

"I'll speak with Axle," the sheriff said, "and get an accounting for the festival sales thus far."

Coco folded her arms over her ample chest. This woman seemed more suspicious to me than anything. I wasn't hearing the usual statements made by family after an unexpected

death. *How did he die? I hope he didn't suffer.* Coco's train of thought was on the show-me-the-money track.

"Mrs. Fisher," I said. "How long have you known Axle?"

"Couple of years," Coco said. "Why?"

"What's his last name?"

Coco screwed up her mouth and looked at the ceiling for a second. "I have no idea."

"Do you know, Sheriff?" I said.

Sheriff Crawford shook his head. "Why do you ask?"

"It's a little strange that no one seems to know." I turned back to Coco. "How well did the two men get along? Even though I didn't know your husband, in the day and a half since he arrived in Lavender, it appeared he had some issues. Would you say he was typically an angry person?"

Coco slapped the tabletop and looked at the sheriff. "Now she's speaking ill of the dead. What gives *her* the right?"

"Hear me out," I said. "Your husband might have made enemies. He seemed to anger easily and that could lead to trouble, even where you least expect it. Something as simple as a cat could get him riled up."

"I thought you said he was already dead when you went after your cat." Coco stared me down.

"That's right," I said. "I'm referring to cats in general."

"Daddy loved cats," Amber said, defiantly. "Stop saying mean things about him."

I raised my brows.

"Sheriff," Coco said, "you find out what secrets this woman is keeping. We need to head back to the hotel now and put Wallie to bed. I'll be back in the mornin' to see what you found out." She motioned to Amber, and the three left quickly. Sheriff Crawford followed close behind, showing them out.

I stayed in my chair, stewing over the woman's ridiculous accusations, thinking it was a good thing Hitchcock wasn't a bad luck cat. If he was, I might have been tempted to sic him on Coco and Amber. The sheriff returned, shaking his head.

"Now I know what you meant," I said. "They're quite unusual."

"Sorry for putting you through that," the sheriff said, "but I felt this was a conversation that needed to happen."

"Why?"

"I had a feeling you'd push Coco's buttons and we'd get a little information. I was right."

"Glad I could help out."

"Do I detect sarcasm?" he said.

"No. Yes, maybe a little. She annoyed the heck out of me, accusing me of things I don't even understand."

"You enjoy helping out with police work, though, you have to admit."

I took a deep breath. "Usually, I do, but I can't believe you gave Coco Fisher the details about the scene. What happened to your standard I-can't-discuss-the-case line? Does it not apply to the widow?"

"I didn't tell her anything," he said. "She came in to identify the body, took one look, and demanded to know who had cuffed her husband and why. We'd already determined handcuffs might have caused the scrape marks we found on the steering wheel."

"But no handcuffs were found in the truck?"

"Nope."

"I guess this does away with any doubt about whether Fisher was murdered."

"Not a shred of doubt left," he said.

Giving me this information must be the sheriff's way of making up for putting me in the same room with Coco. I began to feel better about the situation.

"Sounds like Coco has experience with cuffs."

"Believe you me, I'll be checking her out further," he said. "What's your take on the widow?"

I thought for a second. "Well, she looked strong enough to strangle the man if she had a mind to. I wonder if she has an alibi."

"She does, and it's solid."

"Hmm." I thought for a few seconds. "You might check out Gabe Brenner, the bacon dude I told you about." I reported what Gabe had to say when he brought me the roses, then felt a flicker of guilt for siccing the sheriff on him.

"Got it," the sheriff said. "I'll have Deputy Ainsley check Brenner out. Meanwhile, you steer clear of him. And Coco."

"How about Amber?"

"Her, too," he said.

"Back to Coco. I get the impression she cares more about what she's looking for than she ever cared about her husband."

The sheriff nodded. "That was my take."

"She knows exactly what Calvin had in his possession and she wants it, whatever it is. Doesn't want us to know what's really going on. Which tells me there might be something illegal afoot."

"That about sums it up," the sheriff said.

"Not that I'm complaining, but why are you running this by me instead of your deputies?"

"They're chasing other leads," he said.

"Hope those leads don't involve me."

"They don't. I spoke with Rita Colletti and she admitted to blowing the rumors out of proportion. I think she'll leave you alone."

"Tia Hartwell's in the clear, too?"

"Can't make any promises there," he said. "How well do you know Miss Hartwell?"

I didn't like his super serious tone. "Not very."

"I hear she looks like you."

I nodded. "Did Rita tell you that?"

"She might have mentioned it." He paused for a moment. "Is there some relationship between you and Miss Hartwell?"

"If we're related, I don't know how. I meant to ask Aunt Rowe about our family tree, but she's so busy with the pumpkin cannon we haven't had a chance to talk."

The sheriff sat back in his chair. "I've been listening to that thing go off, but Rowe never mentioned it to me."

"She didn't want you to try talking her out of it," I said. "You'll have to check out her performance. It's quite remarkable."

He shook his head. "So long as they're not shooting her out of the cannon."

"Not so far," I said. "Maybe tomorrow."

We shared a chuckle, then I said, "Back to the investigation. What will you do now?"

He paused as if deciding how open he could be. Then he shrugged and said, "Keep a close watch on Coco Fisher for one thing. She's after something valuable, her husband's dead, and I'll lay odds there's some connection between the two."

"Follow the money," I said.

The sheriff nodded. "You took the words right out of my mouth."

16

FELT UNSETTLED AS I left the sheriff's office. While I knew he didn't suspect *me* of anything, Tia was on his list. I didn't like that, even though the sheriff made a good point: I hardly knew her. My opinion was based on pure emotion. The same thing that might cause a mother to take drastic action to protect her family.

Maybe Tia didn't trust the system, didn't feel her family could survive a CPS investigation intact. Still, it would take a cold, hard personality to kill a man, then stick around and keep up the façade of the sweet artist sketching people for a living. If I'd bumped someone off, I'd want to run and hide. Some criminals are cunning and cool enough to avoid drawing suspicion. What if Tia was one of them?

Since I was already in town, I decided to do a drive-by of the library parking lot. See if Tia had parked there for the night once again.

I turned onto Bottlebrush Lane and coasted. A dim street lamp illuminated the parking lot. Sure enough, I spotted

Tia's green Honda. She was a mom trying her best to make a life for herself and her son. Yes, she had a possible motive for getting rid of Fisher, but I believed someone had a better one, or at least thought they did.

I tried to look at the situation like a villain, something I do on a regular basis when writing a mystery. Someone had handcuffed Fisher to the steering wheel. Unless the killer was in law enforcement and carried cuffs on a daily basis, that meant the act was premeditated. Where had the cuffs come from? Why did the killer need to use them? To hold Fisher still to smother him with a pillow? To steal whatever the widow was looking for? If theft was the motive, then why kill him?

My ringing phone scared the bejeebers out of me. I hit the brake and glanced at the screen. Luke Griffin. I pulled to the curb at a spot where Tia wouldn't see my car if she happened to be looking and answered with a smile in my voice.

"Hey there."

"Hey yourself," he said.

Country music came over the line from his end. "Where are you?" I said.

"At the cottages. Stopped to see you, but you're not home." The music came through more clearly, as if he'd walked closer to speakers—Luke Bryan singing "That's My Kind of Night." I wouldn't mind playing out those lyrics for real with my Luke, but it sounded like he had a crowd on his end. The vendors had come home to roost for the night.

"I'm headed back there now." I gave him a quick rundown of my visit to the sheriff's office. The music faded out. Luke was moving.

"If the sheriff wants more suspects, he should come over here," he said. "There's a big guy toasting Fisher's death."

I didn't need much imagination to figure out who that might be.

"And a woman downing shot for shot right along with him," he added.

"Oh my. Aunt Rowe brought in food for the guests. I didn't know she stocked the liquor cabinet."

"She didn't have to," he said. "Looks like they have plenty of their own. Your aunt might consider hiring a security team. Angie and I are patrolling, just in case things get out of hand, and Hitchcock's tailing us."

Luke's yellow Labrador retriever was a sweet dog who tolerated Hitchcock's attempts to rile her. "Are you serious?" I said. "About the security team, I mean."

"About fifty percent. Thomas is here, keeping an eye on everybody. They're a rowdy bunch."

Who would have thought the folks who sold innocent things like candles and salt-and-pepper shakers would be such hard partiers? I took my foot off the brake and resumed driving. "I'll be there in fifteen."

"We'll see you shortly."

Even though I was eager to join my main men—Hitchcock and Luke—my thoughts still drifted back to Tia. I slowed on a straight stretch of road and punched my speed dial for Tyanne. We didn't see as much of each other as we did before I started spending time with Luke, and I missed our one-on-one time.

"Don't tell me," she said when she answered. "You got the call from your agent."

"Nope, not yet." Her comment made me realize I hadn't checked my emails in a while. I told myself that Kree Vanderpool would call if and when she had big news. "Are you busy, or do you have a minute to talk?"

"I'm soaking my aching feet," she said. "This was one long day, and the festival will be even busier tomorrow."

"You always swear by the comfort of Crocs," I said.

"There's a limit."

"Maybe try tennis shoes tomorrow," I said. "Anyway, I have a hypothetical question."

"Is this for your book?" Ty said.

Her one-track mind.

"You wish. No, it's not."

"What I heard about you finding a body wasn't hypothetical, was it?" she said in a wistful tone.

"I was hoping you missed that news."

"How could I? At least they're not saying you killed him."

"Yeah, that's a relief, but Rita Colletti's offering to represent me after I'm charged with murder, and the dead man's wife thinks I stole something from him that she wants back."

"Dear Lord, is this your overactive imagination at work?" she said.

"Unfortunately not. These are facts."

"As if I didn't already worry enough about you," she said. "What's the hypothetical?"

"Let's say someone threatened your family. In this scenario, things aren't nice and comfortable the way you have them now. You don't have a house, not much money, and you're on your own with the kids."

"Bite your tongue," she said.

"I know, right? But hear me out. Somebody threatens to do something that may result in the kids being taken away."

"I don't like this scenario."

"Of course not. Let's just say it's a mother's worst nightmare. Here's the question: How far would you go to protect your family?"

"As far as I had to," she said. "So maybe I'd call the sheriff first, talk to him."

"What if you were in a strange town where you didn't know anyone?"

"Hmm. It depends."

"What if the threat came from a nasty person and you wouldn't put anything past him?"

"Are you trying to get me to say I'd kill to keep my family safe?" she said.

"Well, yeah, kind of. What's your answer?"

"As a last resort, maybe." Tyanne sighed. "You're inserting yourself into the murder investigation, aren't you?"

"Not on purpose," I said.

"Then back away and let the sheriff do his job."

"But he—"

"Do you have any information that the sheriff doesn't already know?"

"Maybe a few bits."

She made a tsk-tsk noise. "Well, then tell him. The sheriff is the one in charge of solving cases. You know you don't have to do it, right?" The sound of children's laughter came over the line. I heard the deep voice of Ty's husband.

"Right," I said. "I'll let you go."

"Come by my booth tomorrow," she said. "You can fill me in on the latest. And, wow, you mentioned that woman who looks like you. You weren't kidding. We can talk about her, too."

I wondered, as I grew closer to the cottages, whether Tyanne had learned something about Tia that I didn't know. But she was busy now, and Luke was waiting.

I turned my thoughts back to what he had told me about the guests. Too bad we couldn't set a curfew for Gabe Brenner. Then I wouldn't need eyes in the back of my head twenty-four-seven. Drinking to someone's death was a pretty gutsy thing for him to do—stupid, even. Maybe he felt safer drinking out here rather than in some bar in town where he'd attract more attention. Still, a dumb thing to do in a town where gossip spread at the speed of light.

As I rounded the bend to Aunt Rowe's house, Luke pushed away from a tree. He looked equally sexy in his off-duty jeans and boots as he did when he wore his uniform.

The wide driveway was full of cars. Doubtful Aunt Rowe would be going out again tonight, so I parked behind hers.

Angie trotted alongside Luke as he headed toward me. I slid out of the car and welcomed his quick kiss and a hug. I lingered in his embrace, savoring the feeling of his strong arms around me. His Lab pushed her nose against

my elbow, wanting her share of the attention, and I broke away to pet her.

"Where's Hitchcock?" I scanned the lawn and didn't see any sign of the cat.

"On the deck, cuddled up with Winnie Moser. He has a sweet spot for that lady." Luke grinned and put his arm around me as we walked toward the house. "Just like I have a sweet spot for this one."

His words melted away some of the day's stress. "The feeling is definitely mutual." I looked ahead warily. "Is the drinking still going on?"

"Nope. Thomas broke them up. We're about to have pie. Want some?"

"It's always a good time for pie. Who's 'we'?"

"Rowe and friends," he said.

The deck came into view, and I saw Maybelle and Winnie sitting at the patio table. Cecil crossed the deck to join his wife. No Aunt Rowe. No Gabe.

"By the way, Thomas mentioned the big guy has a thing for you." Luke looked at me with raised brows.

"Unfortunately true. He showed up and took an instant liking to me for some unknown reason."

"Not hard to believe," Luke said, "but he should back off if he knows what's good for him."

It was sweet that he cared, but I'd seen Gabe throw that mighty punch at Fisher the day before and didn't want Luke tangling with the big bruiser. He took my hand and we climbed the deck stairs. Hitchcock jumped off Winnie's lap and ran to me before spotting Angie. When he did, he leapt up to sit on the deck railing where he could keep an eye on the dog.

Maybelle waved. "Oh my goodness, Sabrina. You've had a hard day. Come sit and put all of today's nastiness out of your head."

Obviously, she'd heard about me finding Fisher's body.

Maybelle pulled out the chair next to her and patted it.

"We were just comparing sales stats. Can you believe my vanilla candles are out-selling pumpkin by a mile? This is the pumpkin festival for goodness' sake. I should have brought more of the vanilla."

Someone died, and she's counting candles.

I told myself Maybelle was purposely keeping the conversation neutral.

"Tomorrow might be the opposite," I said. "You never know."

She shrugged. "Good point."

"We're taste-testing desserts," Cecil said. "Best part of the day. Winnie and I didn't sell enough to speak of."

"Oh, hon." Winnie touched his arm. "You know we come here for the fun and companionship."

"I am going to buy those cat shakers from you," I said. "I meant to do that today."

"No hurry, dear." Winnie waved a hand and looked at Luke. "You wanted the pumpkin mousse pie, am I right?"

"Yes, ma'am," Luke said, and we sat.

Hitchcock walked back and forth along the railing, taunting the dog.

"Where's Aunt Rowe?" I said.

"She had a real blast tonight with that cannon." Maybelle giggled. "Blast, get it?"

I nodded and tried to quell the anxiety that came with thoughts of Aunt Rowe being anywhere near the cannon. "Is she okay?"

"Oh, sure," Winnie said. "She's fine. She has a visitor in there with her right now."

"Herr Schmidt?" I guessed.

The women shook their heads in unison.

"I didn't see who went in," Cecil said. "Heard a voice sounded like a woman."

"Schmidt hasn't been around much today," Maybelle said. "Isn't that odd?"

I remembered last seeing the man when he'd stalked off after learning of Fisher's death.

"Probably wore out from ordering us around," Cecil said. "Guy's a pain in the neck."

Winnie looked at her husband. "Don't go bad-mouthing people for no good reason. Hard enough we're dealing with a murder in our midst."

"Schmidt was upset when he heard about Fisher," I said. "Were they friends?"

Winnie shrugged. Cecil said, "Hard time picturing Schmidt having friends."

Luke said, "From the little drinking celebration we just witnessed, I don't suppose many people liked Fisher."

"He was very sweet to me," Winnie said. "A real gentleman."

Cecil gave her a look. "The guy was a schmoozer."

The Pure Velvet lady—Britt—came through the back door in time to hear his words and added, "He was a louse. Always has been." I watched her teeter across the deck and figured she wouldn't be able to walk a straight line to save her life. I guessed she was the woman toasting Fisher's demise. I was curious to know more about Britt's relationship with the victim, but I didn't want to ask questions in front of everyone. Instead, I scanned the pies, which were obviously not store-bought.

"Where did these come from?" I said.

"Rowe brought them from some friends of hers in town. They're trying out recipes for Sunday's baking contest, and she promised to take them our comments."

"They could save themselves the time," Luke said, scooping up a forkful of mousse. "Don't care how good these taste, I predict Sabrina will win."

Everyone turned to me.

"What are you entering in the contest, Sabrina?" Winnie said.

"Um . . ." I looked around the table, then at Luke. The

sweet hint of pride in his voice made me feel warm and fuzzy inside.

"I haven't decided yet. Then there's the problem of Aunt Rowe's kitchen being too crowded to bake in right now."

"You could use my kitchen," Luke said, "and I'd be right there to taste-test whatever you might want to try between now and contest time." He grinned.

The invitation to bake in his kitchen struck me as super personal. Should I go for it? I decided to avoid the issue for now. "Taste-testing involves a lot of extra calories."

"I'll risk it," he said with a grin.

We ate pie while a Brooks & Dunn tune segued to George Strait singing "Heartland." Britt sang along, off-key. I noticed Hitchcock had moved to the windowsill by Aunt Rowe's office. He looked like an eavesdropper with an ear to the glass, and I read his expression as worried.

I glanced at Luke and pushed my chair back. "Excuse me. I need to check on Aunt Rowe."

"What is it?" he said.

"Nothing, I hope."

I went in and hurried down the hall to the closed office door. Saw Luke coming in behind me.

"Thought I'd make sure it's not the big guy in there with your aunt," he said in a low voice.

I pressed a finger to my lips and leaned closer to the door. Heard a voice.

"We will search all the cottages, Miss Flowers," a woman said. "Mark my words."

Luke had come up beside me, and we exchanged a glance.

"My guests have a right to privacy," Aunt Rowe said. "No warrant. No search."

I pressed my ear closer. "I can get the warrant," the woman said, "so I'll be back. And I'll be sure to tell Sheriff Crawford you're impeding our investigation."

Realization struck me belatedly, and I looked at Luke. "It's Rosales," I whispered.

"I never saw her come in," he said.

No good would come of the deputy spotting Luke and me together. Movement sounded behind the door, and panic lurched to my throat.

I turned and pushed at Luke. "Quick. Hide."

The door opened, and there she stood in street clothes, dangling earrings, and red lipstick. If Luke and I had paid attention to the cars outside instead of having eyes only for each other, we might have noticed her SUV in the group.

Rosales stared at each of us in turn, her eyes narrowing. "I have excellent hearing," she said, "and it's a little late to hide. Warden Griffin, I advise you to steer clear of these people. They may be harboring a murderer."

She swept down the hall and out the door without a backward glance.

17

TEN MINUTES AFTER Rosales left, Aunt Rowe, Luke, and I holed up in Aunt Rowe's office, away from the prying eyes and ears of the guests.

"I don't think Rosales will get her warrant," Aunt Rowe said. "She's grasping at straws." Hitchcock lounged on the back of Aunt Rowe's chair, his tail curled down into her hair. Angie lay obediently next to Luke with her chin resting on her front paws. Laughter and music drifted in from the deck. The pie-eaters were whooping it up, but I sure didn't feel like partying.

"Did Rosales say what she's hoping to find?" I said.

"I'm not sure she knows," Aunt Rowe said. "Wouldn't tell me if she did."

"This could be connected to what happened tonight at Sheriff Crawford's office." I went through my strange encounter with Coco Fisher. "Maybe Rosales came here to search for whatever the wife is missing."

"She can't search the whole town," Luke said, "especially not with so many tourists around."

"Maybe she believes what Coco said and thinks I took something from Calvin. Why else would she come here?" I looked at Aunt Rowe. "You have any ideas?"

Aunt Rowe paused. "I'm not sure you want to know."

"Yes, I do."

"Okay then." She sighed. "Rosales is following a lead she got from your mother."

I replayed the scene when Gabe showed up at the door with roses and wasn't surprised that his words had caused Mom to call the sheriff's department.

Luke looked at me. "Your mother's here?"

"Not anymore, and that's a good thing. Trust me."

There was no telling what words might come out of my mother's mouth in any situation, and I wasn't ready to take the chance she'd scare Luke off.

"You don't want me to meet her?" he said.

Aunt Rowe said, "I'm sure Sabrina would be proud to introduce you to her mother. Not necessarily the other way around."

"Why's that?" he said.

"She's, hmm, what's the right word, Aunt Rowe? Haughty?"

"That's a good one." Aunt Rowe nodded and added, "Hoity-toity."

"Controlling," I said.

"I'm starting to form a picture," Luke said.

Aunt Rowe smiled. "You'll get your chance to confirm the picture soon enough."

I faked a shudder. "Oh, I hope not."

"She'll be back," Aunt Rowe said. "Soon, I predict."

"What? Why?"

"She didn't get what she wanted from me yet," Aunt Rowe said.

The stress of the day was quickly catching up with me.

I loved my mother, but she was sometimes difficult and better dealt with in small doses. The thought of her showing up twice in the same week that I'd found a body was too much to take. "What does she want?"

"A favor," Aunt Rowe said. "I happen to have a very influential friend in Houston."

"Does this have something to do with Dave running for judge?" I said.

"Yup," Aunt Rowe said.

"Who's Dave?" Luke said.

I put my head on the back of my chair and stared at the ceiling. "My stepfather. Dave Harrison, attorney, head of the law firm where I used to work, Rita Colletti's former partner, now a candidate for some judgeship or other." I straightened and looked at him. "Which I couldn't care less about, even though I'm rambling on."

Luke turned to Aunt Rowe. "What does she want you to do?"

"Ask my friend to endorse Dave in the race," she said.

"And I'm supposed to pose for a family portrait." I looked at my aunt. "What'd you tell her?"

"That I didn't even know Dave, since she hasn't brought him to any family functions and given me a proper introduction." Aunt Rowe snorted. "Not that I ever invite them."

"You know she wouldn't come anyway." I crossed my arms over my chest.

Hitchcock jumped from Aunt Rowe's chair to the desk to my lap. Angie looked up as the cat pushed his head against my chin. I stroked his back. "She didn't ask for you to be in the family portrait, buddy. You're the lucky one."

"Mrreow." Hitchcock turned in circles before settling on my lap. The dog sighed and put her head down again.

Luke had paid close attention to what Aunt Rowe and I had said about Mom. He had a great relationship with his mother, and I hoped he didn't think less of me for not appreciating mine.

"Luke," Aunt Rowe said, "you'll understand when you meet Brenda."

"Thank you for being on my side." I smiled at her.

"Always." Aunt Rowe raised her arms over her head in a stretch. "I knew there was something up as soon as Brenda came in here this afternoon and returned the emerald pendant I've been asking her about for years."

My jaw dropped. "Grandma's? The one she's always denied having?"

"Twenty years of denials." Aunt Rowe nodded. "It's now in my possession and locked up safe and sound."

"The picture's developing," Luke said. "If your mom's heading back, maybe I should leave town." He chuckled.

"Wouldn't blame you." I felt embarrassed that Mom would stoop to lying about the pendant all these years.

Luke shook his head. "I'm not going anywhere. What if Rosales is right and the killer's here at the cottages?"

"Brenda phoned me after she called the sheriff's department," Aunt Rowe said. "Gabe Brenner seems like such a doofus, I can't picture him committing this crime."

Luke wanted to know everything, so I filled him in.

"This guy's a stalker, Sabrina," he said. "Following you. Thinking he needs to protect you. The flowers. Drinking to Fisher's death. These are bad signs."

"I know they are." Even though I'd thought the same thing, I hesitated to put the label on Gabe. "He's definitely odd, and I told the sheriff about him."

"That's a start," Luke said, "but Brenner's still here, and I don't like that."

"The sheriff will check him out. Maybe he just has poor judgment. Lots of people do."

"Thomas is watching Brenner, too," Aunt Rowe said.

I turned to her. "Do you think Gabe's the person Rosales is after?"

She shrugged. "Her suspicions seem to be all over the map."

"Huh. This search she wants to conduct, is it concentrated on Gabe's cottage?"

Aunt Rowe averted her gaze and began straightening the papers on her desk. "Rosales didn't mention Gabe by name."

"Did she specify what she's after?" I said.

Aunt Rowe lifted a stack of paper, tapped the edge on the desk, then faced me.

After a moment, she said, "I worry that she's after you, but I've been thinking. What about that gal who looks like you?"

"Tia Hartwell," Luke said.

Aunt Rowe nodded. "Whatever witnesses may have reported could be about Tia, not Sabrina. So Rosales comes to Sabrina because, well, she's always wanted to put one over on Sabrina, even though it could be Tia she's really after."

Luke grinned. "I totally follow that logic."

"Aunt Rowe," I said, "I've been wanting to talk to you about Tia."

"Why? You think she killed Fisher?"

"No." I hesitated for a moment to consider whether or not to bring this up in front of Luke. Decided "why not?" "Do you think she's related to us? To me?"

Aunt Rowe raised her brows. "I'm sure she's not, unless it's way down the line somewhere."

"People think we're sisters," I said.

"Well, that's not the case. Remember, I've been around since before your parents met. Your only sibling's your brother."

How can you be sure?

I didn't voice the thought, and Aunt Rowe went on.

"I may not have a twin," she said, "but did you know I found out there are five Rowena Flowerses in Texas alone?"

"Five Aunt Rowes?" I laughed. "Whew."

"That's enough." Aunt Rowe stood. "Now I need to get out there and taste those pies, if there's any left."

* * *

IN the Monte Carlo cottage a few minutes later, I told Luke, "It's official. Rosales is the stalker here. Why won't that woman leave me—leave us—alone?"

Hitchcock lifted his head from the crunchy tuna treats I'd given him. "Mrreow."

Angie lay by the fireplace hearth gnawing on a bone Luke had brought in from his truck and didn't comment.

I opened the refrigerator. "Care for some wine? It's open." I took out a bottle of white wine from a local vineyard and removed the stopper.

"Sure," he said and took two glasses from the top shelf. "I get it that you're ticked off. I'm not thrilled with Rosales's behavior, either. She's out of line."

"That's an understatement." I poured the wine, and we took our glasses to the sofa and sat.

I worried, especially because Rosales was investigating my involvement in a murder even before she'd spotted me with Luke. Usually, the woman acted out after she saw us together. She'd changed her *modus operandi*, and I wondered what might have set her off. Someone had reported something to her. Saw something suspicious. Mixed me up with—

Tia.

Aunt Rowe had made a valid point.

"Rosales is annoying, but she's not stupid," I said.

"Okay," Luke said. "Meaning?"

"She came here because Mom reported Gabe Brenner's suspicious words. We don't know who she's talked to about the crime or what they said."

"Probably lots of folks," Luke said. "I'm guessing she's been at this since early this morning."

"She must have gone home to freshen up because she thought she might see you," I said. "The case officially began over twelve hours ago."

"You know the best chances of solving a crime are—"

"Yeah, I know, and even more when you have lots of strangers in town and you want to solve the case before people start leaving to go home. Or disappear into the ether if they don't have a home to speak of."

His brow creased. "You're talking about Tia."

I nodded. "I hate to see her getting mixed up in this because Fisher didn't like her and Damon."

"What if she *was* involved?" Luke said.

I slumped against the sofa cushions. "The truth needs to come out, whether it's about Tia, or Axle, or Fisher's widow, or even the daughter. The only person in this mess that I can vouch for is myself. I didn't do it. So come on, Deputy, and search my place. You won't find a thing."

"You hope," Luke said.

I frowned and my heart began racing. "What's that supposed to mean?"

"Mrreow," Hitchcock said, then turned and trotted into the bedroom. The dog sat up and looked at Luke, waiting for a signal, though she clearly wanted to chase the cat.

"Maybe we should take a look around here and make sure no one has planted any evidence."

I frowned. "That's a horrible thought."

"I agree, but I'd rather not take chances. Let's check it out. Looks like Hitchcock is getting a head start."

We could see into the bedroom from where we sat. Hitchcock raced in a circle on top of the comforter, then pawed at the covers. In seconds, he was under them and moving down toward the bed's footboard.

Angie had moved to the bedroom doorway and looked back at us.

"You want to help us sniff out some clues, Angie?" I said.

"Before we start our search," Luke said, "I want to say one more thing."

"What?" I turned to him.

He put a finger under my chin and tipped my head up to

gaze into my eyes. "I'm worried about Brenner, and I'd feel a lot better if you'd let me and Angie keep a lookout tonight."

"You mean like in an old western, where you sit by the window with your rifle at the ready?" I said lightly.

Did he want me to invite him to spend the night?

"We can bunk down in the truck bed," he said. "In my line of work, we do it more often than you'd think. Nobody'd even see us. Unless, of course, there's trouble."

I tamped down a twinge of disappointment. If I invited Luke to spend the night with me, he would. But these circumstances—with an unsolved murder and a stalker nearby—were less than ideal for a romantic evening.

I nodded. "I get the feeling, Warden Griffin, that nothing I could possibly say would stop you."

18

I WOKE THE NEXT morning to the soothing sound of Hitchcock purring on the pillow next to my head. I got up and
went to the living room, where I found the blanket I'd lent
to Luke folded neatly on the easy chair near the door. The
fact that he'd spent the better part of the night on the lookout
for intruders made me feel as cared for as if he'd spent the
night by my side. I felt a share of guilt, though, for causing
the poor guy to miss out on a decent night's rest.

We had searched my cottage the night before, looking
for anything that might have been planted. Anything that
could possibly be connected to the crime. We found nothing
suspicious. Everything was either a memento of Aunt Rowe's
trip to Monte Carlo or had moved with me from Houston
the year before.

I padded into my kitchen and found a note from Luke
next to the coffeepot.

*Have a great writing day. I'm working a long shift. Good
idea to keep your door locked. L*

A not-so-subtle way of telling me what he thought I should do today. The man knew me well enough to realize I wouldn't sit still until the mystery of who killed Calvin Fisher was solved, but I couldn't blame him for trying.

I poured a cup of coffee and leaned against the kitchen counter, sipping the hot beverage. I wondered if Coco Fisher was already up and grilling the sheriff to see if he'd coaxed any information from me. Whether Rosales was having any luck getting a search warrant. Just in case she came back here with one, I decided to have a second look around to make sure we hadn't missed anything in last night's search. The place wasn't very big, so it wouldn't take long.

Hitchcock wandered out from the bedroom and stretched. It wasn't like him to sleep late, and I surmised he'd spent part of the night on guard with Luke and his dog. The thought of the three of them sitting together in the bed of Luke's truck made me giggle.

I fed the cat and went through the cottage painstakingly. Found nothing. Refilled my mug and took it to my laptop. Settled myself in front of the computer and struggled through the next scene in my manuscript. Some days are great for writing; some aren't. This one was difficult because my focus was so torn.

I gave up an hour into it and spent a few minutes checking my emails.

Nothing from Kree Vanderpool.

I stood and took my coffee out to the deck. The weather was perfect for a festival, with bright sun and a predicted high in the mid-seventies. No doubt the vendors were already in town and set up for a busy tourist-filled Saturday. Hitchcock came up beside me, then leapt to the deck railing and sat to watch me.

"In a few days these guests will be gone," I told him. "The festival will end, and life will go back to normal."

"Mrreow."

"Whether or not the murder is solved." I sipped my coffee

and thought about how unsettled I would feel if everyone left and we still didn't know what happened or why. I paced. "The sheriff is following the money."

I stopped and glanced at Hitchcock, who appeared to be pacing along the railing to mimic me. I smiled and stopped walking to face him.

"Of course, Coco cares about the money. She has those four mouths to feed. That doesn't necessarily mean her husband was killed over money. What about all the other people here? He wasn't a likeable man."

The cat didn't respond.

I sat on the bench to think. Hitchcock jumped from the railing to the bench and sat beside me. I stroked his head absently. How many vendors had a link to Fisher because they'd attended other events with him? They could have additional connections as well. Someone might have witnessed something relevant to the crime. While the sheriff was busy following the money, I could talk to these people. I'd have to do it now, before they left town. Before Rosales drummed up a reason to pin me with the crime. I didn't even need a cover story. I could simply blend in with the tourists and strike up conversations.

I slid my index finger back and forth along Hitchcock's chin, and his motor started up. After a minute of relaxing along with the purr, I stood.

"C'mon, buddy. Let's go shopping."

THE streets in town were already crowded by the time we arrived. I snagged a parking space, turned off the car, and reached down to the passenger-side floorboard to pick up my tote and Hitchcock's harness. I held them up and looked at him sitting in the seat next to me.

"Which one, Hitchcock?"

He appeared to mull over the choices.

"We'll try the tote first. See how that works." I dropped

the harness into the tote, then held it open. With a little gentle coaxing from me, Hitchcock jumped in.

"Good boy. Here we go."

Somehow it seemed as if the number of booths had multiplied since the day before. Maybe the sheer number of tourists made the whole festival appear larger. We headed down Foxtail Lane, a street I hadn't covered the day before. One booth sold Halloween masks, another featured lotions, bar soap, and bath salts made with lavender. A third boasted products to attract the male tourist: Caps and shirts imprinted with hunting slogans and pictures of wildlife. Knives of many shapes and sizes. I scanned the side table that held a variety of metal items. Belt buckles. Whistles. Chains.

I stopped walking.

Handcuffs.

Half a dozen sets in a box marked "Nickel-Plated Solid Steel." I glanced at the man inside the booth who was demonstrating the easy open and close of a pocket knife for a customer.

He noticed me and said, "Help you with something?"

I shook my head. "Not right now. Thanks."

I kept walking, wondering whether I should question him. *When did you arrive in Lavender? What day and time did you open your booth? How many pairs of handcuffs have you sold and to whom?*

Who the heck buys handcuffs anyway?

I didn't know if the killer already owned handcuffs or bought them special when the need arose. It was certainly interesting to discover that they were readily available. A piece to add to the puzzle.

Hitchcock poked his head out of the tote when a lady with a German shepherd walked by.

"Behave yourself," I said. "We're going to see Winnie and her black cat salt-and-pepper shakers."

"Mrreow," Hitchcock said.

On the way to Promenade Street, we passed a section of

lawn cordoned off for games. A sign announced that the pumpkin toss would begin at eleven. A mound of pumpkins sat ready and waiting. Next to them, rows of tables held entries for the pumpkin-painting contest along with the name and address of each entrant.

I found Cecil and Winnie behind their display of shakers. Today, Winnie wore a bright purple shirt covered with little appliqued orange pumpkins. She and her husband were intent on the goings-on at the jewelry booth across the way. Following their gaze, I saw Coco Fisher handling purchases for customers right along with Axle. Odd for the grieving widow to be out and about like this, but maybe the work helped to get her mind off things. I wondered where the kids were.

Winnie noticed me and brightened. "Well, hello, Sabrina and Hitchcock."

I looked down at the tote and saw that Hitchcock was halfway out, his head even with my shoulder.

"Hi, Winnie," I said. "Came to finally check out those cat shakers you have."

"Oh, yes, I put them aside for you. One sec." She practically disappeared under the table skirt, and I turned to Cecil.

"How's your morning so far?" I said.

"Fair," he said. "Sold a few things. Nothin' like them." He tipped his head toward the jewelry display.

"I'm surprised they're open," I said, "and even more surprised to see Fisher's wife here, under the circumstances."

"I didn't know he had a wife." Cecil stood and puttered with rearranging the display on his table.

"I didn't either until late yesterday," I said, "but that's her over there. They have four kids, too."

"Jeez, four of 'em?" Cecil said.

"Yup. I met her last night." I glanced over at Coco and muttered, "I better get out of her sight before she starts accusing me again."

"Accusing you?" Cecil said. "What's she accusing you of?"

"Stealing something from her husband's possessions, or

taking something from him before he died. She wasn't very specific."

Winnie straightened from her search under the table and said, "Here they are."

The shakers she held stood about five inches tall. One black cat wore a white collar, the other a gray collar.

"They remind me of Hitchcock and Merlin," I said. "I'd love to buy them. How much are they?"

She gave me a price, and Cecil collected my money as Winnie wrapped the shakers in tissue. A woman stopped to browse, and Cecil started a conversation with her.

Winnie leaned closer to me and said, "I heard the most disturbing talk this morning."

"About what?"

She looked me straight in the eye. "There's a man saying Tia might be arrested."

"What man?"

She looked at her husband, who was still in conversation with the shopper. "Cecil doesn't like me talking about this. Says it's not our business and we should keep quiet, but I can't quit worrying."

"I understand. I'm a worrier, too. Who's the man?"

"His name's George," she said, "and he's the husband of a lady who sells gift baskets, but he never seems to lift a finger to help her. She's always carrying boxes and setting everything up all by herself, and the whole while he sits out by their RV, smoking like a chimney. He's nothing like my sweet Cecil."

I made a hurry-up-and-tell-me motion with my hand. "I met George, Winnie. What else is he saying?"

"That he saw Tia in the field. You know, over where you found the body. But she's not the only one who ever went over there, and it makes me so mad that he's talkin' about her like this."

"Me, too, but believe me, Tia is not the only person suspected."

Winnie straightened, her eyes wide. "Who else?"

"I can't speak for the sheriff," I said. "But you knew Fisher to a certain extent. A guy like him might have enemies."

"I could believe that," she said thoughtfully.

I glanced at the jewelry booth again. Axle No-Last-Name wasn't in sight. A couple of women browsed the jewelry, but Coco wasn't paying them any mind. Her attention was on a stack of boxes sitting behind the counter. She dug through the one on top. When she raised her head, I quickly turned back to Winnie so the widow wouldn't notice me looking at her.

"Thanks for the shakers." I took my wrapped purchase from Winnie and slid it into the tote beside the cat. "Hitchcock and I are off to continue our shopping. Try not to worry about Tia. I'll check on her."

Winnie thanked me and joined her husband.

I took a circuitous route around a booth selling handmade baby blankets to come up behind the jewelry booth, and I spotted Herr Schmidt standing with Axle, their heads together as if in a serious discussion.

They stood in a position behind a truck, where Coco wouldn't be privy to their words, and I couldn't help but be curious about what the two of them had to say to each other. I slipped around the opposite side of the truck and pretended to browse hand-painted signs with cutesy sayings like "Home Is Where the Harley Is" and "Life Is Better in Flip-Flops." I couldn't see the men from where I stood. In spite of other nearby conversations and laughter, I could hear them clearly enough to make out their words.

"Enough with the excuses. We had a deal." Schmidt's whiny voice.

"You made the deal with Cal," Axle said, "so we got complications."

"I expect you to uphold the bargain."

"Yeah, yeah," Axle said. "I *told* you to give me some time."

"I'm not a particularly patient man," Schmidt said.

At least he recognized his weaknesses.

"I have the woman griping at me now. Give me a chance to get her off my back, then I'll make contact."

"I won't wait much longer," Schmidt said.

"You'll wait however long it takes. I don't see you got much choice." No longer in salesman mode, Axle practically growled the words.

Schmidt huffed and said, "Tonight. Or else."

Jeez Louise. I'd have thought a man like Schmidt would be shaking in his shoes at dealing with Axle, and here he was, threatening the scary man.

Or else what?

I sensed they were about to make a move and darted around the wall holding the signs. Found myself staring at one that said "Oh My Stars."

Fitting.

Hitchcock trilled near my ear. I whispered, "It's okay, buddy."

I peered out from behind the wall and determined that the conversation had broken up. What kind of deal had Calvin Fisher made with Herr Schmidt? It had to be something related to the meeting they were supposed to have had the morning before. And now Schmidt was looking to Axle to carry out some sort of bargain. A bargain that it seemed Coco was not privy to.

I blew out the breath I'd been holding and tried to calm my heart rate. My worry meter had amped up, only this time it wasn't Tia I was worried about. I couldn't keep my imagination from running wild about what Axle planned to do to get Coco off his back.

19

HEADED STRAIGHT FOR Tyanne's book booth. I had to get some of this information off my chest and listen to the voice of reason. She could usually calm me in any circumstance, and that's exactly what I needed now.

As I approached my friend's booth, I counted half a dozen people browsing the shelves. Ty's part-time employee, an older woman named Billie, worked the sales counter. Ethan was arranging books on a shelf. I spotted Tyanne with a girl looking at the middle-grade chapter books, so I went around to the back of the booth to give Hitchcock a break from the tote. I knelt to release him onto the grass and took out the harness.

"Sorry, bud. Too many people around today. I need to keep you safe."

"Mrreow."

That didn't sound like a complaint, and I was able to hook him up with minimal resistance.

"He's in a cooperative mood," Tyanne said, coming up behind us.

"Yes, he is," I said, standing. "And I'm grateful."

When Ty got a good look at my face, she said, "I see new stress lines. What's going on?"

"Too much," I said. "The dead man's wife thinks he gave me something that she wants, but I have no idea what she's talking about. Rosales plans to search the cottages, I don't know why. And Henry Schmidt is hyped up about some deal he supposedly made with Fisher before the man died. I'm sure there's more I'm forgetting."

"Good Lord," Ty said. "I have something to tell you, too. I was thinking about taking a coffee break anyway. How about a visit to Hot Stuff?"

I lifted the hand holding Hitchcock's lead. "I'm always happy for coffee, but I can't go in there with Hitchcock."

"They set up bistro tables on the sidewalk for the festival," she said. "Lime green and yellow. They're really cute."

"How'd I miss that?"

"Maybe because your every thought is completely immersed in that book you're writing," Ty said.

I grinned at her sarcasm as she turned to take drink orders from Ethan and Billie. She told them she'd be back in thirty, and we took off.

I decided the sidewalks were too precarious for a cat on a leash and carried Hitchcock. After we'd walked a few yards, I looked at Ty's feet. She wore bright red Crocs that coordinated with her jeans and red-and-white-striped top. A stretchy red headband held her short blond curls away from her face. "You look very patriotic, but I thought you were going to wear tennies today."

"These will be fine," she said. "I have on really cushy socks."

I nodded. "What did you want to talk about? Have you been hearing rumors about the murder?"

"No," she said. "It's about your not-so-secret admirer. Gabe Brenner."

I rolled my eyes. "Now what?"

"He came by my booth first thing this morning."

"To buy a book?" I said hopefully.

"No, to obsess about you some more," she said. "He really disturbs me."

I'd hoped Tyanne would calm me down, and now she was telling me things that added to my distress. "What did he say?"

"At first, he was looking for your book. Somehow, he knows you're a writer. Did you tell him that?"

I shook my head.

"When I explained that your book isn't published yet, he told me he wants to write a book himself."

I couldn't wrap my head around that image. "A book about what?"

"He's interested in spy novels and mentioned authors by name. Clancy, Ludlum, Forsyth."

"That's surprising, but good for him."

We arrived at Hot Stuff just in time to grab a table outside as two women stood to leave. "Shake Your Booty" by KC and the Sunshine Band came through the speakers loud and clear.

"He wants you to teach him," Ty said.

I put Hitchcock down beside my chair. "I hope you're not talking about this song."

"No. How to write," Ty said. "Gabe wants to learn how to write a book, and he went on and on about learning from you."

I didn't want any sort of ongoing contact with Gabe, and my stomach lurched at the thought. "That's not going to happen."

"I should hope not."

Max came out of the shop door, spotted us, and waved. He walked in our direction, weaving around the tables on his way.

"Hello, Max," Tyanne said when he walked up.

"Hi, ladies and Hitchcock. What can I get for y'all?"

We placed our orders and Tyanne mentioned the drinks that she wanted to take back with her.

"Comin' right up," he said and headed back inside.

Ty said, "I tried to sell Gabe a how-to-write-a-novel book, but he didn't bite."

"If he brings this up with me, I'll suggest the same thing."

"I think the whole idea's a ruse to cozy up to you," she said.

"Maybe so. He certainly got my attention yesterday." I told her what Gabe had said about my troublemaker being gone. "Before you get all worked up about this, I already reported the conversation to the sheriff."

Her eyes wide, she leaned in and spoke in a low tone—as if anyone could hear her over the blaring music. "This guy's behavior is nothing to take lightly. Do you think he killed that man?"

"Do you?" I said. "It sounds like you had a longer conversation with him today than I ever have."

"It's possible, but he doesn't seem like the brightest bulb in the pack."

"I agree. Luke witnessed him toasting Fisher's death last night in front of a dozen witnesses."

Tyanne shook her head. "What a dumb thing for him to do."

"I agree, but that's not what has me going this morning."

Max delivered our drinks and promised to be back with the to-go order in a few minutes, then went on to tend to other customers.

"What's the latest?" Ty lifted her drink and blew on the steaming cup.

Hitchcock tugged at the leash, and I looked up to see a woman with a tiny terrier of some sort. I pulled the cat closer to me and looped the end of his lead around my thigh as I thought about where to begin.

"How well do you know Henry Schmidt?" I said.

"Well enough to be glad he's not in charge of everything around this town. He'd drive us all batty with his rules."

"What about his personal life? I know he used to teach

German, but that's about all I know. Is he old enough to retire?"

"You don't have to be a certain age," she said. "Anyone who decides they want to retire can, though they usually wait until they have enough money saved up. As far as Schmidt goes, I have no idea."

"You know where he lives?"

"That I *do* know. You remember Dawson's Peak?"

"Sure." She and I had made the climb up the peak with a group of seniors shortly after our high school graduation, then put tubes in the river to ride the nearby rapids.

"He built a place up there. One of those houses you can spot from the road."

"I've noticed them. They look expensive." I sipped my coffee thoughtfully. "He have a family?"

"I think he lives alone. From what I've heard, he rarely shows his face around town, except during the festival."

"Kind of weird for a reclusive guy to get involved with the festival at all."

"Why are you asking all these questions about Schmidt?"

To bring her up to speed, I told her about the conversation I'd overheard between Axle and Schmidt, then filled her in on my meeting with Fisher's family the evening before at the sheriff's office. "I don't have a clue what Coco Fisher thinks her husband gave to me or whether these men might have something to do with whatever's missing."

"I saw a woman with four kids this morning," Ty said. "A teenager, a toddler, and two babies that looked like twins."

"That had to be Coco," I said. "Was she short and blond?"

Ty shook her head. "Tall and dark."

I frowned. "She said something about her sister watching two of the kids last night. Sisters don't always look alike, but something's off. For one, why is this grieving widow out selling jewelry this morning? Wouldn't you think she'd have details to tend to after what happened? And what's she searching for, and why does she think I have it?"

Tyanne looked at a spot over my shoulder, and a voice came from behind me.

"Dear Sabrina, you have all the powers you need to find the answers yourself, along with the aid of your special cat."

The words were spoken with the inflection of Glinda the Good Witch telling Dorothy she always had the power to go back to Kansas. I only knew one person who thought I possessed witchlike powers.

Sure enough, I turned and found Twila Baxter, all in black, looming over me.

20

HITCHCOCK JUMPED UP on the bistro table and stared at Twila as if he meant to respond to her comment about our powers. Tyanne didn't bat an eye at Twila's eerie words. She knew all about my past experiences with the older woman.

"Good morning," I said. "How's the antiques business going?" She knew good and well I didn't believe anything she said about special powers or Hitchcock being a legendary cat.

"Business is fine, my dear," Twila said. "This promises to be a busy weekend, but I'm so delighted to have found you here."

Here as in here at Hot Stuff? In town? What?

Tyanne said, "Would you like to join us?"

I figured my friend was concerned for the woman's well-being, given her flushed complexion and the fact that her curly white hair was frizzed out of control. Twila appeared

to have over-exerted herself by walking the four blocks to the coffee shop.

Ty pulled an empty chair from the next table and Twila sank into it.

"I can't stay long," she said. "Ernie expects me shortly, and I thought I'd take him some cappuccino." Twila raised a hand and signaled Max. He delivered a tray of drinks to a nearby table, then came our way.

"Miss Twila," he said, ignoring the fact that a black cat adorned our table. "What can I get for you?"

"I'd like a caramel latte and a cappuccino to go."

I sipped my coffee and exchanged a look with Ty while Max jotted down Twila's order.

"I was sorry to hear about your son's friend," Max said.

"Thank you." Twila nodded. "I will tell him."

Max tsk-tsked. "Hate to see crime hit so close to home."

"It's certainly a shame," Twila said and turned to us as Max walked away. "Now, what I wanted to speak to you about—"

"Wait. Was your son a friend of Calvin Fisher's?" I remembered seeing Fisher at Eddie Baxter's tent.

"Yes," she said. "Eddie and Cal have been friends for a very long time."

"How did they know each other?" Tyanne said.

Twila ran a hand over her hair in an attempt to smooth it down. "They were in the same motorcycle gang."

Visions of the two men in black leather, riding their cycles into town in a cloud of dust, flashed through my head. "Like Hells Angels?"

Twila giggled. "You might say so, but I don't think they had a name for themselves. Or maybe not one they would repeat to me."

"Have you talked with Eddie since the, um, since Cal's death?" I said.

"Oh, yes. He's in shock."

"Does he have any idea what happened?"

"He has an opinion," Twila said, "but the boy isn't thinking straight. I'm sure that poor young woman is not to blame."

My heart rate sped up.

"Who's he blaming?" Tyanne said.

"The artist," Twila said. "That sweet young lady with the gentle spirit and the exceptional little boy. Eddie claims he heard her threaten Calvin's life."

"If that's so, there must be something we don't know," I said. "Maybe Fisher provoked her and she snapped back at him without thinking. Certainly doesn't mean she took action."

"I agree, dear," Twila said. "She isn't the sort to take a life. Don't worry. The truth shall prevail."

"I'll drink to that." Ty picked up her coffee mug in a toast.

Twila put a hand on Hitchcock's head, and the cat sat still, as if frozen by the woman's touch. She turned her gaze on me. "My dear, before I forget, I want to invite you and Hitchcock both to join me for dinner on a very special occasion. Halloween evening."

Good grief. I remembered very well Twila's claim that her dead husband had showed up on Halloween eight years ago, and the woman expected a reenactment anytime now.

"I, um—"

"She can't," Ty blurted. "Sabrina has Halloween plans with my kids."

We had discussed no such thing—not yet anyway—but I credited Ty for her quick thinking.

"That's right," I said. "Can't disappoint the little ones."

Twila's mouth drooped. "I was so counting on you and Hitchcock."

"Mrreow." His spell seemingly broken, Hitchcock moved closer to the woman.

She looked into the cat's eyes. "Maybe *you* could join me for Halloween dinner while Sabrina is busy elsewhere," she said.

I sat up straighter. "I won't leave Hitchcock out of my

sight on Halloween. That's the most dangerous day of the year for black cats."

Twila said, "But you're the only chance my poor Connie has to escape the state he's trapped in. His soul can't find rest."

Tyanne raised her brows and stayed silent.

I didn't know what had ever put such a thing in Twila's head. Nothing I could say would change her mind. However, an interesting idea came to me.

I turned to Twila. "So you think my cat would bring you good luck, is that right?"

"Yes, of course."

"Then where does Eddie get the idea that cats are bad luck?"

"I certainly did not teach him that," she said.

"I'm very unhappy about his bad-luck-cat-themed tent."

"I understand," she said, "and I apologize for his behavior. He didn't get any such idea from me."

"Do you think you could convince him to make some changes?"

Twila's lips thinned. After a moment, she said, "What kind of changes?"

"Removing all references to cats and bad luck from his tent," I said. "He can sell good luck charms, period. No need to refer to any cat or to display that picture that looks like Hitchcock."

"Mrrrreeeeeooooow," Hitchcock added forcefully.

Customers at the tables closest to us heard the cat over the song "I'm So Excited" playing on the jukebox and peered at us.

"I doubt Eddie will listen to me," Twila said. "He always was a willful child and has not improved with age."

"If you can convince him to make those changes—and, oh, one more thing. If you can convince him to keep quiet about Tia Hartwell, that would be even better. There's no need for an innocent woman to be raked over the coals by the sheriff or his deputies."

I was doing plenty of internal waffling about whether or not I thought Tia was involved in Fisher's death, but I sincerely wanted her to be innocent. Better if Eddie kept his two cents to himself.

"So, will you agree?" I asked Twila.

The woman's eyes twinkled behind her glasses. "Yes, I will, assuming there is something in this bargain for me."

"Okay," I said. "If you can talk sense into Eddie, then Hitchcock and I will join you for dinner on Halloween." I crossed my arms over my chest and waited for Twila's response.

Tyanne looked at me like I'd lost my mind. "What about my kids?"

Twila smiled at me and stood. "That would be wonderful, dear. I'll go talk with Eddie right now."

Max came out with two cups in a cardboard tray. Twila met him halfway, took the drinks, and after a wave to us headed out.

Tyanne stared at me. "*What* are you doing?"

"The kids don't really expect me at Halloween, and if you wanted to plan something, I can come over before or after I go see Twila."

"To save her dead husband's soul?" she said in disbelief. "Really?"

"Well, there's not actually going to be any soul saving, if that's what you're asking, but if it makes her feel better . . ." I shrugged.

"You mean if it will convince her to do what you want, which includes silencing a witness who heard Tia threaten Calvin Fisher."

"Allegedly," I said.

Ty pushed her chair away from the table. "I need to get back to work."

"You're upset."

"Of course I am." She looked at me. "You know, Sabrina, if you spent more time writing you'd have less time to become emotionally involved in other people's problems."

"Do you think Tia killed the man?" I said in a low voice.

"I don't *know* her," Ty said, "and neither do you."

"I know she's alone in the world, and she could use somebody on her side."

"Why does that someone need to be you?" she said. "And if you're going to say it's because the two of you look alike, that's not good enough."

"She has Damon to take care of, and she isn't getting any kind of support. The boy has a deadbeat dad."

"If you want to help with that particular problem, I could understand, but you don't have to handle it personally."

I pressed my lips together. I'd gone to Ty for her calming influence, but sometimes I hated it when she was right.

"Get your pal Rita to deal with the support issue," she went on, "so you can keep your focus on what's most important."

The writing *was* important, but I found it impossible to ignore everything else. I had to admit that what Ty said made a lot of sense. Rita Colletti had offered to help Tia and me because she thought we'd end up needing legal representation related to Fisher's death. A child-support case wasn't what she had in mind, but it wouldn't hurt to ask, and she was a shark in family court.

I smiled at Ty. "Thanks for caring, and you make a good point. I'll go to see Rita about this problem."

"And when will you focus on your book?"

"Soon," I said.

21

NEVER EXPECTED TO search out Rita Colletti willingly. After glancing at the business card she offered me the other day, I had only a vague idea where to find the woman. Ty solved that problem in short order by drawing a little map on a napkin for me before she left to go back to work.

So much for that excuse.

Hitchcock and I left Hot Stuff and headed in the general direction of the lawyer's office. Since this was Saturday, I figured I had a fifty-fifty chance of finding her there. When I'd worked for the woman, she never took a day off, but the workload here in Lavender was bound to be much lighter.

The laughter of children and the sweet aroma of cotton candy filled the air as Hitchcock and I walked down the sidewalk. I thought back to my work at the law office and the intake process for new cases. The initial client call usually divulged more facts than those I knew about Tia's situation. Step two was the conflicts check to make sure the

lawyer had no reason to turn down the case. Hmm. I didn't know Damon's father's name.

I didn't even know the jurisdiction this case would fall under. I wondered which county Tia and Damon lived in. How did that work if they truly lived in their car and didn't even *have* an address?

I had no idea.

"Maybe I should run this whole idea by Tia before I talk to Rita," I muttered and looked at Hitchcock, walking beside me. "What do you think?"

"Mrreow," he said.

We headed toward the artist's booth and made it halfway when I heard someone hollering.

"Sabrina. Hitchcock. Yoo-hoo." Maybelle waved to me from behind her candle display. Winnie was there, too. It would be rude, I decided, to ignore them, so we walked over and exchanged greetings.

Sabrina Tate, master of procrastination.

Winnie lit a cigarette while Maybelle turned to me and began her sales spiel on the candles.

"The apple spice is very pleasing," she said. "A classic fall scent. What I'm burning now is buttercream." She fanned the air over the candle to force the scent in my direction. "Smells just like homemade frosting, doesn't it?"

Hitchcock lifted his nose, sampling the scent.

"Your kitty likes it," Maybelle said.

I grinned. "Smells good enough to eat. Are the pumpkin candles selling any better today?"

The woman didn't appear to have heard my question. Her eyes narrowed as she focused on Winnie. "That godawful smoke is ruining the pretty candle smells," Maybelle said. "I thought you were supposed to be switching to that e-cigarette Cecil bought you."

"I am." Winnie frowned. "Cecil wants me to give these up in the worst way." She waved her hand holding the cigarette.

"But I *need* the tobacco, Maybelle. I can't go cold turkey, and who wants to smoke something the flavor of blackberries anyway?"

"So you're deceiving your husband," Maybelle said.

"I don't mean to," Winnie whined, "but I can't help it. Please don't tell him, either of you." She wore a pleading expression.

I put my hands up. "Hey, don't look at me. I see nothing."

Winnie's cigarette smoking wouldn't be news to Cecil. As lovey-dovey as the two were with each other, and unless he'd completely lost his sense of smell, he would surely recognize the tobacco scent emanating from her. Now I knew for sure, though, why Winnie spent so much time away from their booth.

"I'll buy one of the pumpkin candles," I told Maybelle to take her attention off Winnie. As I paid for my purchase and Maybelle wrapped it, I asked Winnie, "Is Calvin Fisher's wife still with Axle selling jewelry?"

Winnie puffed on her cigarette and blew the smoke away from me. "She's there, and now she's got her whole passel of kids over there, too. I'm not sure if she's workin' or just tellin' everybody who'll listen about their bad fortune. I feel so sorry for those little ones, I can hardly stand it."

"You'd think she could come up with a sitter or something," I said, "so the kids wouldn't have to hang around and be bored."

"She left 'em with Axle for a little bit," Winnie said. "The sheriff came by, but she saw him first and took off like her hair was on fire."

"You mean she purposely avoided him?"

"Sure as God made little green apples," Winnie said.

Maybelle frowned. "That's odd."

"I thought so, too, and she stayed gone the whole time the sheriff was there talkin' with that oldest girl. Soon's the sheriff left, here comes Mama. I swear she was watchin' for him to leave."

"Very odd," I said.

"I'm goin' back to check on the latest." Winnie looked at me. "You want me to report back to you?"

I shook my head. "No, that's okay."

"Are you investigating?" Maybelle said. "'Cause I know you write those books, and you know how to solve a crime."

I laughed. "No, I really don't. I was just curious."

In spite of my words, Winnie said, "I'll let you know if I see anything else suspicious."

She waved and took off in the direction of her booth.

After the other woman left, Maybelle leaned close to me. "Now, if the sheriff came a-calling on that facial woman, she *should* run, after the show she put on last night."

"What happened last night?" I said, though I already had a pretty good idea.

Maybelle glanced at some women checking out her candles and spoke quietly. "It was like Britt was celebrating the fact that you-know-who is gone. Bad idea."

"I agree. Do you know what kind of issue she had with him?"

Maybelle shook her head. "No clue."

I nodded toward the shoppers. "You go on and tend to your customers. I'll see you later."

I now had a greater interest in Britt, who seemed like a viable suspect in Fisher's death. Had the sheriff already learned about her, I wondered, or had the woman managed to slip under his radar? Surely someone had thought to mention Britt's use of the word "cyanide" in connection with Fisher. I could seek her out and get the woman talking under the guise of buying facial products. Probably wouldn't hurt to stop cleaning my face with a plain old bar of soap.

My thoughts were hopping around like a rabbit, the way they too often do when I sit down to write. In order for anything good to come out, I had to focus.

First things first. I picked up Hitchcock and hurried the rest of the way to Tia's booth. When we arrived, Tia wasn't there.

"She had to leave for a few minutes," Lorene called to me from the next booth. "I'm keepin' an eye on Damon."

I waved to acknowledge her words and wondered who was keeping an eye on the merchandise with Tia gone. I'd hate to think someone could pilfer a painting from the booth, even an inexpensive one. I had the distinct impression every five bucks would mean a lot to this little family. At the moment, I didn't see any browsers. I put Hitchcock down, keeping a hold on the end of his leash, and walked over to Damon.

The boy stood under the shade of the car's open hatchback. Merlin sat on the tailgate next to a pumpkin and jars of paint sitting on an outspread newspaper. Hitchcock placed his front paws on the car's bumper, then batted at Merlin. Damon held a brush poised over the one eye painted on the pumpkin thus far.

"Looks like you're entering a contest," I said.

The boy looked up shyly and nodded.

"That eyeball looks perfect."

He grinned. "Mama taught me how to paint faces."

After a few seconds of fending off Hitchcock's attempts to start something, Merlin launched himself off the car and jumped on top of Hitchcock. The two cats commenced rolling around in the grass. No way Hitchcock would run off while the other cat was here, so I released his leash and left them to wrestle.

"I think you're going to be as good an artist as your mom," I told Damon. "Where is she?"

"She had to go talk to some lady," he said.

"Did she tell you the lady's name?"

He shook his head and dipped his brush into a jar of royal blue paint.

"I'll bet you paint better than other kids," I said to see how Damon would answer.

He simply nodded.

"Do you enjoy driving around to these festivals?"

Another nod.

The cats disentangled and jumped apart to give each other the eye. I could tell the play session wasn't over. I wondered how much information I could get from the boy about their living situation.

I looked at him. "Damon's a cool name."

"Thanks."

"Are you named after your dad?"

"Nope, his name's . . ." The boy hesitated and he scrunched up his face as he thought about this. "Mitch," he said.

"That's a cool name, too. Probably short for Mitchell."

"Yes, ma'am," Damon said.

The boy didn't show any particular emotion as he stood back from the pumpkin to inspect the eye he'd painted.

"Where does your dad live?" I said, deciding to press him just a little bit more.

Damon shrugged.

A gasp caught my attention, then, "Sabrina, is that you?"

I turned and saw Mom standing by the wall displaying Tia's floral sketches. Mom wore a cranberry business suit with a white top and low-heeled pumps. Very un-festival-like.

"What are you doing here?" I said.

"Shopping," she said.

Like she would seriously consider such a thing. "You look more like you're headed to a board meeting."

She looked down at her clothes and shrugged. "Dave thought we might have some photo ops."

"That Dave. He's always on the ball." I looked around. "Where is he?"

Mom waved an arm. "He ran into somebody he recognized. Imagine that, all the way out here."

She left off the words I felt sure she was thinking—*in the middle of nowhere.*

Mom looked at Damon, who seemed oblivious to us as he began to paint the second eye on the pumpkin. "Who's this little guy?"

"Damon Hartwell," I said, and that caused the boy to

turn and inspect my mother. "And that's Merlin, his cat, rolling around under the car with Hitchcock."

Mom glanced at the cats, then back to the boy.

"Hello, Damon," she said with a smile before turning to me. "How do you two know each other?"

"We met here at the festival," I said. "I guess you've returned to Lavender to see Aunt Rowe."

Mom hesitated before answering. "We may speak with her," she said. "If we can pry her away from all the pumpkins and that cannon. For heaven's sake, I don't understand—"

She stopped talking and her jaw dropped. Her eyes widened, and I turned to see what had caused her reaction.

Tia stood behind me, though she wasn't paying any attention to me or Mom. She was looking at Damon. "That's a wonderful job with the eyes, honey. You're such a good artist."

"Who. Is. This?" Mom looked between Tia and me, obviously struck by our similarities.

"Tia," I said.

"Yes?" Tia said and turned to us. "Oh, hi, Sabrina. Thanks for keeping Damon company."

"You know each other?" Mom said.

"We just met," Tia said.

Mom put a hand to the side of her face as if she'd developed a sudden toothache and looked at me. Her surprised expression was morphing into something else.

"How long have you known about her?" she said to me.

I held out my arms. "Like she said, we just met."

Mom's complexion was reddening to match the color of her suit. "I *always* suspected your father cheated on me," she said with barely contained anger. "I never knew about *her.*"

22

DAMON KEPT PAINTING his pumpkin as if he were all by himself in an artist's studio. The boy had far better focus than I did. Mom's words replayed in my head like a song set to "Repeat." I'd have given anything at that moment to unhear them. Dad wasn't a cheater.

Was he?

Mom continued to stare at Tia with a stricken expression. The younger woman's brows drew together over red-rimmed eyes as she looked from Mom to me. She'd either been crying or was on the brink of tears.

"Sabrina, who *is* this woman?" Tia said.

I sighed. I should have gone straight to Rita's office and avoided this whole scene. Mom might have never seen Tia. But I had started this ball of fate rolling, and now I had to deal with the situation.

"She's my mother," I said. "Disregard whatever you heard. She's confused."

"Don't be rude," Mom said, then addressed Tia. "Where do you live, miss? What was your name again?"

Tia repeated her name and glanced toward her easel and the empty chair she usually occupied. "Look, I need to get to work."

"Where are you from?" Mom said.

"Kerrville, originally," Tia said, "but I'm not whoever you think I am."

Mom held out a hand and swept it from Tia's head to her feet. "Obviously, you are."

"Ma'am," Tia said, "I don't need any more trouble."

"Mom, let's go. Leave her alone."

Mom looked at me pointedly. "Your father went on those trips to a ranch that just so happens to be in *Kerrville*." She turned to Tia. "Y'all's father."

My stomach lurched, but I refused to give Mom the benefit of the doubt. "Dad is gone, and I don't appreciate your tainting my good memories. Let's get out of here. Tia needs to work."

"Forgive me if my manners aren't up to par," Mom said in what my brother and I used to call her Mrs. Snippy voice. "Coming face-to-face with my late husband's illegitimate child is quite a shock."

Tia propped her hands on her hips and tears welled in her eyes. "If you're referring to me, you're quite mistaken. What is this, kick-Tia-around day? First the deputy's accusations, now this."

"What deputy?" I said.

Tia shook her head. "Never mind. I have customers waiting."

Several bars of oompah-pah music came over the loudspeakers, followed by Aunt Rowe's voice.

"Good afternoon, ladies and gentlemen," she said. "Welcome to Lavender's Pumpkin Days. Judging for the sixteenth annual pumpkin carving contest begins at one. Cutoff for entries is twelve-thirty. Extra pumpkins and tools are available."

As Aunt Rowe went on to give more information about the contest, Tia spoke to Damon and walked over to her easel, where she greeted a customer. Aunt Rowe finished her announcement, and the music continued to play.

Mom hadn't moved, and I could tell by looking at her that her agitation level was still high.

"Leave it alone," I said.

"But—"

"Brenda, let's go." Dave appeared, striding briskly toward us. "Hello, Sabrina."

He walked to me and gave me a perfunctory pat on the shoulder. "How are you?"

I was fine before Mom showed up.

"I'm okay," I told him. "Busy."

He didn't care to wait for my response and had already gone to Mom and taken her arm. "Rowe is over by the bandstand. This'll be a good time to catch her."

"Dave's right," I said. "You don't want to miss this window of opportunity." If Aunt Rowe had heard Mom's conversation with Tia, she would chew them both up and spit them out before they got a chance to ask her for a favor. She might do that anyway.

Mom appeared to be mulling over her choices as she glanced from me to Dave to Tia, back to Dave.

"We'll talk later," she finally said and left with my step-father.

I rolled my tense shoulders when they walked away and went to retrieve the end of Hitchcock's leash. The cats had obviously played themselves out and lay sprawled in the shade of the car bumper near Damon. The boy had finished painting the second eye on his pumpkin and was working on an ear.

I watched as Tia sold a bluebonnets painting to a woman. Naturally, anyone who saw me and Tia together would wonder if we were related—that had been my first thought when I saw her. Mom's reaction, though, was way over the top and

I wanted nothing to do with her view of the matter. What I wanted was to know more about Tia's talk with the deputy, so I picked Hitchcock up and approached the easel.

"I apologize for my mom."

Tia looked up with a frown that told me she wished I would leave.

"Do you paint cats?" I said.

Tia looked at Hitchcock.

"I mean sketch them, if I can get him to hold still long enough."

"You want to buy a sketch?" she said.

I looked at the small white sign hanging from her table. Twenty bucks seemed more than fair and completely worth it for a chance to continue our conversation.

"Yes, I do."

She indicated the chair and described how I should sit and where I should place my arms. "You want me to sketch both of you, right? Or did you want the cat by himself?"

She was all business, as if I were a complete stranger, which wasn't that far from the truth. "Both would be nice," I said.

"With or without his harness?"

"I can remove the harness."

She shook her head. "No need. I'll pretend it's invisible."

"Okay."

A family stopped to watch as Tia got started. A small girl jabbered about the kitty and Hitchcock's ears twitched. I didn't appreciate the audience, but after a minute they moved on. If I wanted to talk, I'd better jump in now while no one was close enough to hear.

"Which deputy spoke with you?" I said.

Tia's gaze lifted from the sketch to me, but her hand kept moving. "The black-haired woman."

"Patricia Rosales," I said. "She's not very nice, though I suppose '*nice*' isn't in her job description."

"She practically accused me of killing that man," Tia said in a near whisper.

"That's how she is, but you shouldn't panic. Last night I felt like she was pointing the finger at me."

"She sounded deadly serious." Tia lowered her hand from the sketch. "She talked about witnesses."

"She's obviously all talk," I said. "If they had evidence worth anything, they would have already arrested someone."

Tears sprang to Tia's eyes. "If they arrest me, what will happen to Damon? He can't go to his father. Mitch doesn't care enough to watch the boy for an hour."

"They aren't going to arrest you," I said with more conviction than I felt.

"I might need a lawyer," she said, continuing to sketch, "but I can't afford one."

"Did you do anything wrong?" I said.

Tia shook her head repeatedly. "No."

"Then let's hope it doesn't come to that, but coincidentally I did want to talk with you about a family-law matter." Hitchcock squirmed in my lap, and I rubbed his chest to keep him still.

Tia's hand stopped moving. "Related to your mother's accusations?"

"No, no. I'm going to do my best to pretend she never brought up the subject. I never heard one thing about my father straying, and I'm pretty sure Aunt Rowe—Dad's sister—would go for the jugular if she heard Mom say otherwise."

Tia grinned. "Your aunt is feisty."

"Yup," I said. "And my mom can be annoying. She jumped to a silly conclusion based on our looks."

"To say the least," Tia said. "Not that I would mind being your sister, but I'm not. There's nothing in my past to suggest my father wasn't my father. He was always there for me, even though we moved often because of his job. He's gone now."

"Mine, too." I hesitated for a second. "And your mother?"

Tia blinked rapidly. "She's in a nursing home with early-onset Alzheimer's."

"I'm sorry."

The woman might not remember my father even if approached with the topic, and did it even matter at this point? I thought not.

"Listen, Tia," I said. "I used to work for a family-law attorney." I explained that Rita might be able to help her with a child support case and have the court order Damon's father to pay all fees. "Would you like me to talk with her about it?"

Tia's lips trembled as she nodded. "I'd appreciate any help I can get."

She gave me the bits of information Rita would need if she took on the support case. More onlookers came along and watched Tia work. When she finished with us, I placed Hitchcock on the grass and stood to stretch. I paid Tia and met her eyes as she handed me the picture. Her work was remarkable given the short amount of time she'd spent.

"I believe whoever's guilty is here in Lavender, and I'm going to convince Rosales it's not one of us," I told her.

Several people milled around the booth and Tia needed to get moving. She smiled at me. "Thank you."

Before we could say more, a teenage girl with a toddler in tow marched up to Tia. She handed Tia a piece of paper, and I caught a glimpse of a family photo on the page. The heading said "Family of Calvin Fisher," though he wasn't in the picture.

"We need your help," the girl intoned. "Our father was taken from us before his time."

Tia scanned the paper in her hand and paled.

I realized belatedly that the teenager was Amber Fisher. The boy with her was probably one of the twins Coco had mentioned at the sheriff's office. Deke.

"May I have a copy, Amber?" I said.

The girl eyed me as if trying to remember where we'd met before and finally handed over a flyer.

"Donations can be made in cash or through our website listed on the page," she said before turning and practically dragging her brother away with her.

Tia and I exchanged a glance.

I couldn't help but wonder when these flyers with the smiling family photo had been printed. It seemed to me that the widow Fisher had arrived in Lavender with a campaign prepared well in advance.

23

WITH HITCHCOCK, THE salt-and-pepper shakers, my new apple-spice candle, and the sketch of me and my cat, my hands were full. I had to at least offload some of these purchases in the car. I'd feel better, though, if I took Hitchcock home where he could be comfortable and take his usual afternoon nap. No need for the cat to traipse around the festival all afternoon, even if I carried him while I asked questions. Lord knew, I had plenty to ask.

On the drive home, I thought about Coco Fisher and what kind of mother would send her children out on a fund-raising mission the day after they learned of their father's death. Then again, what *was* the proper timing of such a thing, if the family was in really dire straits?

I didn't want to be insensitive, but Coco seemed like an enigma, crying over her lost husband, selling jewelry, sending the kids out to collect money. I couldn't predict or explain this woman's actions.

When I got back to the cottages, I noted the atmosphere was in its usual pre-festival state. Quiet and peaceful. Thomas, doing some work beside the Venice cottage with hedge clippers, waved as I drove by. Aunt Rowe's golf cart stood by the storage room, undoubtedly parked there by Glenda, who'd be making her rounds to restock the cottages with fresh towels and supplies.

I parked at the Monte Carlo cottage, and Hitchcock jumped over my lap and out through the driver's side the second I pushed the door open. He was up on the deck and through the cat door by the time I stood. I opened the back car door to retrieve my tote and the sketch I'd laid carefully on the seat.

I straightened and closed the door. Held the sketch up to admire it.

"That sure is beautiful."

I jumped at the voice coming from behind me and spun to see Gabe Brenner standing not five feet away.

My heart thudded. "What are you doing here? Isn't it, like, lunchtime? Your busy time?"

He grinned. "I got plenty of help with the cookin'."

"Oh."

"Bacon's sellin' like hotcakes today," he said. "Fair amount of stuffed jalapeños, too, and we're runnin' low on salt. Come back here for the extra case."

The thought of all that salt—on top of bacon and jalapeños—made my mouth pucker.

"I'm guessing your salt is at the Melbourne cottage, not here," I said.

"Right." He chuckled as if I'd told an especially funny joke.

Had he really come back to pick up supplies or had he watched me leave the festival and followed? I forced my breathing to slow.

Get away from him.

I turned toward my cottage. "I have to run. Nice seeing you."

"Sabrina, wait."

I looked back to see that he'd come a couple feet closer. But he *had* stopped, so it wasn't as if he meant to grab me or do anything equally scary. No need to race inside screaming.

I hoped.

"What is it?"

"I talked to your friend about book writing. She said you'd be able to help me."

No, she didn't.

"She told me you talked," I said, "but I'm sure she didn't promise you any of my time. I'm very busy, Gabe, and I'm not a teacher."

"But you have experience," he said. "You know how to get 'er done, and I sure could use a boost in the right direction."

"There's probably someone near your home better equipped to help you," I said.

"But I want you."

His expression was an odd combination of admiration and something else I didn't care to define. I shivered involuntarily.

I heard the cat door and turned to see Hitchcock on the deck.

"Mrrreeeooowww," he said. "Mrreow."

"I'm being summoned," I said. "See you later."

I quick-stepped up the walk with the key in my hand. Hitchcock went through the big door with me. The second we were safely inside I slammed and locked the door. After the bright sun outside, the cottage interior seemed dark. I noticed the living room curtains were drawn. I usually opened them when I got up in the morning, but I was admittedly distracted today.

My vision adjusted slowly, and I noticed Hitchcock had jumped up on my writing table to sit beside my laptop.

"Mrreow," he said.

"Not now," I said. "I can't write while my heart's racing.

Where'd that guy come from anyway? I didn't see his vehicle, and the thought of him lurking out there on foot freaks me out."

"Mrreow," Hitchcock repeated.

I walked to the kitchen sink and opened the shutters to look out. "It's okay. He's gone now. I think."

I turned back to the cat, and my foot brushed against something.

I looked down and saw my kitchen towel on the floor instead of next to the sink where it belonged. And something else. Potholders from the drawer next to the cooktop. I looked up. The drawer was open. I squinted as I looked around the kitchen and realized all of the drawers and kitchen cabinet doors stood open.

I walked to the wall switch, flicked it on, and gasped. The place had been ransacked.

My heart rate climbed to marathon speed in a split second.

Call for help.

I wasn't going to risk Deputy Rosales responding to a 911 call, so I dialed Sheriff Crawford's personal cell number. When he answered, I told him about returning home to find Gabe Brenner outside and the ransacked cottage.

"Are you sure you're alone?" the sheriff said.

"It's just me and Hitchcock. He'd let me know in a second if the intruder was still here."

"I'm sure he would. Were the doors and windows locked when you got home?"

"The doors were locked. I haven't checked the windows."

"Don't touch anything," he said. "I'll be there shortly."

I didn't want to go outside because Gabe might be out there, so I called Glenda and Thomas and asked them to come to me. The sheriff would want to know if anyone had seen anything important, and they might have something to report. While I waited for them, I did a visual check of

the windows and found the latches on one in the bedroom open. I didn't think I'd left it that way, but I couldn't be certain.

My arms and legs felt jittery as I stood in the bedroom and imagined an intruder going through my things. Had Gabe Brenner been in here touching my clothes, playing out fantasies in his I-want-to-be-a-writer imagination?

Scary.

I made a pass around the cottage to see if I could identify anything missing. After my two recent searches of the place, I was super familiar with what was where. My fingerprints were obviously everywhere already, but I followed the sheriff's instructions and didn't touch anything. Nothing stuck out except for an impression that every item had been slightly moved.

A knock sounded at the door, and I heard, "Sabrina, it's Thomas."

I went to the door and let him in. He took one look and said, "Holy cow. How did this happen?"

"You tell me. I was at the festival."

Hitchcock was now lounging on the back of the sofa, and Thomas cast a leery glance in the cat's direction.

"He did not cause this bad luck," I said.

"I know he didn't," Thomas said. "But who did? I've been around all day, and I didn't see anyone hanging around."

"It's okay, Thomas. This isn't your fault." I told him about my short conversation with Gabe Brenner and my worry that the man had been the person inside my cottage.

"I saw Brenner come and go in a white pickup," Thomas said. "He wasn't here but ten minutes, fifteen tops."

"My place is small," I said. "That would be long enough to do this."

"But why would he?" Thomas said. "Seeing as he wants you to do him a favor and teach him how to write."

"So he says. That might be a complete fabrication."

Thomas said, "Wouldn't be the first guy who lied to get what he wants."

"Good point."

"So who else is in the running?" Thomas said. "Bet you have ideas."

"Last night Rosales wanted to search every cottage here. Maybe she got a warrant."

"They'd give us notice. With Rowena at the festival, they'd have come to me or Glenda. I haven't seen anybody," he said again.

I caught sight of the golf cart through a side window and opened my door for Glenda. Thomas walked around the living room, eyeing the window locks, then went into the bedroom.

"My goodness gracious," Glenda said when she saw the mess. She pointed to my laptop. "You're lucky this is still here. Is anything missing?"

"Not that I can tell," I said.

"Someone made a mess for the sake of making a mess?" she said. "That's weird."

I agreed. "You see anybody around in the last couple of hours?"

"Not since I saw a certain someone sneaking out of here before the crack of dawn," she said in a low voice and winked.

I explained that Luke had actually spent the night out in his truck watching for intruders, but I'm not sure Glenda believed me.

"Have any of the other cottages had a problem?" I said.

Glenda shook her head. "Not the ones I've seen so far. I'm about halfway through them."

The sheriff showed up five minutes later with a uniformed young lady he introduced as a fingerprint technician. He gave her instructions, and she went into the bedroom to begin her work.

"Sorry to make your job harder, Glenda," the sheriff said, "but we have to dust for prints. The perp may have come prepared and worn gloves, but we might get lucky."

"Are you going to do this at every cottage?" Glenda said.

The sheriff looked at her sharply. "Were there other break-ins?"

"No, I don't think so," she said. "Let me run and check the cottages I haven't already been to this morning."

Sheriff Crawford nodded. "You do that."

Glenda scurried off, and the sheriff turned to Thomas. "Tell me about this morning. What you were doing, what you saw; more important, who you saw and when."

Thomas launched into a rundown of his day so far, the chores he'd done, what time each of the vendors took off for town, who left with whom, and Gabe's return a short while ago. The sheriff interrupted him every so often to request even more detail than he'd already given.

I paced the living room as they talked. Given the fact that the sheriff had an open murder case to deal with, it seemed like he was spending an inordinate amount of time on this case of much smaller magnitude. Not that I didn't appreciate him dropping everything and rushing over here. I did, but something was off.

Hitchcock sat tall on a sofa cushion, his eyes following me back and forth, back and forth. He reminded me of one of those cat clocks with eyes that move in time with the second hand. I wished, not for the first time, that there was a way I could know what the cat was thinking. When Thomas finished outlining his day, Sheriff Crawford excused him and Thomas left the cottage.

The tech moved from the bedroom into the kitchen to collect prints there.

The sheriff turned to me. "Okay, Sabrina. Please tell me everything that Brenner said to you when you got back here, before you came inside."

I tried to ignore the tech and the fingerprint dust she was leaving all over my kitchen. I repeated my tale, filling in details about Gabe's prior conversation with Tyanne about his desire to write a book.

"Did he mention Calvin Fisher today?" the sheriff said.

I shook my head. "No, he didn't."

"Are you sure?" The sheriff's dark eyes homed in on my face as if he was searching for a sign that I was telling the truth—or not.

"I'm positive," I said. "He talked about writing. That was it. Oh, and he mentioned the salt he'd come back to pick up."

"Salt?"

"Yes, for his cooking."

"Did you see the salt?"

I shook my head. "No, he said they were running low and he'd come back to get the extra case. Thomas saw him come and saw him leave. I didn't."

"Where was Brenner, exactly, when you first saw him?"

"Standing behind me on the sidewalk. Between my car and the deck."

"Why don't you tell me everything about this morning, from the time you got up?"

I sighed. "What does all that have to do with somebody coming in here after I left? I can promise you that the break-in did not happen while I was still at home this morning. It happened *after* I went to the festival."

"Are you questioning my ability to run an investigation?" the sheriff said.

"No, I'm just frustrated."

"I know the feeling."

My phone buzzed, and I pulled it from my pocket to read an incoming text from Glenda.

"No other break-ins," I told the sheriff. "Glenda says she checked all the cottages."

He rolled his shoulders and smoothed his mustache. "So you're the lucky one."

"Looks that way."

"Has Brenner given you any personal details about his life?" the sheriff said.

I made a face. "Only about the food he sells. Believe me, I don't care to know—"

I stopped talking when I noticed the intense concentration on Sheriff Crawford's face. This was about more than this break-in.

"Something tells me you know plenty about Brenner," I said.

The sheriff nodded. "Matter of fact, I do. I told you I'd have Deputy Ainsley check him out, and he has."

"What did he learn?"

"Brenner lives in Lufkin, Texas, with his mother. He's twenty-nine. Started out at SMU after high school, played football, had a serious knee injury, and went back home. Works at a restaurant."

I wondered why he thought I needed to know all of this.

The sheriff continued. "On top of the bum-knee problem, doctors diagnosed him with late onset juvenile diabetes. He takes multiple insulin injections a day."

I wondered what the health information had to do with anything. The sheriff was building up to something, so I stayed quiet and waited.

"Back in Lufkin, several complaints have been filed against Brenner. Young women reporting him for unwanted attention, writing love notes, calling at inappropriate times, etc."

"He stalked them?" I said.

"His actions don't exactly meet the legal definition of stalking. However, he was found guilty of assaulting the male friend of one of these young women. Man ended up in the hospital with a broken nose and fractured ribs."

"I wonder what the guy did to deserve it?"

The sheriff frowned. "What makes you ask?"

I shrugged. "I think of Gabe as the type who strikes out to protect, not for the sake of striking out."

"And that makes it okay?"

"No, I'm just saying."

"All right. You're allowed your opinion." He cleared his throat. "I'm going to begin by asking him about this break-in."

"Even if he isn't the one who broke in," I said, "he was clearly right here. He might have seen someone else who—" I stopped, and my brain rewound the sheriff's words. "What do you mean 'begin'?"

Sheriff Crawford didn't respond.

"You think Gabe killed Calvin Fisher?" I didn't know why this surprised me. I'd seen Gabe punch Fisher in the face with quite a bit of force. I had a feeling he had the strength to do a lot more than what he'd exhibited in the grocery store parking lot. But the dead man had showed no signs of a beating. No marks on his face, at least.

Bottom line? Gabe scared me, but I didn't believe he was the one who killed Fisher.

The sheriff's expression told me he thought differently.

"Does Deputy Ainsley also think Gabe committed murder?"

"He—no, *we*—believe Brenner needs to be taken in and questioned."

The tech had moved carefully around us, doing her work quietly. She paused to pet Hitchcock, then slipped out the front door.

I frowned at the sheriff. "One big problem sticks out in my mind about your theory."

"What's that?"

"Someone as big and strong as Gabe wouldn't need handcuffs to control Fisher. And, by the way, I saw a festival booth that's selling cuffs, which means they're readily available for anyone who decided that they *did*, in fact, need help to control the victim."

"You can use that in your next plot," the sheriff said. "Continue to steer clear of Brenner, just in case you see him before we pick him up." He turned to go, then paused and looked at me. "Maybe take extra precautions and stay somewhere else tonight, even if I have Brenner under lock and key by then. You could stay with Rowe at the house."

He opened the door and left.

My stomach felt sick as I thought about the sheriff's theory. I couldn't explain why I wasn't buying Gabe Brenner as the killer.

I turned to look at Hitchcock. The cat was completely sacked out on the sofa cushion. We were safe here—otherwise my smart kitty would be up and patrolling. I didn't think we needed to spend the night elsewhere. Right now, all I wanted to do was go back to the festival to conduct my own interrogation and find the truth.

24

ON MY WAY back to the festival I realized I'd forgotten to ask the sheriff if Coco Fisher returned this morning to quiz him further about me and/or her husband's missing possessions. She'd probably been too busy getting the kids lined up for their fund-raising drive. Maybe her thoughts jumped around from topic to topic the way mine did.

I was not relieved to know the sheriff was closing in on a solution to Fisher's murder. Thankfully, he wasn't targeting Tia. Try as I might, though, I couldn't accept the possibility that Gabe was the guilty party. Yes, he was a weird guy. He had a creepy fixation on me, and my skin crawled when I was in his presence. That didn't make him a killer. Plus, there were so many other pieces that didn't fit into the puzzle where Gabe was concerned.

I didn't want the man to be arrested for murder simply because I brought him to the sheriff's attention for an entirely different reason. If Gabe turned out to be the person who'd

searched my cottage, I'd be surprised, even though he'd been right there on the premises. An unwelcome thought struck me. What if he came inside simply to put his hands on my personal belongings? The very idea made me cringe. Maybe I should quit coming to the man's defense, but accusing him of murder just didn't feel right. Maybe I could learn something to point me in a better direction.

After I'd driven around town in search of a parking space, one finally opened and I pulled in before someone else could snatch it. I would have quite a hike to cover the ground I wanted to cover, but at least the weather had held and the air carried a gentle breeze. On my agenda for questioning were Britt Cramer, Axle No-Last-Name, and Eddie Baxter, Fisher's long-time friend. I was glad Hitchcock hadn't balked at being left at home. I had locked the cat door and felt reasonably assured that he'd stay there until I returned.

I decided Britt, Gabe's drinking partner from the night before, should be my first subject. On my way to looking for her facial-products booth, I passed Rita Colletti's office. Funny how her name had slipped my mind when I reviewed my mental to-do list. Frosted-glass windows flanked a red front door that could have used a fresh coat of paint. Block lettering on a white placard attached to the door showed the firm's name and phone number. Knocking and ringing the bell produced no answer, and the door was locked. I shrugged and scribbled a note to slide under the door. I could have texted Rita, but that might have produced an immediate response. I didn't want to go there when my mind was already fixed on Britt.

I found the Pure Velvet Facial Transformation Systems booth on Oleander Lane. Britt was easy to spot in a bright orange poncho with fringe over off-white slacks. She wore a multicolored necklace of giant beads, and her blond curls were teased out in a Texas-sized hairdo that coordinated nicely with the big necklace. Her eyes were bleary, though, and I guessed she hadn't yet recovered from last night's partying.

"Good afternoon," she said with a smile when she saw me. "May I interest you in a Pure Velvet transformation?"

Behind her, a wallboard held before and after pictures of women who claimed the Pure Velvet products had made them appear ten years younger. Next to the wallboard, another woman—Britt's employee, I assumed—smeared goop on a customer's face.

My skin felt fine as it was, but I told myself "in for a penny, in for a pound" and smiled at Britt. "I would love to be transformed."

Taken out of this universe would have sounded even better right about now, but I was sure such a request was beyond Britt's powers.

She invited me to sit on an empty stool next to the display table and draped a plastic cape around me.

"My name is Britt," she said as though we'd never met. "What's yours?"

"You remember me, don't you?" I said. "From the party last night?"

Britt squinted for a second, then forced her eyes open wide as if she realized the squinting would cause wrinkles. "Oh, Sabrina," she said, surprising me. "I didn't know you were there. At the party, I mean. Not that I remember much." She held fingertips to her forehead. "I'm not quite recovered from the whole event."

"I'm not surprised," I said, continuing with the ruse. "You and Gabe were busy knocking 'em back."

Britt glanced at the others as if to assure herself they weren't hearing our conversation, but the women were gabbing about moisturizers. Britt turned back to me.

"Guilty," she said with an embarrassed smile. "I admit to overdoing it. Now tell me a bit about your facial routine."

"Not much to tell," I said. "Jump in the shower, soap up, rinse off, pat dry."

"You use *soap* on your face?" Her eyes widened with mock horror. "Regular soap?"

"I'm afraid so."

She leaned down to peer at my complexion, so close that I could clearly see the red-lined whites of her eyes. I'd have been surprised if she didn't have a killer headache.

Britt straightened and said, "You're a very lucky woman." She turned to the table beside her and picked up a bottle and a cotton ball. "Your skin has held up very well in the face of neglect."

Her words sounded unnecessarily rude, but I reminded myself I wasn't really here because of my skin. Britt dabbed the cotton with solution from the bottle and began tapping it across my face.

"I'm hoping my skin will cooperate a good while longer," I said, "though one never knows how much time one has left. Just look at what happened to poor Calvin Fisher."

Britt stopped patting. "Huh. What'd he ever do to make you feel sorry for him?"

"Um, he was murdered," I said. "That usually generates some sympathy for the dead person."

"Not from me, it doesn't," she said.

"Then maybe for the family?"

"I don't know much of anything about Cal's family," she said forcefully. "Jeez, now you've got me all worked up. I might need a shot of something to calm me down."

"Maybe not everyone liked the man," I said, "but he didn't deserve to die."

She glared at me. "Oh, he didn't, did he? How well did you know good ol' Cal?"

"I didn't. I live here, and he didn't. I'm not sure where he's from. Do you know?"

"I'm sure he didn't keep me updated with address changes over the years," she said.

"So you knew where he lived at some point?" I said.

"I may have," she said. "In another lifetime."

"You knew him well."

"Let's just say far too well," she said. "The man was a parasite."

She continued the cotton ball treatment. "This is toner," she said. "There are a couple of steps you would ordinarily use before this—twice a day. The makeup remover and the foaming cleanser. We're not equipped here for those steps, and since you're not wearing any makeup . . ."

She may as well have been saying "blah, blah, blah." My mind was back on "*parasite.*"

"You have quite a vocabulary when it comes to describing Cal," I said. "Last night you called him a louse, you mentioned giving him a cyanide facial, and now he's a parasite. How did you come by all this experience with the man?"

"We met a long time ago," she said. "In a time I'd rather forget."

"Did you date him?"

She shook her head.

"Marry him?"

"Thank the Lord, no," she said.

"Live with him?" I guessed.

"Stop it," she said. "Please. I don't want to talk about him."

Something in her tone brought out my empathetic side. I kept quiet while Britt smoothed something green and slimy on my face, then covered that layer with a white, frothy substance that reminded me of beaten egg whites.

When I spoke again, the stuff on my face had begun to harden, and I felt the mask cracking alongside my mouth. I decided to change my approach slightly. "Do you know Coco Fisher?"

"No." Britt inspected my face. "When we remove this, we'll pull impurities from your complexion, and—"

"You know, Britt, it wasn't a good idea to celebrate Cal's death in public in front of witnesses. That behavior tends to make you look suspicious."

"I wasn't the only person celebrating," she said.

"What do you know about the other guy, Gabe Brenner?"

She shrugged. "I never met him before. He made some kind of a toast, said the world was a better place without Cal in it, and I agreed. I started drinking along with him, and I honestly don't remember much else."

The woman looked a lot smarter than she acted.

"Have the authorities come by to speak with you?" I said.

She stepped back and glared at me. "Are you interested at *all* in Pure Velvet?"

"Well." I looked into her eyes and determined she was hurting. From something that Fisher had done in the past? Something I'd said? I wasn't sure. I reminded myself that I *did* need someone to wipe the gunk off my face and I ought to play nice.

I swallowed. "I wouldn't mind beginning a reasonable skin-treatment regimen, but you can't expect me to start with the ten-step process. That's not gonna happen."

Britt found a smile. "Not a problem. We can start with the cleanse, tone, moisturize package."

"How much is that?" I asked, even though Fisher was what I really wanted to discuss.

"Eighty-seven dollars including tax," Britt said.

I gulped and made a decision.

"If I buy the package, would you consider answering a few more questions?"

"That depends," Britt said.

THIRTY minutes later, I left Britt's booth. I had to admit my skin felt great. She'd taken me through another five steps at least, then convinced me I really should opt to add the eye cream to my three-step package. I reminded myself that the age of forty was in my near future and succumbed to the sales pitch. I didn't relish the thought of seeing extra lines in my magnifying mirror.

I was out one hundred and twelve dollars, including tax, but she'd let me ask more questions.

She'd heard Cal married a few years ago, possibly three or four. She didn't know he had children. With those facts, I concluded that Amber must be Coco's child from a prior relationship. Britt saw Cal from time to time at other events, and she always steered clear. She refused to elaborate on the reason for her deep-seated dislike of him.

She knew other vendors had issues with Fisher. Gabe Brenner hadn't said anything self-incriminating to her. She didn't know Tia Hartwell personally, and she hadn't heard anything about Tia wishing to do away with Fisher. She didn't know a thing about Axle or his business relationship with Cal.

Britt closed with: "Look, Sabrina. I'm not one bit sorry he's dead, but I didn't kill him, if that's what you really want to know."

That *was* one of the things I wanted to know, and she'd said the words with a sincere expression and tone. Was she telling me the truth?

While my skin might benefit from the time I'd spent with Britt, I didn't have much more data to help me find out who had killed Calvin Fisher and why. The good news was that I hadn't learned anything that could hurt Tia, either.

Time to move on to the next character in Fisher's life— Axle No-Last-Name.

25

I MEANT TO HEAD straight for the late Calvin Fisher's jewelry booth, but my rumbling stomach reminded me I'd skipped right past lunch. The mixed scents of French fries, hot dogs, sausage on a stick, and even the deep-fried bacon, had finally cut through my focus.

Wait, me? Focused? This might be a small miracle.

I worried about the wisdom of interrupting my clear train of thought to eat. I needed food, though. Otherwise, I'd get weak and—

For Pete's sake, Sabrina, eat. Now.

Calliope music played in the area surrounding the food trucks and made me think of the times Dad had taken me to the circus when it came to Houston. Thinking about him could have distracted me for sure, so I forced myself to concentrate on the food.

I stopped at the first stand I reached and got in line to buy a chili dog. Decided to get two while I was at it, then

realized there was no way I could eat something so messy while standing.

Picnic tables sat nearby under a grove of live oaks, the perfect solution for my dilemma. I headed that way and was almost on top of Rita Colletti before I heard her call my name. The lawyer wore jeans and a festival T-shirt, and I realized this was the first time I'd seen her dressed casually. She sat at a large table by herself and waved me over.

Ordinarily, running into Rita was a bad thing. Fortuitous today, though, since I had something I wanted to discuss with her.

"Grab a seat," Rita said when I reached her. "Got your note. You decide you need representation after all?"

I swung my legs over the bench seat and took a swig of my soft drink. "Nope. It's something else, but let me get a start on this food first so I don't pass out from hunger."

"Go ahead," she said. "I'm not goin' anywhere."

Rita had two sticks of what looked like veggie shish ke-bab on the plate in front of her. Onions, bell peppers, mush-rooms. Looked good, but I needed protein to keep me going. Not that the hot dog with meat-based chili was anything to brag about.

I opted to cut my food using the plasticware I'd picked up. Otherwise, I'd end up wearing half of the chili. I stabbed a chunk of meat and bun with the tiny fork, dragged it through the chili, and stuffed it into my mouth.

"What do you hear about the murder investigation?" Rita said the moment I took the bite.

"Ummmm," I said and pointed the fork at my full mouth.

Rita popped a miniscule piece of bell pepper into her mouth and swallowed. "They're saying Fisher died from an injection."

I stopped chewing and washed the food down with an-other swallow of my drink. "What kind of injection?"

"Don't know yet," she said. "Heard they found the cap to

a syringe in his truck. Wife doesn't know anything about Fisher ever having a syringe, so they're working on the assumption the killer brought it with him." She worked a mushroom off the kebab. "Or her."

I flashed back to the sheriff's discussion about Gabe and his diabetes injections. Was this why the sheriff had focused on him?

That and the fact that he'd told me my troublemaker was gone. He *had* said it with what could have been considered a self-congratulatory tone, but I still didn't think Gabe had committed murder. I wanted the truth to come out, and I believed the sheriff was like a dog barking up the wrong tree.

"Maybe Fisher was a drug user," I said. "He might have hidden his drugs from his wife."

"Possible," Rita said.

My mind raced as I took another bite of hot dog. There were other uses for syringes, weren't there? I remembered watching a video of a woman using a large syringe to decorate cookies with frosting. The really big ones could be used to baste a turkey. I doubted that was the type of syringe Rita was referring to, though. With all the stuff for sale at the festival, could someone be selling syringes right here on the streets of Lavender?

Nah. That's far-fetched.

"I see the wheels turning," Rita said. "What are you thinking?"

I shrugged and shoved more food into my mouth. Ate it quickly and said, "Did they find needle marks on Fisher's body?"

"I don't have that information," Rita said.

"What does that mean exactly?" I said. "The medical examiner hasn't given that bit of news to Deputy Rosales yet so she could spread it all over town?"

"I'm not answering that," Rita said.

I had a snarky response ready, but I took a bite of hot dog instead. As I chewed, I checked out Rita's T-shirt.

"What's with the shirt?" I said. "That's not your style."

"I'm helping your aunt with the contests," she said and twisted so I could see the big word "JUDGE" on the back of the shirt. Underneath, in smaller print, "Colletti Law Firm" was printed along with the office address and phone number.

"Ah, you're advertising," I said.

"Need to build up the clientele," she said, "now that I'm settled here and officially divorced from the Houston firm."

I guessed Rita and Dave had finalized the paperwork to dissolve Rita from the partnership, but I didn't care to know the details. Though the thought of her living in Lavender from now on made me groan inwardly, I figured this was a good time to tell her about Tia's situation. Rita listened attentively while I told her about Tia's ex-husband's failure to pay child support.

"It's a case," Rita said, "but I'd rather be her attorney for the murder charge."

I glared at her. "She isn't being charged with murder."

"Not yet." Rita took a bite of grilled onion and chewed slowly before swallowing.

"Forget I said anything." Why had I even bothered to bring this up?

"I'd like to represent whoever gets charged," Rita said. "A murder case is a murder case."

"And all you care about is the publicity," I said. "How could I have forgotten that lovely fact about working with you?"

I stood and picked up my drink and my plate.

"Have a great afternoon, Rita." I stomped across the grass to the congregation of trash bins and set my cup on top of one while I gobbled down the second hot dog without cutting it up. When I finished, chili was running down my hand. I looked around to see if anyone was watching, didn't notice any lookers, and licked the mess off. Grabbed my drink and guzzled it before throwing away my trash.

That woman had the power to aggravate me more than anyone else I knew. Except people who thought my cat brought bad luck. I tried to chill. Rita had the right to make a living however she chose. She was making sound financial judgment calls for someone growing a new business. I wished she had picked a different small Texas town.

I found a restroom to scrub my hands and noticed chili on my shirt when I glanced in the mirror. I did my best to rinse the stain and emerged a few minutes later wearing a dark, wet blotch. I heard the pumpkin cannon going off, which told me where I could find Aunt Rowe. Surely, Mom and Dave were finished sucking up to my aunt by now. After dealing with Rita, I did not want to run into them.

On my way across the square, I spotted Amber Fisher with not only the little boy she'd had with her earlier but a similar-sized girl, plus the older child, Coco, and another adult. The woman with dark hair Tyanne had mentioned earlier.

Coco wore tight shorts, tennis shoes, a visor to shield her face from the sun, and a fanny pack with a water bottle attached. She looked like a coach gathering her team in a huddle. Amber and the two women each held a sheaf of papers. I didn't know what other people would think of them, but I found their behavior odd.

I bypassed the "team" and approached the pumpkin cannon. Aunt Rowe and Thorn stood up on the trailer. Herr Schmidt stood nearby and appeared to be watching Coco and her "team." I wondered what kind of rules he had for dealing with people who wanted to use the festival grounds for fund-raising. I didn't care what they were doing, and certainly not about any rules, but this would give me a good reason to start a conversation with Schmidt. Not that he'd tell me anything about his relationship with Calvin Fisher or the do-or-die conversation he'd had with Axle earlier, but I might learn something useful.

I walked up to the man. "Hey there, Herr Schmidt. The pumpkin cannon seems to be a big hit with the crowd. I'm glad you let Aunt Rowe keep it."

He gave me a dour look. "She wouldn't take no for an answer, and we're not out of the woods yet. She's taking a risk with every pumpkin that flies out of that thing."

"Life is full of risks," I said. "Just look at what happened to Calvin Fisher. He was a friend of yours, wasn't he?"

Schmidt startled at the question. "Me? No, not exactly."

I put a hand on my chest. "Sorry, I'm not sure where I got that idea." I waited a moment, then snapped my fingers. "Probably because you were so eager to find him yesterday morning. You had Deputy Rosales hunting him down for you."

Schmidt seemed to be avoiding my gaze.

"Why was it so important for you to find him?" I said.

"Uh, I don't recall," Schmidt said. "Must have been something about his booth rental."

"Right." I nodded. "Maybe he wasn't following your rules exactly the way you wanted. Do you write out citations for people who aren't following the festival rule book?"

Schmidt frowned. "There are no citations."

"It's probably better that there aren't. Otherwise, you'd probably cite Fisher's family."

Schmidt played dumb. "Excuse me?"

I gestured to Coco and the children. "Coco Fisher arrived in town last night. Looks like she and Calvin's children are holding a fund-raiser."

Schmidt's brows drew together. "They are?"

"I'm pretty sure." I pulled the folded sheet of paper Amber had given me from my pocket. "They're passing these out."

Schmidt hemmed and hawed for a few seconds, then said, "Well, that's not ordinarily something I would condone. Under the circumstances—"

"Do you have rules about such things?" I said.

"Not exactly, but—"

"It's unusual for the family themselves to be the ones asking for donations. I usually see such things handled by friends or the community in general. Of course, they aren't from around here. Maybe there's a similar drive going on back home, wherever that is. Do you know where they live?"

"I do not," Schmidt said.

I thought about the remarks he'd made to Axle about the deal he had with Fisher. Something about the scary tone of his voice made me afraid to ask him directly what he and Axle planned.

Instead, I said, "Aunt Rowe and I have a little something special for you. In appreciation for all of the work you did on this festival."

"A gift?" he said with awe in his voice as if no one had ever given him anything in his life.

I felt guilty, but pressed on. "Right. We'd like to get together with you tonight, later, after the festival, and give it to you in a special ceremony."

Your imagination's working overtime, Sabrina. Where is this coming from?

Schmidt frowned. "I'm busy tonight. No ceremony is necessary."

I wanted to know what he had planned, so I said, "We could make the presentation at your home this evening if you prefer."

He frowned. "Tonight will simply not work."

"Perhaps in the morning, then? Or right after the festival ends?"

"I'll let you know." I could practically see the sweat rings growing under the man's arms. He was a nervous wreck. He glanced at his watch. "I really must be going. We'll talk. Later."

"Later, then." I gave him a little wave. "Bye-bye."

As the man scuttled across the lawn to another boom from the pumpkin cannon, I decided that I had to know what he and Axle had cooked up for that evening. A bit of surveillance seemed to be in order.

26

WHEN I TURNED to watch Aunt Rowe stuff another pumpkin into the cannon, I saw Sheriff Crawford striding across the lawn toward me.

Oh Lord. What does he want?

I reprimanded myself immediately for the bad attitude. The sheriff was always available to help when I needed him. The least I could do was be civil. I pasted on a smile. He reached me and nodded with a tip of his Texas Rangers ball cap.

"Afternoon, Sabrina," he said.

"We meet again."

"Wish I could say I'm surprised to see you out here after I warned you to be extra careful," he said, "but I'm not surprised at all."

"I didn't want to miss out on the festivities," I said.

"Uh-huh." He paused and looked in the direction Schmidt had gone. "What did you say to Henry Schmidt to send him scurrying off with his tail between his legs?"

"Nothing special," I said. "Normal chit-chat."

"Sabrina," the sheriff said in a stern-parent tone.

I looked up at him and squinted against the sun. "Did you know Schmidt was looking for Calvin Fisher the morning I found the body?"

"No, I didn't," he said.

"Well, he was. You can ask Deputy Rosales."

"What does she have to do with it?"

"She came into Eddie Baxter's tent while I was there talking with him and asked if we'd seen—"

"*You* went into the bad luck cat tent?" He sounded like I'd just told him I'd walked a circus tightrope.

"I was lodging a complaint about his cat theme," I said, "but that's not the point. Rosales came in while I was there and said she was searching for Fisher because Schmidt had a meeting scheduled with him for that morning. Fisher was a no-show."

"Huh," the sheriff said. "Why was Schmidt meeting with Fisher?"

"Good question, but I don't know the answer. You could find out from Rosales."

"I may do that," he said.

"You might also ask her why she's talking about the syringe cap found in Fisher's truck."

Surprise flickered across his face. "I don't believe my deputy is gossiping about evidence."

I shrugged. "Believe what you want."

"Did you hear this bit of information from Deputy Rosales personally?" he said.

"No, I didn't. She's very busy, and I try not to bother her."

"Uh-huh," he repeated. "Who told you about the syringe cap?"

"Rita Colletti."

"Her again."

"She's annoying, right? Can you believe I worked for that woman for eight years?"

"Hardly," he said.

"I'm surprised to see *you* out here," I said, changing the subject. "I thought you'd be off stringing Gabe Brenner up by his toenails by now."

The sheriff smoothed his mustache and turned to face the cannon. He was clearly watching Aunt Rowe as she strutted along the stage with her eye on Thorn like a cheerleader showing off for the football team.

"About Brenner," the sheriff said, never taking his eyes off Aunt Rowe. "Turns out he has an alibi."

"What is it?" I didn't expect him to answer me.

"He was with his mother. She arrived in Lavender around eight that night and went straight to the Melbourne cottage to help her son prep food to cook on Friday. Ended up spending the night. And, please, jump right in if you have any information or knowledge to contradict her report."

"I didn't know anything about his mother being here," I said. "Luke told me he saw Gabe partying that night at Aunt Rowe's."

"He was, until Mama called and told him to get his butt back to the Melbourne cottage, they had work to do. Her words. She says they cut up four tubs full of bacon."

"Jeez Louise," I said. "What a job."

After downing Lord knows how many shots of alcohol, Gabe was lucky he hadn't sliced off a finger in the process. Glenda would need some heavy-duty air freshener in the Melbourne cottage to get rid of the raw-meat smell.

"Mrs. Brenner claims Gabe passed out soon as they were through. She stayed the night and was with him until after you found Fisher's body."

"Good. Then he checks out," I said. "I didn't think he did it anyway."

"Unless Mama straight-up lied to a law-enforcement officer," the sheriff said, "in which case, Mama and son are both in trouble. For now, I had to release him."

He had a point. Mothers had been known to lie to save their children, but I didn't comment further. The sheriff's gaze was still glued to the cannon and Aunt Rowe. He tipped his head toward me and spoke directly into my ear as if he was sharing top secret information. "Who *is* that man up there with Rowe?"

"I'm assuming he's Thorn, her personal trainer, based on the ad on the back of his shirt. Never met the man."

"Huh," the sheriff said. "She talks about that trainer a lot."

"Guess you never met him, either."

He shook his head. "They seem awful friendly."

"She works out with him several times a week, but like I said, I never met him. She's keeping him all to herself."

He looked at me and frowned. "What's that mean?"

"I was joking, but I think somebody's jealous."

"I'm not—" He paused, and I sensed he realized he was about to tell a lie.

"You can admit it to me," I said, "even if you don't want to tell Aunt Rowe."

"Telling Rowe anything doesn't do me a whole hell of a lot of good," he said. "She's not interested."

"Oh, I think she is." I grinned at him. He looked at the cannon. Aunt Rowe held a pumpkin and kept strutting around Thorn with a teasing expression on her face. I had a feeling she was laying it on extra thick because she knew good and well the sheriff was watching her every move.

"I have work to do," Sheriff Crawford said. "You watch your back."

He walked away, but I saw him turn to look at Aunt Rowe when the cannon went off. I thought about what it would be like if—or should I say when?—Aunt Rowe stopped brushing him off and admitted that she wanted to spend more time with the man. I decided I'd be happy to see them together. Then I went to catch Tyanne up on recent events.

* * *

M Y friend was busy chatting up customers at her book-store booth. She spotted me and said, "Here's the future best-selling author now."

A woman with an armload of books turned to me excit-edly. "Are you Sabrina?"

I smiled and nodded.

"Ohmigod, it's so good to meet you. I'm Deloris Baker, and I can't wait to buy your book. Tyanne told me all about it."

"She's very optimistic," I said.

"No, I'm realistic," Ty said. "I have a feeling that book will be published before you know it, which means—"

I nodded. "I know what it means, Ty, and I'm working on the next book every morning. That's my best creative time."

Well, almost every morning.

Deloris produced a colorful cloth-covered notebook from her purse. "Would you mind signing my autograph book, Sabrina? I collect author autographs, and I have others from their prepublication days, too. If it's not too much trouble, could you add today's date?" She pulled out a pen and of-fered it to me.

I took the pen and the book from her. "I'm honored, Deloris. This is the first time anyone's asked me for an autograph."

"I'll bet it's not the last," the woman said, excitement shining in her eyes as she watched me sign her book. "Best of luck on your first published novel and many more."

Tyanne grinned at me as Ethan came to the counter to handle Deloris's purchases.

"How'd that feel?" Ty said.

"Amazing," I said, and I meant it.

"Get used to the glow," she said. "I predict you're going to be doing a lot more of that, and soon."

"If giving one person an autograph feels so awesome, I

can't imagine what it would be like to hold my own published book."

"Time will tell," she said. "I think you'll have a lot more fun working as a published author than you did in that law office. Speaking of which, have you talked with Rita yet?"

"About Tia's child-support case? Yes. I should have known better. Rita's only interested in representing Tia if she's charged with murder."

Ty looked horrified. "Murder? Really?"

"Yup, and, oh, get this. My mother came face-to-face with Tia."

"Your mother's here? In Lavender?"

"Surprise," I said. "She's here, and after one look at Tia she jumped to the conclusion that Tia is my father's illegitimate daughter."

Ty stared at me. "Wow, that's a big leap."

"Tell me about it."

"Did your parents have marriage trouble, like, twenty-something years ago?"

I shrugged. "If they did, I never suspected, but I'm not buying Mom's claim and neither is Tia."

"Why is your mother even here?" Ty said. "I can't see her getting into the whole festival scene."

"She's not." I explained what Aunt Rowe told me about the judicial campaign.

Ty chuckled. "I can picture your aunt making them work extra hard for her endorsement."

"Me, too."

"Do you need me to invite you to dinner so you'll have an excuse to avoid campaign-strategy meetings?" Tyanne teased.

"I already have a plan for tonight," I said. "You think Bryan would mind staying with the kids for a few hours?"

"He already planned to take them to a movie to give me a break," she said. "What do you have in mind?"

"Something mysterious."

"I don't like that plotting expression," Ty said. "Not when it involves me."

"It'll be fun, just like old times," I said. "Trust me."

I pretended not to notice when she rolled her eyes.

27

I F I HOPED to convince Tyanne to accompany me on a surveillance mission tonight, I needed to be ready with a credible reason. I didn't think the "tonight or else" comment I'd heard Schmidt make to Axle would convince her we needed to follow the men to see what they were up to. That might work for a movie plot, but not in our ordinary, usually boring, Lavender, Texas, world.

It might help if I could learn more about the Fisher-Axle-Schmidt relationship, and the only way I could think of to do that was to talk with the scary man himself—Axle No-Last-Name.

On the way to the jewelry booth, I spotted Coco Fisher and crew approaching pedestrians along the main drag through town. I felt relieved that I saw no sign that Axle had physically harmed the woman to "get her off his back." At the same time, I was glad she'd be out of the way when I went to talk to him. I was surprised she hadn't hunted me down today. I expected more questions about the mysterious

something she thought her husband had handed off to me before he died. Then again, maybe she'd found what she was looking for.

I approached the jewelry booth from the side opposite Winnie and Cecil Moser. No need to get into another conversation with the couple at this point. Winnie would likely ask me a dozen questions about my day. I didn't want to shun the chatty lady, but at the moment, I wanted to keep my mind on track.

I watched Axle from a distance for a moment before I convinced myself to approach the booth. I began by casually browsing the variety of bracelets for sale. He had every style imaginable—bangle, charm, silver, gold, beaded, stretchy.

Through the fringe of my lashes, I watched Axle as he helped a woman decide which pair of earrings to purchase— the dangling turquoise or silver double hoops. Axle was about six feet tall and hefty, seriously one of the last people I would ever envision helping this woman choose a pair of earrings.

He wore baggy jeans with knee rips and a white T-shirt that exposed tattooed biceps. His longish dark hair was pulled back and held with an elastic band to reveal dark bushy brows. When he smiled at the customer, his stern demeanor softened.

After handling the customer's earring purchase, he moved along behind the counter, asking others if they needed help. When he asked me, I said, "How's business today?"

That made him inspect me more closely, and I was almost sorry I'd said anything. Having his dark piercing eyes on me felt intimidating.

"Business is good," he said after what seemed like a full minute.

"Sorry about your friend Calvin," I said.

"Thanks. You wanna buy a bracelet?"

"I haven't decided yet."

"I got my eye on you," he said.

The way he said it offended me, as if I needed watching. "What do you mean by that?"

"We got some shoplifting going on around here," he said. "Gotta keep my eyes open."

"I'm not a thief," I said.

"Good." He walked in the other direction, continuing to converse with customers, though I doubted he was accusing any of them of shoplifting. The nerve. I hadn't done anything to make him suspicious, had I? But the man kept watching me, and now I was getting cold feet about asking him any substantive questions.

He handled a few more transactions. When there was a lull in shoppers, he returned to me.

"You're taking a long time making up your mind," he said.

I shrugged. "I'm indecisive."

He studied me thoroughly, then had a light bulb moment. "You're the dame who found Cal in his truck. The one with the cat."

"You don't see a cat, do you?"

"Good thing," Axle said. "Cats are trouble, always puttin' their noses where they don't belong."

"I don't think it's fair to put the nosy label on a cat," I said. "Lots of people are nosy, too."

He shrugged. "True."

"How's Coco doing?"

He frowned. "Why you askin' about her?"

"Yesterday she was upset, looking for something, asking me about it. Today she's out with Calvin's kids asking for donations."

Axle threw his head back with a big belly laugh. "Yeah, Coco and the kids."

"Why's that funny?"

He sobered as if a switch turned off. "It's not. Look, cut the bull. Did Cal agree to give you a cut or what?"

I put down the bracelet I'd been looking at. "A cut of what?"

"You know." He looked around furtively and lowered his voice. "Good thing you came to your senses and gave the stuff back."

"What stuff?"

"Don't play dumb," he said. "Coco told me you were holding the stuff. Good thing you gave it back. Just in time, too. That was smart, but now you're not so smart to come over here and squeeze me for a cut."

I swallowed hard. "I'm not sure what you think—"

"Can it," he said. "Listen, the meet is tonight at nine. We can talk after, before Coco gets her fingers in the mix."

My knees were practically knocking together, and I wondered what the heck I'd gotten myself into.

"Coco doesn't know about the meet?" I said.

He grinned, but it was a cruel grin, not the happy smile he showed the customers.

"What Coco doesn't know won't hurt her," he said.

I heard the cackle of a group of women coming up behind me, then "Hey, Sabrina. Color me surprised, finding you shopping for jewelry."

Aunt Rowe.

I turned and faced her.

She took one look at me and said, "What's wrong?"

I heard Axle asking someone if he could help her with the necklaces.

Aunt Rowe continued to study me. She took one of my hands. "You feel clammy. What did that guy say to you?"

"I'm not sure I understood him," I said. "He wasn't making much sense."

Her eyes narrowed. "This is that dead guy's booth."

I nodded.

"Then who's the dude running the show?"

"His name's Axle."

Her expression changed and brightened. "You're investigating, aren't you?"

Keeping hold of her hand, I walked away from the booth.

"I thought I was, but Axle thinks I know more than I know. He and Schmidt are up to something."

"Henry and that guy?" She cocked her head toward Axle. I nodded.

"Like what?"

"I'm trying to figure it out," I said. "Something shady, I'm sure."

"You think Henry Schmidt, the guy who follows every rule ever made, is doing something that's not aboveboard?"

"There's a decent chance," I said.

"Huh. That'd be something to see. I could use that when he's peppering me with his rules and regulations."

I had to smile. "I'll be sure to let you know whenever I figure this out. And by the way, we need to find a gift for Herr Schmidt. A thank-you for all the festival work he's done."

Aunt Rowe's brows rose. "You want me to give Schmidt a gift? For crying out loud, why would I do that?"

"Because I told him we had a gift for him. It's a long story."

"Is this what you and Jeb were talking about?" she said. "Back at the pumpkin cannon?"

"No."

"Were you talking about the break-in at your place?" she said. "Glenda filled me in. Thank goodness it was only a minor disturbance and no real damage, other than her having to clean up all that fingerprint mess."

"No, we weren't talking about that, either." My brain was rerunning Axle's remarks, trying to figure out what he thought I had done when, in fact, I hadn't done anything. At least nothing on purpose.

"I figure the break-in is the reason you brought Hitchcock over here with you instead of leaving him at home," Aunt Rowe said.

That pulled me back to the present. "But he *is* at home. I didn't bring him."

"Somebody did," she said. "He's with the artist."

"Tia?"

She nodded. "Her little boy was taking his painted pumpkin over for the contest. He had two cats with him. Hitchcock and the one that looks like Hitchcock's shadow. They're following that boy around like he's the Pied Piper."

28

WALKED WITH AUNT Rowe to the contest-judging area, where a good-sized group of people had congregated. Pumpkins were lined up on four long folding tables, awaiting judging. "Monster Mash" played from a boom box sitting at the end of one table. I scanned our surroundings, looking for Damon and the cats.

"I don't understand how Hitchcock could be here," I said to Aunt Rowe. "I latched the cat door to make sure he'd stay home."

"Your cat's a Houdini," Aunt Rowe said. "Maybe he slipped out when Glenda went in to clean up that fingerprint powder."

I'd bet that's exactly what happened. I could imagine Hitchcock waiting patiently by the door for any chance to escape. That still didn't explain how he got here. Most everyone at the cottages involved with the festival had driven over early this morning and would stay until it was time to close up shop.

"There's my team of judges." Aunt Rowe checked her watch. "Right on time."

I looked in the direction she was waving and saw Rita Colletti standing with Daisy from McKetta's Barbeque and Max from Hot Stuff. I considered going over to speak with Daisy and Max, but then I spotted Damon.

Sure enough, both black cats were right there with him, sitting as obediently as a well-behaved dog might sit by the boy's feet. Lorene, the woman from the booth next to Tia's, stood with them. She was easy to pick out with her red curls and turquoise glasses. I hurried over, tamping down my anxiety. I didn't want the boy to feel as if he'd done something wrong.

"Hello, Lorene, Damon, Merlin," I said, "and you, Hitchcock."

My cat looked up at me and blinked slowly. The little devil appeared to be smiling.

"Mrreow," he said.

"Hi," Damon said. "I entered my pumpkin in the contest."

"That's great," I said. "Good luck."

Aunt Rowe made an announcement that the judging of the pumpkin painting contest was about to begin. Any others who wanted to enter needed to submit their pumpkin in the next five minutes.

"This little fella made the best darn painted pumpkin I ever did see in my life," Lorene said, "and I've seen plenty."

I grinned. "I caught a glimpse when he'd only done the eyes, and it already looked great. He inherited his mother's talent." I looked around us. "Where is Tia?"

"She was busy doin' her sketches," Lorene said, "and I got a cousin here watchin' my stuff. Tia wanted to see the contest, but didn't want to turn folks away, so I volunteered to keep an eye on Damon."

I nodded with understanding. Tia wanted—no, *needed*—to make as much money as she could while she had the chance.

"You hear anything from your agent yet?" Lorene said. "I've been putting in a word for you in my prayers. I'm just so excited for you to find out when that book will be published."

The woman got almost giddy with excitement whenever she mentioned my book. I realized I purposely wasn't allowing myself to expect anything, lest I be disappointed. If good news came from Kree Vanderpool, then people would see me jumping up and down.

I smiled at her. "Thanks. Every little bit helps."

"Oh, look, Damon," Lorene said. "The judging started."

I turned to see Aunt Rowe and the other judges walking slowly alongside the tables. Each of them held a clipboard and a pen, and they jotted on their papers as they moved down the row.

"Oh Lordy, I can't wait to find out if you're gonna win anything," Lorene said. "Here, rub on this a bit." She pulled something from her pocket and held what looked like a smooth stone out for Damon to touch. "This'll give you good luck."

"Mrrreeeooowww." Hitchcock butted his head against Lorene's leg.

"You wanna play, kitty?" Lorene said.

I scowled at the stone and wondered if she'd bought it from Eddie Baxter. "I think he's trying to tell you that he'll bring Damon good luck. Along with Merlin. We don't believe that black cats are bad luck, do we, Damon?"

"No, ma'am," Damon said. The boy glanced at Lorene's hand but didn't move to touch her stone. Instead, he reached down and picked up Merlin. The boy turned back to watch the judges, holding his cat tight.

I had to grin. He was my kind of kid.

Lorene stuffed her stone back into her pocket, and Hitchcock left her to move closer to me. Apparently my cat wanted nothing to do with the woman who believed a stone could bring good luck.

Lorene didn't argue the point. "I'm gonna take a picture

for your mama if you win. Sabrina, look at this picture I took of Damon standing with his pumpkin. It's a good one."

She scrolled to the picture and passed the phone to me so I could get a good look.

I checked the picture and enlarged the image so I could see the pumpkin better. "That really is good work, Damon," I said. I looked again and noticed Coco Fisher in the background standing with a man. I enlarged the picture some more and recognized Herr Schmidt. The two of them appeared to be in a discussion, each with very serious expressions, not the happy-go-lucky faces of others in the shot. I highly doubted they were chatting about the pumpkin painting contest.

I handed the phone back to Lorene and scanned the area for Schmidt or Coco. No sign of them.

Aunt Rowe turned her microphone back on. "The judges have come to a decision on first, second, and third place in the pumpkin painting contest. Will all contestants please come up and stand with your pumpkins, and we will announce the winners."

"Ooh, Damon, aren't you so excited?" Lorene said. "Here, let me hold the cat for you."

Damon handed Merlin to Lorene and made his way through the audience to the tables.

Lorene leaned toward me. "I hope for that poor boy's sake his mama doesn't end up in jail for killing that man."

I looked at her sharply. "Why would you even suggest such a thing?"

"That man told me," she said, then added, "Oh, look at Damon. Isn't he such a little cutie? I think he has a really good chance of winning, don't you?"

She watched the boy as he approached the table where his pumpkin rested.

"Lorene, what man?"

She tore her gaze away from Damon for a split second to look at me. "The man in that black tent, the one I bought

the good luck stone from. Sorry, I know you don't believe in such—"

"I don't care about the stone. What did he say about Tia?" I moved to block her view of Damon so she'd have to pay attention to me.

Lorene pushed her glasses up on her nose. "He said the dead guy and Tia had a feud that went way back, and when he turned up dead, the good luck guy knew right away whodunit. Now, I didn't believe one word of—"

"That's not fair." I blew out a frustrated breath and turned to pick up Hitchcock.

"I didn't believe him," she said.

"C'mon, buddy," I said to Hitchcock. "Let's go show Eddie Baxter what bad luck feels like."

"Aren't you gonna wait and see if Damon wins?" Lorene said.

"You can take a picture for me," I said.

E DDIE Baxter's tent was a good eight blocks from the pumpkin judging, and I was breathing plenty hard by the time I reached his place. I didn't like the idea of taking Hitchcock into the tent with me, but I simply couldn't wait to confront Baxter. I had to find out what on earth had convinced this guy that Tia was guilty of murder.

I stopped by the entrance to catch my breath and checked out the signs on the front of the tent. Twila had managed to convince Eddie to remove the picture that looked like Hitchcock and the reference to a bad luck cat. I was pleased about that, but my aggravation over him telling people Tia was a killer far overshadowed the good.

"Well, he took the picture down," I said to Hitchcock, "so Twila will expect us to join her for Halloween dinner."

"Mrreow," he said.

I shrugged. "A bargain's a bargain. Let's go see what this dipwad son of hers is up to."

Hitchcock trilled as I pushed aside the black cloth covering the doorway and walked into the tent. Battery-powered candles and a single strand of white lights draped from the ceiling cast a dim glow over the interior. Music that reminded me of the séancelike tunes Twila played in her antiques store came through speakers mounted to the top corners of the tent.

More than a dozen people browsed inside. I hoped to high heaven Eddie wasn't telling all of them that the artist outside doing sketches was in reality a killer. I hoped, too, that none of these patrons would turn on me for bringing a black cat into the midst of the good luck charms. Although, if they believed in such things, then Eddie's sales might pick up if shoppers spotted the cat.

I scanned the area and saw him talking with a woman across the way. Another woman worked behind the counter, handling transactions for customers. A man near me reached for a sign hanging on a pegboard wall. The sign said "Lucky Horseshoe" inside a picture of a horseshoe. That was kind of cute. Near the wall filled with wooden signs, black totes hung from a hook. Printed on the front, along with a green four-leaf clover, were words in white—"Luck Is Believing You're Lucky."

Perfect.

I grabbed one of the totes. I was in no mood to support Eddie's business venture, but I'd feel a lot better if Hitchcock was less visible.

I looped the tote over my arm and held Hitchcock's back legs together as I urged him into the bag feetfirst. "In you go."

He gave me a look but acquiesced, and I let out a pent-up breath. I headed for Eddie and waited behind the woman he was currently helping. When they finished their conversation, I stepped up.

"Hello, Eddie," I said. "I'd like to buy this tote."

He looked at me and took a few seconds to realize who I was. "Hey, you're the one who blackmailed my mom."

"What?" I rolled my eyes. "I did no such thing."

"She came over here and said I had to take down my signs or you wouldn't help her with something." His face screwed up. "I forget what it was she said she wanted from you, but it's still blackmail."

"That's ridiculous. How much is the tote?"

He looked at the bag hanging from my arm. "What you got in there? You shoplifting?"

"Right, like I would point this out to you if I'd filled it with stolen merchandise."

"Can't be too careful," Eddie said.

Hitchcock poked his head out of the tote. "Mrreow."

Eddie jumped as if the cat had bitten him.

"Jeez, that's the—"

"Don't you say it." I held a finger in his face. "Not one word."

"Or what?" he said. "You'll put a spell on me?"

"Now you are really ticking me off," I said. "We need to talk."

"About what?"

"First I want to pay for this tote so you don't accuse me of stealing. Lord knows you're quick to accuse innocent people of things."

Eddie didn't seem to grasp what I was talking about. He stared at Hitchcock as if he were afraid of a cat attack. "Ten bucks," he said.

I pulled out my money and paid him. "Can we step outside for a minute?" I said.

He looked like he was afraid to say no and motioned to his helper to watch the counter.

"What's this about?" he said, squinting as we stepped outside into the bright afternoon.

"Your friend Calvin Fisher."

"He's dead," Eddie said.

"I know that. You and he were friends for a long time."

"Yeah. So?"

"Did he come to this festival every year?"

"Yeah, for the last ten maybe."

"Why are you saying my friend Tia Hartwell killed him?"

"'Cause I think she did."

"You *think*? And that makes it okay for you to blab your dumb opinion to anybody who'll listen?"

Eddie's eyes were wide as he looked from me to Hitchcock.

"Look, I'm just talkin'," he said. "Don't hold it against me."

"This is very serious," I said. "What makes you *think* Tia would have done this?"

"She and Cal had trouble from way back," he said.

"How far back?"

Eddie pulled his lower lip between his teeth. "In the spring sometime. San Angelo, that was it. They were at a bazaar, and they really got into it. Arguing and stuff. Her kid was giving Cal fits. Him and the cat both. They have a black cat, too."

He eyed Hitchcock again.

"I know. His name is Merlin. What did the boy and the cat do?"

"He said the kid got underneath his table and into his stash."

"What stash? What does that mean?"

Eddie shrugged. "I dunno. His stuff. His products. Whatever."

I didn't get the feeling that Fisher would have referred to his stock of costume jewelry as his stash. "What else did he say about the boy?"

"Something like 'The kid saw my stash, and I told her I'd shut him up one way or another.'"

"Dear Lord," I said. "Fisher threatened to hurt the little boy?"

"Nah, he wouldn't do that," Eddie said. "He just wanted her to keep the kid away from him. He was talkin' big."

"Yeah," I muttered. "He probably talked big to the wrong

person at the wrong time, but I don't think it was Tia. Tell me more about his stash."

Eddie held his hands up. "Look, I dunno what Cal was into, and I'd rather not know. I figure I'm better off not knowin'."

I frowned at him. "You think he was doing something illegal?"

"Lady, I'm just tryin' to make an honest livin' here. I don't appreciate people like you wastin' my time."

"One more thing," I said, "then I'll let you go."

Eddie stuffed his hands in his pockets and seemed like he'd relaxed his wariness about his proximity to Hitchcock. "What?"

"Have you seen Calvin's wife and kids since they arrived in town?"

"Kids?" Eddie busted up laughing. "Listen, I don't know what kind of game Coco and that daughter of hers are playin' here. I saw them with those little ones, but they ain't Cal's. He don't have kids, least none he knew about."

29

BACKTRACKED THE WAY I'd come and noticed the contest crowd had dissipated. The painted pumpkins were still on display, and I took a quick detour past the tables. Damon's pumpkin had received a red second-place ribbon.

Not bad.

I would congratulate the boy when I saw him, which would be soon. I wanted to know exactly what he saw that had so greatly agitated Calvin Fisher this past spring. Hitchcock squirmed. I held the tote in front of me and adjusted the fabric so half of the cat's body was inside, half out. He looked around happily as I headed back to Tia's booth.

Sheriff Crawford was told about Fisher's children before the family ever arrived in Lavender. What was up with that? Did Coco think having children would push Fisher's murder case to the top of the to-be-solved list? That didn't even make sense. There was always a chance the truth would come out, and why pretend to have children at all? Unless the our-family-breadwinner-is-gone-and-we-need-help gig

was too good to pass up. For all I knew, Coco could have used this scam before in other towns. The kids might belong to the dark-haired woman I'd seen with Coco and they were in the scam together.

When I came within sight of Tia, I stopped walking. She was working, and her sketch in progress looked very familiar. I studied the likeness for two seconds, then stepped forward quickly to see the customer.

Mom.

Good grief. Could she not leave well enough alone? Did she have to come back here to harp on Tia about her crazy assumption that Tia was Dad's daughter and my sister?

"Sabrina," Mom said when she spotted me. "What are you doing here?"

"Checking up on you, I guess. I hope you're not harassing Tia."

"She's fine, Sabrina," Tia said, "and I'm glad to see you have Hitchcock. Damon told me you took him with you when you left the contest. I was afraid he'd run off."

"No worries." I knelt and let the cat out of the bag—literally—and he ran to Merlin, who appeared to be chasing a bug in the grass. Damon sat nearby with his back against a tree, his sketch pad on his crossed legs.

"I saw Winnie Moser, and she was looking for you," Tia said.

"What did she want?" I watched Hitchcock join in the bug-chasing fun with Merlin.

"To apologize for bringing Hitchcock to the festival. She had to run back to their cottage for something and didn't know the cat had jumped into her car until she got back here."

The cat mystery solved.

I grinned. "He does that a lot."

Mom said, "You may need to keep him in a locked cage. Otherwise, you'll never know where the animal is."

"I'm not locking him in a cage, Mom."

"Just trying to be helpful," she said.

"I'm surprised you're still in Lavender. The town must be growing on you."

Or you didn't get what you wanted from Aunt Rowe yet. She gave me a withering glance.

"Brenda," Tia said. "Where's the smile?"

Mom showed her teeth, though her expression wasn't exactly happy.

I turned to Tia. "I saw Damon placed second in the contest. I need to congratulate him."

Tia smiled. "Go on. I think he's drawing a picture of his pumpkin with the ribbon."

I walked over to the boy, feeling slightly guilty that I wanted to quiz him about Fisher without telling his mother first. I decided it would be okay to simply start the conversation and see where it led. With that plan made, I sat cross-legged on the grass next to Damon. He was, in fact, drawing a likeness of his painted pumpkin.

"Congrats on winning second place," I said when he looked up at me.

He gave me his shy smile. "Thanks."

"Sorry I had to leave just before the winner was announced, but I went back and took a close look at your pumpkin. I think you should have won first place."

"The winner was much better than me," he said.

"I'll bet that person was older than you, too."

He shrugged.

"Your sketches are so good. What else have you drawn?"

He flipped back a few pages, and I admired several pictures of Merlin before deciding how I wanted to approach the topic I'd come to discuss.

"Sometimes people give me a hard time because Hitchcock is a black cat," I said, "and they don't like black cats. Do you ever have that problem?"

"Sometimes," he said, "but that's dumb."

"Not everybody's as smart as you and me when it comes to knowing cats."

He turned back to his sketch in progress and continued working.

"Did you have problems like that with the man who sold jewelry?" I said. "Did he complain about Merlin?"

Damon rolled his eyes. "All the time. That's why Mama said we didn't want to be near him anymore."

"Did he ever get angry with you?"

Damon looked up from the pad. He glanced at his mother, who was busy chatting with Mom. Lord only knew what the two were finding to talk about. Damon returned his gaze to me.

"Did he?" I urged.

The boy nodded slightly.

"Do you know why he was angry?"

"Because I was under his table," Damon said.

I leaned forward with elbows on my knees and looked at the boy. "Did you see something you shouldn't have seen?"

Damon shook his head quickly. "No."

Tia said, "Why are you asking him these questions?"

I looked up, startled. The woman stood in front of us. She must have supersonic hearing to have heard my questions from where she was with Mom.

"I wouldn't ask if it wasn't important, Tia," I said. "People are blaming you."

"Blaming her for what?" Mom had followed Tia to where Damon and I sat in the grass.

I scrambled to my feet and tried to silence Mom with a stare. She realized belatedly I was talking about the recent murder.

"Ohhhhh," Mom said, drawing the word into four syllables.

"I was the one who got under the table," Damon said. "I was looking for Merlin. Mama didn't do anything."

"Honey," Tia said, "you don't have to talk about this."

"I don't want them to blame you," he said.

"Does he know what we're talking about?" Mom said.

I looked at her. "*We* are not talking about anything. I only meant to ask Damon a simple question."

"I know that man died," the boy said, "and I don't want them to take Mama to jail."

Tia inhaled sharply. "Damon, it's okay. I'm not going anywhere."

"Why ever would they arrest Tia?" Mom said. "I've only known the girl for a short while, and I can tell that would be completely preposterous."

Maybe I'd inherited the tendency to jump to conclusions about people without having all the facts. I marveled at Mom's change of heart and wondered what had happened to make her Tia's champion.

"I saw things under that man's table," Damon said. "He had jewelry in a bunch of fancy boxes."

"He sells jewelry, Damon," I said. "That's not a big deal. He was being mean if he got angry with you for seeing his jewelry."

"He had a lot of money, too," the boy said.

I wondered what would seem like "a lot" to a boy Damon's age.

"How much money?" Mom said. "This much?" She held thumb and forefinger an inch apart.

Damon shook his head and held his arms spread as far as he could reach. "Like this much. A whole backpack full."

Mom gasped.

I looked at Tia. "Is all this related to the comment I heard Fisher make to you about playing innocent?"

Tia slowly released her breath. "Fisher got a look at Damon's sketchbook. He'd drawn a picture of the jewelry and money he saw under the table. He's a very good artist, and there was no mistaking what the drawing was about."

"I can imagine," I said.

Tia continued, "When I told Fisher that Damon didn't

see anything, I hadn't looked at his sketch. Fisher got even nastier. That's when he started telling me where I was allowed to go to work and where I wasn't allowed."

"How or why did he decide some towns were okay and others weren't?" I said.

Tia shrugged. "I never could figure that out."

She urged Damon to go back to his sketch and walked me a few yards from the boy. Mom followed us, and I didn't bother trying to get her to back off.

"What Damon's telling you happened half a year ago," Tia said. "I don't see why it has anything to do with what happened this week."

"Apparently, Fisher told his friends what Damon did and saw back in San Angelo and mentioned he'd threatened you. So now they think you're the likely killer."

"We'll have to set them straight," Mom said.

Tia looked at Mom with disbelief. "Yesterday you were a bit threatening yourself. Why would you want to help me now?"

"Because I like you," Mom said, "and you *do* remind me of my late husband." Mom looked at me. "I always wanted you to have a sister, Sabrina, but it just never happened. Or maybe it did."

I exchanged a glance with Tia.

"I don't think we're sisters, Mom."

Tia said, "Not that I would mind being Sabrina's sister— that might be very nice—but I'm not, Brenda. Really."

"Whatever." Mom waved a hand. "Tia, you didn't cause this nasty man's death. Do you want me to have a word with Jeb about this?"

"Who's Jeb?" Tia said.

"The sheriff," I said. "Mom and Aunt Rowe have known him for a very long time."

Eyebrows raised, Tia looked at Mom. "He would take your word and believe whatever you tell him?"

"He might," said someone behind me, "but I wouldn't."

I recognized Deputy Rosales's voice before I turned and saw her standing there.

"I SHOULDN'T have provoked Rosales," I told Aunt Rowe later at her house, "but I couldn't help myself. I accused her of breaking into my cottage. She said she would sue me for slander."

"Sounds like a regular cat fight." Aunt Rowe sat and stretched her legs out on the chaise in her bedroom. She looked at my cat, who sat in the doorway watching us. "No offense meant, Hitchcock."

I plopped down on the bed and crossed my arms. Aunt Rowe leaned back against the chaise and closed her eyes. We were both taking a brief respite from the festival. She would go back before long for the evening's pumpkin-cannon festivities. I was changing into dark clothes for my surveillance of Herr Schmidt and Axle. Tyanne didn't know exactly what I had planned, but she expected that I'd pick her up as soon as she closed her booth for the night. I hoped Rosales wouldn't go back and pester Tia again.

"I might have made things worse for Tia by mouthing off," I said. "Rosales had already grilled her earlier, then she came back to put the fear of God into the poor woman. She seemed like she was trying to bully Tia into a confession, so I got between them and said Tia wasn't talking without her lawyer present."

"Does she have a lawyer?" Aunt Rowe said.

"Not exactly, but by then Damon was crying. He told Rosales to leave his mama alone, and she backed down."

"Good for him," Aunt Rowe said. "I passed the deputy this afternoon at the festival, and she wouldn't even look at me. She's steamed 'cause she didn't get that warrant she wanted to search the cottages."

"Do you know what she's after?"

"Not a clue."

"I don't know why she's dead set on Tia's guilt. Mom and I are convinced she's innocent."

Aunt Rowe opened her eyes and looked at me. "You and your mother agree on something? That might be a first."

"True."

"Why is Brenda still in town? I told her I'd talk to my friend about Dave's campaign just to get her out of my space. Thought she'd head straight home. What's her interest in Tia anyway?"

I could have gone into the whole story, beginning with Mom's accusations about Dad, but Aunt Rowe was trying to rest.

"Far be it from me to figure out that woman," I said.

My phone buzzed and I pulled up a text from Luke, the last of a row of texts he'd sent me throughout the day. I smiled at the phone.

"From your sweetie, huh?" Aunt Rowe said.

I glanced at her and found her peeking at me with one open eye. "How'd you guess?"

She grinned knowingly. "You two getting together tonight?"

"Doesn't look like it." I read the text aloud. "'Tied up tonight. After guys who started deer season early. Stay safe.'"

I texted back. "You, too. I'm with Aunt Rowe."

That was absolutely the truth at this moment.

"So what are you up to this evening?" Aunt Rowe said.

"Tyanne and I have plans."

Also true.

After a beat, I said, "How well do you know Henry Schmidt?"

"Well enough to know I'll be glad when he goes back to his hidey-hole after the festival."

"What do you mean by that?"

"He's like a hermit," she said. "Stays up on that hill in that house. All by himself, from what I hear. Him and his collections."

"What kind of collections?"

Aunt Rowe shrugged. "I'm not sure. Stamps? Coins? All I know is what I hear. The man's a rule fanatic who collects stuff. Why? You want this gift we're supposed to be giving him to be a perfect fit?"

"I forgot all about the gift."

She turned to stare at me. "What's goin' through that head of yours?"

"Still puzzling over what Schmidt and Calvin Fisher's buddy are up to." I didn't want to tell her I meant to follow up on that very issue tonight, but Aunt Rowe was no dummy.

"You and Tyanne watch your backs," she said, "and don't do anything I wouldn't do."

I had to laugh. Her comment gave me a wide berth.

30

GOT BACK TO the festival around dinnertime and cruised past the jewelry booth first to make sure Axle was still there and accounted for. He was busy selling jewelry, and he was alone. I stood at a distance for a few minutes, studying the table and its ground-length cover. Why was Fisher so concerned about what Damon had seen the day he'd slid under the tablecloth? Did Axle know about the event? Did Coco? I wondered where she and the children were, but I didn't hang around because I didn't want Axle to notice me. Cecil and Winnie had spotted me, though, and I waved to them as I turned and headed to the food trucks.

I knew good and well that I was taking advantage of Tyanne by expecting her to accompany me on my mission tonight after her full day of working. The fajita tacos and iced drinks I picked up could definitely be classified as a bribe. When the festival closed down and Axle left his booth, I wanted us to be ready to follow him however long it took to find out what he and Schmidt were doing.

Ethan was beginning to pack up the books for the night when I got to Ty's booth. He sniffed the air when I walked up behind him and turned before I said a word.

He homed in on the food sack. "For me?" he said with a smile.

"I have enough if you want some," I said. "Figured Ty would have gone all day without food."

My friend looked up from her tablet, where it appeared she'd been tallying up the day's sales. "I had a slushie," she said defensively. "And that coffee you and I had earlier."

"How nutritious," I said and handed her the sack I'd brought. "Chicken fajita tacos with extra tomato, no sour cream, just the way you like them."

She grinned. "You're buttering me up, and here I thought we were going out for dinner. Like grown-ups, without the kids."

"We can do that tomorrow if you like," I said. "Tonight I have an important mission."

Ethan unfolded the top of the sack and breathed in deeply. "Like a James Bond kind of mission?" he said.

"Something like," I said.

Ty accepted the first taco out of the sack. "What does this mission entail?"

I thought back to our trips to Dawson's Peak as seventeen-year-olds. "Visiting our past," I said.

We ate the tacos and finished packing up the books that would be unpacked again in the morning for day four of the festival. Twenty minutes later, as the sunny day dissolved into streaks of yellows and pinks across the fall sky, we sat in my car behind Axle, who drove a beat-up gray Dodge pickup. Ty wore a black hoodie I'd brought to cover her colorful shirt. We'd made a stop at her car, where she traded her Crocs for a pair of sneakers she carried with her in case of emergency. This didn't qualify, but I warned her we'd be doing a bit of walking.

Axle took the turn I thought he might take and headed in the general direction of Dawson's Peak.

"Tell me again why you think this guy needs to be followed," Ty said, "'cause if you think he killed his co-worker, then I say we're turning around now."

"I don't think he killed Fisher," I said. "Axle and Henry Schmidt have made some kind of bargain."

"About what?"

"I don't know."

"Then why do we care?"

"Axle thinks I'm trying to get a cut of the profit."

"Profit from what?"

"I don't know."

"For Pete's sake, Sabrina, what do you hope to accomplish here?"

"We're going to watch and see if we can figure this mystery out by seeing what they do next."

I caught her rolling her eyes.

"It's not like we're in foreign territory," I said. "I did a drive-by and cased the joint earlier. When I knew Herr Schmidt was at the festival and not at his house."

"Did you actually say '*case the joint*'? You do realize that this is real life and we're not in your fictional world?"

"Of course," I said. "Smart aleck."

"How'd you know exactly where Schmidt was when you cased the joint?"

"Aunt Rowe told me."

"Your aunt is in on this?"

"Umm." The way my answer came out could have been construed as a yes or a no.

Ty correctly interpreted it as a no. "Does she have any idea what you're doing?"

I shook my head.

"Does anyone know?"

More head shaking.

"I'm sending my husband a text, so at least somebody will have an inkling where I am and where to start looking if I don't get back home tonight."

"C'mon, Ty, give me some credit. I'm not planning to do anything that would put you in jeopardy."

"Be real," she said. "In this day and age, no one ever knows if they'll arrive home safe and sound at the end of a day."

Sad but true.

Axle slowed at the foot of a long drive that went up to Dawson's Peak. He turned in—no surprise—and I followed, leaving more than ample space between our vehicles.

"He's going to see your lights following him," Ty said. "Then what?"

"I'm not going in very far," I said. "I'm parking on River Road."

We both knew River Road well, as did every other person who'd grown up in the area or visited often, as I had.

"But you want to see what they're doing up at the house," she said.

"Yup." I pulled off the main road onto River Road and went to the area that would hold about a dozen parked cars. Tonight, we were here alone. "We'll go the rest of the way on foot."

"Seriously?" Ty said. "You should have added some of your homemade chocolate chunk cookies to the bribe if you wanted me to exert myself this much after the day I've had."

"How about a rain check on the cookies?" I pulled two flashlights from the door pocket and handed one to Ty.

We climbed out and spent a few seconds listening to the awesome sound of the rushing river. Then we trekked up a well-beaten path that ran perpendicular to the main road. We only had the equivalent of four or five city blocks to walk, but it was all uphill. By the time the house came into view, I was thoroughly winded. I heard Ty breathing heavily behind me.

Axle's truck was parked in front of the upscale rock-sided structure.

I turned to Ty. "Schmidt has a really nice place here."

She nodded. "Now what?"

"House is pretty lit up," I said. "Let's walk around the outside. See what we can see."

"Like a couple of Peeping Toms?" she whispered.

"Exactly."

We flicked our flashlights off. As we crept across the manicured lawn surrounding the house, guided by the glow from the house windows, I hoped the fanatical Schmidt hadn't installed any motion sensors to trip an alarm or turn on outside lights. When I reached the edge of the house, I realized I'd been holding my breath, and I gulped for air.

"You all right?" Ty said behind me.

"Yeah."

"We could turn around and go back," she suggested.

I shook my head and sidestepped bushes in the front flower bed to cross the porch and peer in the window beside the front door.

No one there.

I went back to Ty. "Let's stick together."

She followed me around the side of the house where we paused to look in each window. Schmidt had a dining table for twelve, a modern and well-kept kitchen, and a living room with a large television set mounted to the wall. Curio cabinets lined another wall, and I wondered if they held his collections.

We made the turn to the back of the house. Ty whispered, "I think we're crazy for coming here."

I shrugged, then paused to look around. The light from the windows cast a dull glow over the backyard, which appeared to be landscaped with elaborate flower gardens. I scanned the stone walks that wended their way through the

beds, birdbaths, and statuary. Night critters serenaded us, and an owl hooted. A collection of ten-foot-tall flagpoles stood along the far side of the yard and flags whipped in the evening breeze.

"Nice place," I said again. "Let's check these windows."

I reached the second window from the corner, peered in, and jumped back fast.

I turned to Ty and pointed. Mouthed, "They're in here."

We eased into a position below the window and inched up slowly. This felt ridiculous, and I almost burst out laughing. But I really wanted to know what these guys were up to, so I raised my head until my eyes were above the sill.

Schmidt, in his usual formal attire, sat behind a large oak desk. Scruffy Axle, in his wrinkled T-shirt, stood on the other side. I found it strange that straitlaced Schmidt would allow himself to occupy the same room as the other man. Something covered the center of the desktop between them. I squinted. Dark fabric—was it velvet?—lay spread out on the desk, covered by sparkling stones. Schmidt picked up a jeweler's loupe and lifted a stone with a green tint.

"I don't think they're dealing with costume jewelry," Ty whispered.

"Shh." I held an index finger to my lips, and we continued to watch the men.

After a few seconds of inspecting the first stone, Schmidt put it down and picked up another. He went through them one at a time and had looked over quite a few when he put down his loupe and placed both hands on the desk.

He pointed at the stones and spoke while giving Axle a palms-up. Axle's response appeared clipped, his expression angry. The windows were too well insulated for us to hear them. With a better angle, I might have been able to read lips, but I didn't need to hear exactly what was said to know that Schmidt was extremely put out. He stood, and I hoped

that guns weren't one of the things he collected. Both men were yelling now.

Ty tugged on my arm as she lowered to the ground. "We should get out of here."

I tended to agree. We backed away from the window and stood near a bed of blazing red bushes.

"What do you make of this?" she said.

"I'd have to guess Axle hoped to make a sale to Schmidt," I said. "Maybe the quality of those stones isn't good enough for Schmidt."

"I'm sure he has rules on the topic," Ty said.

"Right." We crept back the way we'd come.

I led the way around to the front porch. We were about to reach the sidewalk when someone jumped out of the bushes in front of me.

"Hold it right there," said Coco Fisher. "I came a long way to put this deal to bed, and you're not getting between me and my money."

I put my hands up the way they do in old westerns, but this was no movie. The woman held what looked like a real revolver. Her hand was way too steady, and I wouldn't have put it past her to take a shot if she thought she needed to. My shock gave way quickly to fear.

"I'm not interested in your money," I said.

"You planning to keep the stone for yourself?" she said.

I frowned. I didn't know what the heck she was talking about, but would she shoot me if I said that?

Coco tipped her head. "Think you can sell it to him yourself, after we're out of the way? That's not happening, bitch."

My mind raced. Were these gems the reason someone killed Fisher? Had Coco killed him herself so she could have all the money? But the sheriff said she had an alibi. And if she wanted to kill her husband, wouldn't she have simply used the gun she held now instead of—

What? I didn't even know what killed the man.

"Sabrina is nothing if not fair," Tyanne said.

I slowly glanced over my shoulder to see that she, too, had her arms up over her head.

Ty continued to address Coco. "If she has something that belongs to you, all you have to do is tell her what it is and I'm sure she'd return it."

Coco barked a laugh. "Yeah, right. Good one."

"I'm quite serious," Ty said.

I turned my head and muttered under my breath, "I don't have anything."

Coco came closer. "You're lying."

And that's when someone came flying out of the bushes to hit Coco low and hard. But not before she got off a shot. The man who'd flown through the air grunted, and the two of them went down in a tangle of arms and legs.

Ty grabbed my arm, and we jumped into the bushes ourselves, hit the ground, and rolled. We ran a few yards and ducked behind some thick pampas grass. Ty had her phone out and was punching in 911.

I lifted my head to try to identify the man struggling with Coco. She was on top of him, whoever he was, and I worried she'd shoot him point-blank. Then I spotted Coco's gun across the porch from where she straddled the man, who appeared to have collapsed.

The front door burst open and Axle raced out. Coco jumped up. Her head seemed to swivel as she scanned the grounds, looking for us, I was sure.

"Let's go," Axle growled and grabbed her arm.

Coco retrieved her weapon, and the two of them took off into the night. Ty and I stood.

Herr Schmidt rushed through the door and stopped dead when he spotted a man bleeding on his porch. Schmidt wasn't holding any weapon, and being that he was supposed to be a pillar of the community, we came out from our hiding spot.

"Help is on the way," Tyanne told Herr Schmidt.

I rushed over to the porch to get a look at Coco's attacker.

I stopped by his body and looked down.

Gabe Brenner. Good Lord, had he followed me again?

31

"THE THING IS, I don't know if Gabe was following me, the way he has before, or if he came to Schmidt's house to participate in the deal they were trying to make."

"Coco acted like you were trying to horn in on the profits," Tyanne said. "Why would she think that?"

"From the time she arrived in Lavender, the woman has claimed I have something she wants. I'm guessing it was those gemstones. She's probably the person who broke into my cottage looking for them."

"Maybe so, but that's not the whole story," Ty said. "She sounded like she still thinks you have something."

"Well, I don't."

"I get that," Ty said.

We were leaving the local hospital emergency room, where we had learned through wheedling a close family friend of Ty's that Gabe was being treated for a minor gunshot wound to the upper arm. The hospital employee had

sworn us to secrecy after telling us Gabe's mother was on her way over.

We skedaddled out to my car after her warning, as we didn't want to run into Mrs. Brenner and have to explain anything about the night's events. I was still trying to figure it all out myself.

I started the engine and relaxed back into the car seat. "We are so lucky Deputy Ainsley showed up instead of Rosales or even the sheriff."

"You said that, like, a dozen times already," Ty said.

"It's true. They wouldn't have bought our story that we came to see Schmidt about the festival. They'd have wanted to know why my car was parked so far down the road. Ainsley didn't seem to notice that little tidbit."

"So maybe he's not the brightest bulb," she said. "He was worried about Gabe bleeding all over the place and Schmidt trying to deny knowledge of the two who got away."

"Wonder if Coco and Axle ran very far, or if they're staying wherever they stayed last night."

She turned to me. "We are *not* going to look for them."

"No, no." I shifted into reverse to back out of the parking space.

"And you are *not* going back to stay alone at your place, where they might show up to get you."

"You're right. I'll bunk with Aunt Rowe."

"You'd better. I could call her to make sure you do."

"That's not necessary. I promise."

I coasted through the parking lot. "I'm sorry, Ty, really so sorry. I never thought we'd be in any kind of danger."

She reached out and put a hand on my arm. "We're all right," she said. "That's what matters."

I braked and turned to her. "Except for the scratches on your face from rolling into the bushes. How will you explain those?"

"I'm telling the truth, the whole truth, and nothing but the truth when I get home," she said. "Will you tell Luke?"

I screwed up my mouth, thinking.

"If you don't, he'll find out anyway," she said.

She was right and I would admit the whole story just as soon as I saw Luke, which might be in the morning.

I delivered Tyanne back to her car, surprised that there were still festival hangers-on in town, even though the booths had closed up for the night hours ago. People stood around the town square socializing.

Ty leaned across the console to give me a hug. "You watch your back, and text me when you're safe and sound in your aunt's house."

"Cross my heart." I made an X across my chest and smiled at my friend.

I drove home and actually felt a little spooked about going into my place for Hitchcock and a few other things I'd need during the night.

"Mrreow." Hitchcock walked across the bathroom vanity and rubbed against me as I collected toiletries to throw into a bag.

"I had a rough night, buddy," I told the cat, "and Herr Schmidt's probably having an even rougher one, being questioned at the sheriff's department. Wonder if he'll tell them how he got involved with that hoodlum Axle in the first place."

The cat trilled a response and followed me around the cottage as I finished gathering my things.

Fifteen minutes later, we entered Aunt Rowe's house through the back door. It was after eleven and all was quiet on the home front. Aunt Rowe's bedroom door was closed, and I didn't want to wake her. Instead, I found a pillow and blanket in the linen closet and made up the sofa in her office. I plugged my phone into the charger and remembered to send Ty a text that I was safe and sound at Aunt Rowe's. She sent a reply within seconds.

"I'm home. Hubby says I can't hang out with you anymore. Kidding."

Seconds after I lay down, Hitchcock was on top of the blanket and nestled against me. His purr was soothing to a certain extent, even as I reviewed the evening's troubling events. Axle and Coco were obviously up to no good. Did it mean they were guilty of murder? Not necessarily. But if they didn't kill Fisher, then who did? With that uncomfortable thought, I drifted off to sleep.

Nightmares about Calvin Fisher fighting with Tia and Coco and Herr Schmidt woke me around three. My stomach rumbled. The fajita taco dinner hadn't been enough to sustain me through everything that had come after. I started thinking about that pumpkin pie I'd meant to bake and had never gotten to. Wondered if I could clear enough room in the kitchen to make it now. I shifted on the sofa and moaned. My limbs ached from the tumble I'd taken through the bushes at Schmidt's house. The whole crazy scene replayed in my head. I checked the lighted face of my watch. Three-thirty in the morning.

Beside me, Hitchcock stretched.

"I know. It's way too early, but I can't stay still."

I swung my legs around and sat up. Hitchcock stood beside me and cocked his head to look at me.

"You may stay here if you like," I told him.

The cat seemed to consider this for a moment, then he turned in circles and settled himself on top of the blanket. I threw on my robe, stuffed my feet into flip-flops, and headed for the kitchen. The room didn't look nearly as full as it had on the first night I'd intended to bake. Obviously, a lot of the food had been eaten over the last few days. I opened the refrigerator and decided Glenda must be keeping the cold trays out in the storage room. My pumpkin sat on the windowsill in the breakfast nook. I was surprised someone hadn't shot it out of the cannon by now.

I checked for the other ingredients I'd need for my Paradise Pumpkin Pie and took out two pie pans, because why make only one when two is just as easy?

After confirming I had everything I'd need, I set about cutting up and peeling the pumpkin for cooking. A lot more work than opening a can of pumpkin, but the task felt therapeutic.

When I had the pumpkin simmering in a large pot on the stove, I started on the piecrusts. My brain was awake enough now to think about the events of the night before. Axle had laid out what I assumed were precious gems for Schmidt to inspect. The scene looked like something from a movie, and those movies always involved stolen gems. So was Axle a jewel thief or did Fisher have the stones before he died? Maybe he made a business of selling stolen merchandise and the costume jewelry booth was a front for what he really had going on behind the scenes. And that's why he had the backpack full of money that Damon saw under the table. The scenario made perfect sense. So who wanted Fisher out of the way more than anyone else? Or was the murder a joint project concocted by Axle and Coco?

I measured the flour for the pie dough and added a bit of salt, then went to the refrigerator for the butter and jumped a mile when I saw a face at the window of the kitchen door. Britt Cramer. The woman smiled and tried the knob, but I'd locked the door behind me when I came in. I went and unlocked it for her.

Britt didn't look like the perky facial-products saleswoman at the moment. Her curly hair was held back in a clip, her face was puffy and makeup-free, and her eyes were slits. She wore a blue T-shirt bearing the Pure Velvet logo over gray pull-on shorts, and she carried a paper grocery sack.

"You're up early," I said.

"I'm not the only one. I saw the lights on and decided to get started." She lifted the brown paper bag. "I'm baking for the contest."

"That's ambitious. Seemed like you had your hands full already with your booth."

Britt shrugged. "I do, but baking relaxes me."

"Me, too. Come on in."

Britt followed me into the kitchen and sniffed the air. "You cooking fresh pumpkin?"

I nodded and headed back to the pie dough. "For my pumpkin pie."

"Are you entering the bake-off, too?"

I shrugged. "Maybe, if the pie turns out okay."

Britt set her sack down on the breakfast table and took out her ingredients, including canned pumpkin. "I don't want to get in your way. You mind if I start a pot of coffee?"

"Help yourself."

The woman obviously knew her way around the kitchen and went straight to the coffee canister. I cut the butter into the flour for my pie dough. Ideally, I'd chill the mixture for several hours before rolling it out, but I was in no mood to wait that long. Thirty minutes, maybe. I wrapped the dough in wax paper and stuck it in the refrigerator.

The coffee started brewing and Britt sat at the breakfast table with her head propped on her fist.

I looked at the things she'd placed on the table. "What are you going to bake?"

"Pumpkin swirl cheesecake."

I grabbed a banana from a bowl on the island and peeled it. When I turned and took a bite, I saw tears were running down Britt's cheeks.

"What's wrong?"

She wiped her face with the back of a hand. "The recipe—" She paused and took a breath, blinked a few times, and took a napkin from the holder on the table to wipe her eyes. "The recipe was my sister's favorite."

I wasn't sure what to say. "It sounds good."

I went to the stove and stuck a fork into the cooking pumpkin. Almost ready.

"I'm going to have more than enough of this cooked pumpkin," I said. "You may use some if you like."

Britt was unwrapping packages of cream cheese and seemed to have gotten over her crying jag. She looked over at me. "Does it taste the same as canned?"

"Better, in my opinion."

She shrugged. "Okay, then. I'll try it. Thanks."

I went back to checking the pumpkin and wondered if she knew anything about Fisher's involvement with the possibly stolen gemstones. She wouldn't be happy if I brought him up, but maybe I could get her interested if I told her about last night.

"Coco Fisher nearly killed me last night," I said.

"She *what*?" Britt's sleepy eyes opened wide.

I poured us each a cup of coffee and we sat down at the table. I told her the bare facts we'd given Deputy Ainsley the night before. "After the shot, Coco and Axle hightailed it out of there. I don't know whether they've been found or not. I stayed here at the house instead of in my cottage just in case they came looking for me again."

"Why would they?" she said.

"I'm sure I have no idea why Coco thought I was involved in the first place. She seemed convinced that Calvin gave me something before he died."

"How did you even get mixed up with that bunch?" she said.

"I was in the wrong place at the wrong time. That's all."

"Like my sister."

I frowned. "What do you mean?"

Her shoulders slumped, and she put her coffee cup down on the table. "Calvin came through our town with a crew working on restoring the electricity after a hurricane blew through. Alicia. What was that, eighty-four?"

"Eighty-three, I think." I remembered the hurricane even though I was very young at the time. "Was he an electrician?"

Britt shook her head. "He was a con man, probably lied about his qualifications. I'm sure they were looking for as many hands as they could get."

I could buy Fisher as a con man. I sipped my coffee and waited for her to go on.

"My sister, Jenna, volunteered to help one day at a Red Cross shelter. She liked doing good deeds. She was such a kind person."

"Was." I didn't like the sound of that.

"Calvin came by while she was there, and they met."

"But he didn't need the help of the Red Cross," I said, "or did he?"

"He said he did. One thing led to another. Fast forward six months, they were engaged." She stopped talking and looked at me. "I'm sorry. You tell me you're nearly shot, and here I am commiserating about my sad past."

"You're fine." I put a hand on her arm. "Go on. I want to hear."

Her eyes welled up again. "Calvin was good at what he did when it came to the con," she said. "Our whole family loved him. He was attentive to Jenna, helpful whenever Dad needed a hand with chores around the house, complimentary of Mom's cooking. We all thought they would be one of those couples who'd do anything for each other, like the Mosers. They are so cute together, don't you think?"

I did think Winnie and Cecil were cute with each other, but I was more interested in hearing about Jenna and Calvin.

After a few seconds, Britt said, "Jenna started making wedding plans, and we were all on board with the happy preparations."

"Did you know anything about Calvin's past, his family?" I said.

"He told us he didn't have family. Lied to our faces as easy as you blink your eyes."

"How'd you find out he was a liar?"

"A friend of mine from school was out of town and ran into him. Couldn't wait to tell me what she saw. I didn't believe her at first."

"What did she see?"

"Calvin with another woman. A woman driving an expensive sports car. Wearing gobs of jewelry."

I sighed. "Did your family have a lot of money?"

"He thought we did." A tear ran down her cheek. "We found out later he'd convinced Jenna to empty her bank account. There wasn't a huge amount, but she gave it all to him. He was supposed to have bought a lot where they'd build a new house one day."

I shook my head. "I'm so sorry. But at least your sister didn't marry him, did she?"

Britt looked me straight in the eye. The tears flowed in earnest now. "No. They didn't get married. He pulled up stakes and pretty much disappeared."

"In retrospect, that might have been a good thing," I said.

"Depends on how you look at it," she said. "If he'd stayed, my dad would've probably killed him. Or I would have."

Her words sounded drastic. Couples split up all the time. Engagements ended. Going on to get married and later divorced might have been worse.

"When did you run into Fisher again?"

"Couple years ago," she said, "at a festival like this one. I'd been working at a bank for a long time, got tired of that. Decided to try the Pure Velvet gig. Probably wouldn't have gone that route if I'd known it would put me within a hundred miles of Calvin Fisher. When I saw him behind that jewelry counter the first time, I wanted to go over and slug him."

Once again, a drastic reaction. I found myself wondering if Britt had purchased a set of handcuffs at this festival.

"Have you heard anything about him dealing in stolen jewels?" I said.

"I don't know anything about what he was involved with," she said. "I don't want to know."

"Do you think your sister had any contact with him after the broken engagement?"

Tears leaked from Britt's eyes, and she shook her head. "She had no contact."

"Are you sure?"

"Positive," she said. "After Calvin left Jenna, she grieved for a long time. Then she killed herself."

32

I JOINED BRITT IN a good cry for a few minutes, then we managed to stand and finish our baking. At half past five we had the kitchen cleaned and went our separate ways. Hitchcock and I headed for my place with the pie I would enter in the bake-off. Britt and I had eaten most of the other one and determined it contest-worthy. Her cheesecake looked great, too, but we talked ourselves out of cutting into that as well. Depression could do a number on a person's appetite, and the story Britt told was certainly depressing.

Not to mention a great motivation for murder.

I thought about Fisher and the nasty way he'd grabbed my arm a few days ago. His wife wasn't much better. I had no doubt she'd have shot me for no good reason. I almost wished she would show her face now. I'd like to clobber her for holding a gun on me *and* for being married to such a jerk. Not really, but it felt better to imagine letting loose.

Back home, I rearranged things in my little refrigerator to fit the pie inside. Then I fed Hitchcock and went off to

the shower while he enjoyed his breakfast. My phone pinged with a text message while I was toweling off.

"Meet at Hot Stuff? Nine am?"

The thought of seeing Luke made me smile, though I had already consumed plenty of coffee. I responded that I'd be there. I might be ready for more caffeine by then.

I chose a pair of skinny jeans that barely zipped after all the pie I'd eaten and added a flared tunic to hide any tummy bulge. Hitchcock usually had a sixth sense for when I was about to put on my tennis shoes, but he wasn't here now. I tied them without the usual cat-chasing-laces game.

I went outside to look for him and was surprised to see some of the vendors were still here. Seemed they were running a little late. I walked toward Aunt Rowe's house, looking left and right for the cat. He could be anywhere, and it would be pure luck if I found him in my cursory search.

Maybelle came walking at a fast pace from the direction of Aunt Rowe's house headed to the Rome cottage, where she was staying. "Mornin', Sabrina. Rowe's kitchen sure smells good, like somebody was baking already this morning. Was that you?"

"Caught," I said. "I decided to enter a pie in the competition."

"Good luck to you," she said. "I have to run. Sunday's always another big tourist day."

"Have you seen Hitchcock?"

"I did," she called back. "He's with Winnie at the Florence cottage. You know that cat has a crush on her?"

"He's good at cozying up with anyone who'll give him treats."

"Smart boy," she said and kept walking.

I slipped around behind the Melbourne cottage. A vehicle sat in the parking slot. Probably belonged to Gabe's mother. I didn't want to run into either one of the Brenners, though I wondered if Gabe had been released from the hospital. He truly might have saved me from being shot last night. I

couldn't quite bring myself to think of the man who was stalking me as a hero, though. Of course, he might have gone to Schmidt's for another reason, but that didn't seem likely.

The Florence cottage was situated close enough to Brenner's that the bacon smell might have wafted over into their space. Maybe that was part of what attracted Hitchcock to the area. I spotted the cat hopping around in the grass between the parking spaces for the two cottages. I wondered what he'd found to play with and hoped it wasn't another grass snake. I'd caught him with those snakes in the past. He was always on the lookout for things that slithered.

The Mosers' Buick was still here, but Cecil and Winnie weren't in sight. They were getting a later start than usual this morning, and I hoped they were okay. The sun was almost completely up, and tourists would begin pouring into town anytime now.

I approached Hitchcock slowly and inspected the grass around him. I caught sight of something shiny in the sunlight. An object glittering, not slithering. What did that cat have now?

"C'mon, boy, let me see." I crept closer to him and stooped down to watch. My phone rang, and I saw that it was Aunt Rowe calling. I swiped my finger across the screen to answer.

"Morning, Aunt Rowe."

"Somebody's been sleeping on my couch," she said. "I figure it was either you, Baby Bear, or Mama Bear."

"It was me. Sorry I forgot all about folding up my bedclothes. But I didn't eat any of your porridge, honest."

She laughed. "Mainly, I just wanted to know you're okay. Got a call from Jeb a minute ago."

"And he told you about my escapade last night?"

"He said you almost got yourself shot," she said, "and that put a scare into me. Had to hear your voice."

"I'm sorry, but I didn't want to wake you when I got in

just to tell you something that would likely have kept you up all night."

"Appreciate the thought," she said.

"What else did the sheriff tell you? Have they found Coco Fisher and Axle?"

"I don't think so, but he didn't want to go into all the details. Where are you now?"

"Between Florence and Melbourne. Hitchcock is out here playing with something he probably shouldn't have."

"What is it?"

"I can't tell yet. He batted it under a car."

"I'm off to the festival shortly," she said.

"What time do the bake-off entries need to be in?"

She told me the contest rules and times. "What are you entering?"

"Are you a judge?"

"I am."

"Then it's a secret."

She laughed. "You always were a smart cookie. I'll see you later."

The call disconnected, and I stuffed the phone back into my jeans pocket. Then I knelt on the ground and looked at Hitchcock, sitting under the Mosers' Buick.

"C'mon, bud," I said. "Out from there. What's so interesting anyway?"

His front paws moved quickly and something rolled toward me. I put a hand out to stop the forward progression and caught the object. Picked it up.

The sun caught the sparkle of the good-sized blue stone. Most likely it had fallen out of a piece of costume jewelry.

Wait, Sabrina. Use your head.

I had watched Herr Schmidt inspecting what appeared to be real gemstones just last night. Coco Fisher was shooting at people. She'd asked me about a stone. Could this be the stone she was looking for? I'd have to turn it over to the sheriff.

A door creaked, and I jerked my head around to look at the Melbourne cottage. Stuffed the stone into my pocket. Gabe Brenner came out to the front stoop and stretched his right arm high above his head. His left was supported in a sling. *I could do without running into that guy now.*

I hunkered down by the Buick and crabbed around to the opposite side. Hitchcock crawled out from under the car and watched me quizzically. I scooped the cat up with one hand and hurried back to our place.

B Y the time I settled Hitchcock in my bedroom and left for town, the Mosers' Buick and the car at Brenner's cottage were both gone. I drove straight to the coffee shop and snagged a nearby parking space on the street. I noticed Luke's truck parked a few spaces away as I hurried into Hot Stuff. "Turn the Beat Around" was playing on the jukebox when I walked in, and I spotted Luke at the table I liked to sit at to write. Which reminded me that more than twenty-four hours had now passed since I'd written a word.

Extenuating circumstances, I told myself, an excuse I used too often. I would make up my word count next week, after Pumpkin Days had ended and things went back to normal.

Luke smiled and stood to greet me, looking very official in his uniform. He put his hands on the sides of my arms and leaned in to kiss me on the cheek. I inhaled his luscious scent, then we sat, and I waved to Max. Noticed a number of other townspeople who had watched with interest as Luke greeted me.

A waitress came over and took our order. When she left, Luke put his hands on the table in front of him and laced his fingers.

"Did you nab the hunters who weren't supposed to be hunting yet?" I said.

"One of them," he said. "We suspect there's a gang of them, based on the number of reported gunshots." He watched me closely.

"Gunshots, right. That reminds me of something I have to tell you."

"Good," he said.

Clearly, he already knew what I was about to say. I rolled my eyes. "It's not my fault Calvin Fisher's crazy wife showed up with a gun."

"And you were visiting Schmidt because . . . ?" He paused and waited.

I wasn't keen on telling him why I'd gone up to Dawson's Peak, but he'd drag the story out of me eventually. May as well give in. "Tyanne and I were doing a little surveillance."

"Because the sheriff can't handle the investigation on his own?" Luke said. "Or why, exactly, did you think you two needed to tackle that project?"

"Ty didn't know any details ahead of time. The idea was all mine. There was no way I could have predicted Coco Fisher or Gabe Brenner would be there."

"Going into the hills on foot at night isn't the best idea to begin with," he said.

The waitress came back with our coffees. I added cream to mine and took a sip. Put the mug back down on the table.

"So what else have you heard?" I said.

"Fisher's wife is in the wind," he said.

"You know, the sheriff told me she had an alibi for the time of her husband's death, but that could have been cooked up. She's all about the money."

"You mean Fisher had a bunch of life insurance?"

"I don't know about that, but she was part of the deal that was going down last night at Schmidt's. Except she was still looking for something. I'll bet she's the one who broke into my place. She thought I had this."

I reached into my pocket and pulled out the blue stone. Glanced around to make sure no one was paying attention, then opened my hand in the middle of the table. The stone glittered under the coffee shop's fluorescent lights.

Luke looked at the stone, then met my gaze. "You *do* have it."

"Not until an hour ago. I'm taking it to the sheriff."

"Where'd you find it?" He reached for the stone. "May I?"

"Of course."

I watched as Luke carefully picked up the stone and rolled it in his palm.

"I found Hitchcock playing with it in the grass between two of the cottages."

He looked up with a smirk. "The cat's a jewel thief?"

"Hitchcock isn't a cat burglar," I said, giggling, "even if he was caught with the goods. He has an attraction to jewelry, though, that's for sure. He once found a necklace that someone hid in my cottage decades ago."

"I remember." Luke rolled the stone in his palm. "Looks real, but I'm no expert. Wonder where the cat found it."

I raised my brows. "He was in the grass near Brenner's cottage."

Luke looked at me. "So Brenner might be up to more than stalking."

"And deep-frying bacon," I said.

"That, too." He picked up the gem with a thumb and a forefinger and reached across the table to hand it back to me.

"Hello, Sabrina," said a man.

I looked up to see Dave Harrison standing next to our table. He looked jaunty in khakis and a blue-and-white striped shirt, as if he were about to go out on a sailboat. Mom, in a similar casual outfit, stood beside him, her gaze fixed on the blue stone Luke was handing to me. Her hand went to her mouth.

"Sabrina. Oh. You—" She looked at Luke and seemed

to take in every detail of him in one quick glance. "You must be Sabrina's young man."

Luke deposited the stone in my hand, then stood and tipped his head. "Yes, ma'am." He shook Mom's hand, then Dave's, and they all introduced themselves while I sat dumbstruck.

"You're Sabrina's folks," Luke said. "Care to join us?"

He wore a big grin, clearly enjoying this chance meeting. I wasn't sure how I felt about it.

Mom sat, her gaze on the fingers that I'd closed around the stone.

"I thought y'all had gone back to Houston," I said after the waitress delivered mugs of coffee to Mom and Dave. "You've finished your business with Aunt Rowe, right?"

"But not with Rita," Dave said. "We have a sticking point in the dissolution papers. She's trying to steal a firm client. I will not agree to that."

"A Houston client?" I said, wondering if Rita planned to divide her time between Lavender and Houston. The firm had always had plenty of clients to go around.

He shook his head. "Someone out here. He contacted Rita for some work, but I originated his company's business and the firm can handle whatever he needs. It wasn't my decision for her to move to this—"

He wisely stopped talking, but I could imagine his next words would not be complimentary of our charming small town.

"Excuse me," I said, "but isn't the client the one who gets to choose his attorney?"

I couldn't believe I was defending Rita, but I felt suddenly proud of her decision to break up, so to speak, with the man seated across the table from me.

"Enough about business," Mom said. "Tell us more about yourself, Luke." She eyed his uniform. "You're a—"

"Texas game warden," he said.

"You deal with animals, fish, and things?" She seemed to be fighting to keep from wrinkling up her nose as she said it.

"Yes, ma'am."

"You have to work on Sundays?"

"Sometimes," he said. "Depends on the schedule and whether we have enforcement issues to deal with."

"And what about that gem I saw you giving Sabrina?" She gave him a wide smile. "Do you two have some news you'd like to share with us?"

I straightened in alarm. "Mom, no. I just found this stone in the grass this morning. Luke never even saw it before."

Mom raised her brows. "In the grass? Really? You don't expect me to believe you can find sapphires lying around any old place."

"I really did find it in the grass, or rather, I found my cat playing with it in the grass." I opened my hand and looked at the stone. "How do you know it's a sapphire?"

She leaned over to get a better look, then picked up the stone. "It looks just like one to me, about five carats."

"That'd be worth thousands," Dave said. "You shouldn't carry it around so carelessly, Sabrina. Do you have insurance on that thing?"

I looked at him. "I'm not being careless. The stone isn't mine. I'm turning it over to the sheriff."

"Why ever would you do that?" Mom said as if she longed to add the sapphire to her personal jewelry collection.

"The stone might be connected to unsolved crimes," Luke said.

"Crimes? Plural?" Mom said. "I knew about the one, but Sabrina, this is turning into a dangerous place. I really wish you'd come back home with us."

I sighed. "I'm not going to do that."

"I thought they would arrest that person," she said. "I reported what he said to you about killing that man."

"I heard about what you reported," I said, "but don't go

saying he killed a man when you don't know what really happened. No one does."

"Yet," Luke added. "The sheriff's office is in the middle of an ongoing investigation, so best not to guess who's guilty."

Mom studied him but said nothing.

"So I need to get this stone to the sheriff," I said. "Matter of fact, I need to get over there right now, and Luke needs to work. Right?"

I turned to Luke and lifted my brows.

He gulped his coffee and stood. "She's right. I'm running late. Good to meet you folks."

I stood, too, but Mom put a hand on my arm. "May I have a word in private, Sabrina?"

The song "Don't Leave Me This Way" came over the sound system as if she'd planned it.

"I'll see you later," I told Luke. I stuffed the supposed sapphire in my pants pocket, then sat back down.

Mom watched Luke leave the coffee shop. "He's very handsome," she said.

"Yes, he is."

"Seems nice enough," Dave said.

"His job, though," Mom said. "It seems—" She hesitated, grasping for words.

"Luke's job is not a concern of yours," I said. "What is it you needed, before I leave to see the sheriff?"

"About your *friend*, the other one: Tia," Mom said. "I was considering asking her to take a DNA test to see if she's related to you."

I was about to balk, but she went on.

"Then I saw her with that fellow."

"What fellow?"

"The one who brought you flowers," she said. "They had their heads together, whispering."

"When was this?" I said, wondering what Tia and Gabe could have discussed.

"Last night," she said. "Dave and I were leaving dinner

with the client. He insisted on going to that local barbeque place." She made a face.

"Where did you see Tia?"

"On the sidewalk, with the man," she said, "and I just have to tell you that after I saw their clandestine meeting and him passing her a handful of cash, I decided that we're really better off not knowing whether she's kin or not."

33

MADE MY WAY to the sheriff's office, eager to get the stone that might be worth thousands out of my pocket. Mom's news kept running through my head. Tia and Gabe. Gabe and Tia. A wad of cash. What the heck was that all about? Hadn't Tia told me she didn't know Gabe? Did the two of them have something to do with the gemstones Axle was showing Schmidt? Had Gabe been at Schmidt's because of the stones and not because he was following me? Did I want to bring any of this up to the sheriff?

Not necessarily.

Just hand over the stone and get out. This whole thing was giving me a giant headache. As I got closer to the sheriff's office, I patted myself on the back for opting to walk over. Church was obviously in session. Cars had maneuvered around the festival booths surrounding the blacktop and packed the lot. These booths weren't yet open for business and probably wouldn't be until services ended.

I pushed through the door into the sheriff's department

office and waved toward Laurelle's desk, only to realize she wasn't there. A younger woman with shoulder-length frizzy hair and cat's-eye glasses sat in Laurelle's chair. Of course, one woman couldn't work twenty-four-seven, but I was so accustomed to seeing Laurelle in her spot whenever I happened to come in that I considered her a permanent fixture.

"Good morning," I said to the new woman. "Is the sheriff in?"

She greeted me and said, "He's on the phone, but I betcha he'll only be a minute longer. I'm Stacy. I'm new here. What's your name?"

I went to her desk and introduced myself.

"You're the one with the cat Laurelle told me about," she said.

"That's me. Hitchcock's at home this morning." At least he'd better be. "I'll bring him to visit you sometime."

"I'd love that," she said. "I just moved here last month 'cause my husband threw me out. Said he wants a divorce."

"Oh no. I'm sorry." That was a big piece of news to throw out to a stranger.

"Me, too," Stacy said, "but maybe it's for the best. I came back here to where I grew up, and my mama's happy about that. Seems like everybody else I knew way back when has moved away."

I smiled at her and glanced toward the sheriff's closed door.

"Found me a great lawyer," she said, "and she could have cost me a bundle. I don't have much, so we made a bargain, and she's gonna represent me. Said she'd take my husband for all he's worth."

I'd often heard Rita make tacky statements like that to clients.

Stacy was still talking, and I replayed her words. When she paused, I said, "What kind of bargain did you make?"

"Oh, that's between me and the lawyer. You know,

attorney-client privilege and all." She waved a hand and her phone rang. She picked it up in a flash.

"Nine-one-one, what is your emergency?" she said.

While she was occupied with the call, I walked down the hall to Sheriff Crawford's office. Put my ear close to the door and listened for a few seconds. Didn't hear any talking and decided to knock.

"Come in," he said.

When I entered the office, he stood to greet me. "Sabrina. Here you are, still not staying safely indoors even after last night's hoopla."

"Things keep happening," I said. "Even when I'm not looking for trouble. You have a minute?"

"You've piqued my curiosity." He sat in his chair and rolled it up to his desk. He sipped from a coffee mug and watched me expectantly.

I pulled the stone from my pocket and sat in one of the visitor chairs. "Hitchcock was playing in the grass this morning at the cottages." I placed the stone on the papers scattered across his desk blotter. "With this."

He put on his reading glasses and leaned forward to get a better look. "Be kind of a coincidence if this is something a kid got out of a gumball machine and dropped by accident," he said.

I nodded. "That's what I thought, and my mother believes it's a real sapphire."

"She a jeweler now?"

"No, but she has lots of experience with expensive jewelry. Her husband says this stone could be worth several thousand."

The sheriff let out a low whistle. "Tell me exactly where you found this."

I described the area where Hitchcock was playing with the stone.

"Outside of Brenner's cottage," the sheriff said.

"Right." I thought for a few seconds before deciding to go on. "He may be the person who dropped this without realizing it."

"He's not in the jewelry business," the sheriff said.

"To our knowledge," I said. "How do you know he's *not* involved with whatever Axle and Coco were doing last night?"

"Brenner admitted he was following you to make sure you were safe. Said he didn't like you going out at night like that by yourself."

I frowned. "Tyanne was with me."

"Brenner's a stalker, Sabrina, and if you want to press charges against him, we might be able to make them stick."

"I might have been shot if he hadn't followed me."

"I know."

"What does he say about the stones Axle was showing to Schmidt?"

"Said he didn't know anything about them."

"Do you believe him?"

The sheriff shrugged. "There's no record of Brenner associating with the others. They didn't live anywhere near each other. Brenner's out of East Texas. The Fishers and Axle Howard are from North Houston."

"Howard," I said. "Axle Howard. Nobody else knew his last name. How'd you get it?"

"Took some prints from the table at the jewelry booth. Easy to get a bead on him after that with his record."

"What kind of record does he have?"

The sheriff sighed. "You never rest."

"I intended to give the stone to you and leave," I said, "but I could have been shot last night. I don't know why Coco Fisher wanted to shoot me, why she was there in the first place, why she thought I might have a stone that might be the stone I just gave you, or why she thought I might have tried to sell the alleged stone or to whom. These things tend to bring out the curiosity in me, even if I try to tamp it down."

"I imagine they do."

"Was Axle trying to sell valuable jewels to Henry Schmidt?"

"Looks that way."

"Where are those stones now?"

"Don't know. Deputy Ainsley reported no jewels found on the premises."

"But Schmidt saw them. He was inspecting them, for crying out loud. What does *he* say about them?"

"Nothing."

"What do you mean, nothing? Has someone questioned him?"

"Of course."

"And he's claiming ignorance of the whole matter?"

The sheriff nodded. "Yup."

"Why would he do that?"

"I'm guessing he doesn't want to admit any involvement with the purchase of stolen gemstones."

I raised my brows. "They were stolen?"

"I'm guessing."

"Isn't that a big leap?"

"Not with the criminal records of the people in question."

"Coco and Axle?"

"Right," the sheriff said. "And Calvin Fisher."

"If all these people have criminal records related to the topic of stolen jewels, then I'd guess the murder is somehow connected to the stolen jewels."

"Makes sense to me," he said.

"Are Coco and Axle still missing?"

He nodded.

"And Calvin's dead, so where does that leave you?"

"In the middle of a frustrating investigation," he said.

I thought back to my talk with Axle Howard the afternoon before. "You know, Coco isn't the only one who made a reference to my wanting to get a cut of the profit. Axle said something like that to me yesterday. He thought I might have made a deal with Calvin. I had no idea what he was talking about."

"What else did he say?"

"You know how Coco was asking me if her husband had given me something to hold on to before he died?"

"I remember," the sheriff said.

"I think Axle believed Calvin actually *had* given me something, but that I had wisely decided to return it. He must have been talking about the jewels he showed to Schmidt."

"Why did they think you had them?"

"Obviously, the jewels must have been missing, but I swear I never had them, and I don't know who did."

The sheriff sat back against his chair. "I don't suppose your cat nabbed the whole sack of jewels and then returned it in the nick of time?"

I grinned. "Hardly."

He twirled one end of his mustache. "One of them broke into your cottage because they thought you had the stuff."

"I figure that's what happened."

"Somebody had their hands on the jewels, but it wasn't you, or your cat, or Coco, or Axle, and obviously not the dead man. Who else could it be?"

I thought about the meeting between Tia and Gabe that Mom had reported. If one of them had supposedly valuable gemstones in their possession, why would they have turned them back over to Axle when they did?

"Penny for your thoughts," the sheriff said.

"It's a good thing this isn't a plot that I came up with, 'cause I feel the way I do when I've written myself into a corner."

He grinned. "Lots of investigations feel that way."

"Have you found out any more on whether it was an injection that killed Fisher?"

He shook his head. "Toxicology reports can take several weeks."

"Well, I got a lead on the source of Rita Colletti's information about the syringe."

"Tell me."

"You might want to have a talk with Stacy."

He frowned. "Our person? Stacy?" He pointed toward the lobby.

"That's the Stacy," I said.

"What does she have to do with anything? She hasn't been in town a month."

"Talk to her," I said. "I think she'll have quite a bit to tell you about her new lawyer."

34

I WASN'T AT ALL surprised that Rita Colletti would ask a sheriff's department employee to give her confidential information about an investigation. I felt a bit sorry to drop poor Stacy in the grease, but it seemed to me the sheriff ought to know if an employee was handing out details she shouldn't. This problem was between them. I wouldn't let the guilt about turning her in get to me.

Taking my best friend to the scene of a shooting was different. Tyanne deserved an apology. I headed to her booth to make sure she'd recovered well from our scare the night before. When I came within a few yards of the bookseller's booth, I realized her husband, Bryan, stood behind the counter with Ethan. I slowed my steps and thought about turning around, but Bryan had looked up and seen me coming. He was medium height and stocky with blond hair, and he usually wore an easy smile. He wasn't smiling today.

"Morning," I said when I got close enough for him to hear me.

He nodded. "Morning, Sabrina. Glad to see you survived the night."

"Yeah," Ethan said excitedly. "I heard about the shooting. Can't believe y'all were right there in the thick of things. Like a scene right out of an adventure novel."

I looked at the boy and willed him to keep quiet about the shooting. He noticed we weren't chiming in and looked from me to Ty's husband. Bryan's expression was a sure sign of his bad mood. Ethan hunched his shoulders and moved to the other side of the booth, where some women were looking at the books.

I stepped closer to the counter. "Bryan, I'm really sorry I asked Ty to tag along with me last night. I had no idea—"

"Because you didn't stop to think," he said. "From what she tells me that's pretty common for you. I mean you not thinking, 'cause if you had thought, you'd have realized you were taking the wife and mother of our family into danger."

Ty's text the night before had said her husband wouldn't let her go anywhere with me. She must have added the word "kidding" so I wouldn't be upset, but she wasn't kidding at all.

My lips quivered at his harsh words. "I'm so sorry, Bryan. If I could take back last night, I would. Is Ty okay?"

"I'm fine." Ty came around a bookshelf with a sack in her hand. "What's going on?" She looked at her husband. "Bryan, what are you doing?"

"Nothing, honey," he said.

Ty looked at me with a questioning expression, but I shook my head and made an everything-is-fine-don't-rock-the-boat gesture with my hand.

She stashed her sack under the table and changed the subject. "Today's bake-off day, and I'm dying to know what you decided to make, Sabrina."

Bryan said, "I'm about to take off. Will you be okay here until I come back for you?"

"I'll be fine." Ty gave him a kiss and sent him on his way, then looked at me. "He's not happy."

"I gathered. Can't really blame him for worrying about you, and I'm sorry."

"You weren't dragging me off against my will," she said, "so stop it. Let's talk about what you baked for the contest."

"I didn't think I'd get a chance to bake anything," I said, "so how do you know I did?"

"It's in your genes. You couldn't live with yourself if we had a bake-off right here in Lavender and you hadn't made something to enter. So, what is it?"

I told her about my early-morning baking session with Britt and what the other woman had shared about the heartache that had led to her sister's suicide.

"Dear Lord, that's awful. There's no telling *what* I would do if something like that happened in my family." She closed her mouth and glanced around, then lowered her voice. "Do you think she killed him?"

"I'm not turning her in to the sheriff," I said. "In fact, I just came from talking with him and didn't even think to mention her."

"It sure is a good enough motive for murder, though," she said.

I agreed and thought about Tia. Both of the women had an excellent motive for wanting Fisher gone.

"What *were* you and the sheriff discussing?" she said.

"Jewel thieves and the fact that Herr Schmidt is denying knowledge of any gemstones."

"We saw him with the stones," she said. "What did the sheriff say about jewel thieves?"

"He didn't tell me much, probably for fear that I'd gab around town what I learned. Which is probably what he'd say I'm doing now."

"I'm not going to post what you tell me on the Internet or anything like that," she said.

"I know, and here's what I think. From the things Sheriff Crawford said, I gathered that both of the Fishers and the other guy, Axle, have criminal records and are involved somehow in selling stolen jewels."

"Oh my goodness," Ty said. "We don't usually have that sort of thing here in Lavender."

"And I guess we don't anymore, either," I said, "since one of them's dead and the other two ran. I doubt we'll see them again. Anyone who planned on buying jewelry from that booth today is out of luck."

She looked at me. "No, they're not. I was over to see Winnie Moser this morning, bought the cutest salt-and-pepper shakers shaped like bookshelves. I'll show you." She bent to take out the sack she'd stashed under the table. "The jewelry booth is open for business."

"Who's running it?"

"The girl who was out collecting money with those younger kids yesterday," she said. "Today she's alone. What's her name? Amber?"

I stayed with Ty long enough to look at her bookshelf shakers—they were very cute—then headed over to the jewelry booth to confirm what she'd reported.

Rather than walk straight up to Amber, who seemed to be handling the sales as competently as any adult could, I stopped with Winnie and Cecil Moser. Today Winnie wore a shirt with ghosts appliqued on black fabric.

"Good morning, Sabrina," she said. "Isn't this weather divine?"

I smiled at her but kept one eye on the girl selling jewelry. "Yes, it is, Winnie. A beautiful fall day."

Cecil stood up from a folding chair behind their table and approached us. "The girl got here about an hour ago," he said. "Don't know what happened to the other two."

"You mean Mrs. Fisher and Axle?"

"Right-o," Cecil said. "Haven't seen hide nor hair of them two."

And he probably wouldn't, but I didn't need to go into the whole story with him.

"Amber is an unusual young lady," Winnie said. "I went over there to look at their things. Asked about her mother, but she wouldn't answer me."

"I have a feeling the little family isn't what they hold themselves out to be."

"What does that mean, dear?" Winnie said.

"I'm not sure what's up with them, but I'm going to figure it out."

"Don't waste your time," Cecil said. "Festival's ending and everybody'll be out of your hair soon enough."

"I'm a mystery writer, Cecil. I can't tolerate an unsolved puzzle." I smiled at them. "Or to see the wrong person take the blame."

Winnie's eyes widened. "You don't think that young girl murdered her father, do you?"

"I don't even think that man *was* her father."

"Oh, dear," Winnie said.

I left them to puzzle over my statement and headed over to speak with Amber. She wore a pink T-shirt with jeans, and she looked a lot more approachable than she had when decked out in all black. She didn't look as surly today, either.

I forced a smile. "They left you in charge, huh?" I said.

She didn't respond.

I scanned the jewelry display and picked up a chunky silver ring with a large green stone. "What's this? Jade?"

She looked at me. "It's fake."

"Oh." I put the ring back and checked the price. "Guess that's why it doesn't cost very much."

"Exactly."

"Are any of your stones real?"

"I don't know." She busied herself straightening necklaces that hung on a wooden dowel.

"Maybe I could ask your mother. Will she be here soon?"

Amber slid her gaze over to me. "No."

"How about Axle Howard?"

"They aren't working today."

"Surely, you haven't been left to handle the booth all by yourself."

"You don't think I'm capable?" she snapped.

"Well, of course you are." I smiled at the girl. "I see you here doing a fine job, but I had a question about real jewels."

"Everything we have is out on the tables," Amber said. "See something you wanna buy, I'll sell it to you."

"Okay, I'll let you know if I find something. I was kind of hoping, though, to ask your mom about this nice blue stone I found. It's a really lovely piece, and I was trying to figure out how much it's worth."

"I already told you she's not here," Amber said, "and I don't expect her."

"Fine. Say hello to her for me." I smiled again. "And hug your brothers and sister for me, wherever they are."

Whoever they are.

I walked away from the girl, my imagination going ninety to nothing. She might have the opportunity to tell Coco about my blue-stone comment; she might not. The sheriff and his deputies were on the lookout for Coco, and the woman had to know it. She would probably not set foot in Lavender again. I figured she and Axle had all the other jewels from Schmidt's house last night. For all I knew, they were out of the country now and unloading the merchandise. Wishful thinking. My common sense warned me that talking about the stone to Amber wasn't the smartest thing I'd ever done. I had to know the truth about these people, though, even if that meant painting a target on my back. I planned to stay at the festival, surrounded by tons of people. There was safety in numbers. Coco wasn't going to burst into a crowd and risk getting herself thrown into jail.

35

G LENDA MET ME outside the coffee shop mid-afternoon
to deliver my chilled pie and Hitchcock, per my request when we'd spoken on the phone earlier. She'd
reported the cat had been making such a racket that she could
hear him howling from outside the Monte Carlo cottage. He
didn't appreciate being left out of today's festivities, and I
missed him. Since I planned to spend several more hours in
town, I wanted him here with me.

Glenda placed the covered pie carrier on a bistro table
and handed the end of Hitchcock's leash to me. "I don't think
I could have managed to get that harness on the little dickens
by myself. Thomas had to help."

I giggled. "Thomas? Seriously?" I picked Hitchcock up
and cuddled him.

She nodded, laughing along with me. "He didn't want to,
but he took one look at my face and knew I meant business."

I grinned. "Thanks for bringing Hitchcock and the pie.
I'm having someone else take my entry over to the bake-off

so Aunt Rowe won't know which is mine. She's not above cheating, you know."

Glenda smirked. "Good thinking. I'll swing by the contest later. Now I'm going to do some early Christmas shopping."

"Have fun, and thanks again."

Glenda left, and Lacy Colter, one of Hot Stuff's waitresses, came out a few minutes later to take care of my pie entry. I put Hitchcock down and shifted my tote on my shoulder, then we made our way to the bake-off site. Hitchcock politely endured petting by several children along the way, and we arrived to find that Luke was already there.

"Mission accomplished," I told him.

He grinned. "Gotta love a gal who plays fair."

"Mrreow." Hitchcock rubbed against Luke's uniform pants.

We laughed, and Luke put an arm around me and pulled me close. Three tables lined with desserts were set up between us and a small platform that served as a stage. A decent-sized crowd had gathered, and I had to look between people to spot Aunt Rowe making her way to the front.

She picked up a microphone and began her announcements, starting with a thanks to everyone who'd made the festival possible. She went on for a few minutes about the fireworks display that would alternate with shots from the pumpkin cannon later in the evening.

"I'll be one of three judges." She introduced Rita Colletti and Henry Schmidt, who stood beside her. "If y'all hang around until we announce the winners, we're gonna pass out free dessert. First come, first served."

That remark brought a round of applause.

As the judges moved to the head of the first table, I turned to Luke. "I'm surprised Schmidt is here after last night."

Luke shrugged. "Maybe he wanted to keep his ear to the ground. Hear what people are saying about him."

"Maybe."

"I don't feel like waiting for dessert," he said, drawing out a small paper sack. "Gotta eat these or they'll melt." He waved the sack in front of my face, teasing.

I grabbed it and looked inside. "Yum. I love malted milk balls."

"I know you do," he said with a smile.

I took a couple pieces and popped one into my mouth. "You know the way to a girl's heart."

Hitchcock made figure eights around our legs and his leash tangled. Luke chuckled at the cat and kissed me on the forehead. I savored the feeling along with the sweetness of the candy, then jumped nervously when I spotted a frowning Gabe Brenner standing to my right. Gabe had one hand stuffed in his pants pocket. He looked uncomfortable with the other arm in the sling.

"Um, hi, Gabe," I said. From the corner of my eye, I glimpsed Luke leaning forward to peer at the other man.

"Sabrina." Gabe edged closer to me and looked Luke up and down. "Who is this?"

Luke stepped between Gabe and me and introduced himself as a Texas game warden, which was completely obvious by the fact that he was wearing his uniform.

Gabe, unfazed by the show of authority, said, "He a friend of yours, Sabrina?"

If Gabe had been watching us together, as I assumed he had, he already knew the answer to that question. I nodded. "He's my boyfriend."

I hadn't ever identified Luke as such, and the words felt awkward. Maybe I should have said "significant other." Either way, Gabe wasn't happy.

"Oh," he said. The word sounded weak and small in a voice that didn't even sound like Gabe's. "I didn't know you had a boyfriend."

"Now you do," Luke said.

"Mrreow," Hitchcock said.

I tensed, not sure what to expect from the men.

Gabe looked down at the cat, then up at Lūke, and said, "You're a lucky man, Mr. Griffin. Sabrina's very special."

Luke nodded. "Yes, she is."

I waited for the other shoe to drop. When nothing happened, I said, "Gabe, my mother saw you with Tia Hartwell last night. How well do you know her?"

"I've seen her around," he said. "In other towns."

"Do you have business with her?"

Gabe shook his head. "She never drew my picture, if that's what you're askin'."

"What do you know about the business between Axle Howard and Henry Schmidt?" I said.

"Nothin'," he said.

I narrowed my eyes in an attempt to convey the seriousness of the discussion. "I don't understand what you were doing at Schmidt's house last night."

Gabe glanced nervously at Luke. "Uh, making sure you were safe."

The same thing he'd told the sheriff. Maybe I should lighten up on the guy. "How's your arm?"

"It'll heal."

I granted him a tiny smile. "Thanks for diverting Coco Fisher's attention."

"She was gonna shoot you," Gabe said.

Maybe not, but thanks to Gabe I didn't have to know.

"I'm glad you're okay." I paused for a moment. The guy had some connection to Tia—what was it? "Did your trip to Schmidt's have anything to do with Tia?"

"Nope."

I scanned the gathering crowd and wondered how I could ask Gabe about the money exchange with Tia. Cecil Moser stood near the bake-off tables. No doubt he wanted to be first in line for the free handouts. Tia and Damon headed our way with Merlin running beside them. I turned back to Gabe and was surprised to find he'd left.

I looked at Luke. "What happened to Gabe?"

"I don't know." He shrugged. "I think he got the point you're not available."

"That's a good thing," I said, "but I had something else I wanted to ask him."

"It's better to let him go," Luke said. "In my opinion."

I didn't reply to that because Tia and her son had reached us.

"Damon heard about the desserts and talked me into taking a break," she said.

"I'm glad he did." I took my tote from my shoulder. "I went out and got y'all a little gift today."

Damon's ears perked up at the word "gift," and he leaned his ever-present sketchbook against a tree to watch me pull out a harness like the one Hitchcock wore.

"I thought this would help you keep track of Merlin," I said.

"Thanks," Damon said, and I showed him, with some struggling on Merlin's part, how to fasten the harness to their cat.

"I appreciate this, but you didn't have to." Tia looked at the cat and giggled. "Merlin's not too crazy about the idea yet."

We all watched Merlin jump around and scratch at the harness, then Hitchcock batted at Merlin and they started wrestling. Aunt Rowe and the other judges proceeded down the tables, tasting desserts and marking scorecards.

Damon watched them. "When can I have dessert?"

Luke checked the progress of the judges and said, "That's a lot of sweets to judge. It's gonna take them a while."

The boy's smile drooped.

Tia said, "What happened to Gabe Brenner? I needed to talk to him."

"Really?" I said. "What's going on?"

She shook her head. "It's a personal matter."

"I'd steer clear," Luke said. "Guy has issues."

"I'll be fine," she said. "Do y'all mind keeping an eye on Damon for a minute?"

"Sure," Luke said. "We'll watch Damon."

"Thanks." She looked at the boy. "Honey, why don't you draw something? It'll make the time go faster."

As his mother walked away, Damon slumped, clearly disappointed about having to wait for his treat.

I watched Tia moving through the crowd and looking around for Gabe. The man was tall enough that he shouldn't have been hard to spot, but what the heck did she have going on with him?

I had been so convinced Tia hadn't killed Fisher. Now an unwelcome thought ran through my head. What if she'd involved someone else to get the deed done? They'd exchanged cash, but Mom said Gabe was handing the wad of cash to Tia, not the other way around.

You're crazy, Sabrina. Tia doesn't have the money to pay a hit man. Plus, Gabe wouldn't have needed the handcuffs to get the job done.

"What's wrong?" Luke touched my chin and turned my face to his. "You're in another world."

"I'm trying to figure out a plot."

"Fictional or real?" he said.

I didn't respond. He likely already knew the answer.

Luke turned to Damon. "Feel like drawing a picture?"

"Nuh-uh." The boy shook his head.

"How about you show us pictures you already drew while we wait?"

Damon seemed to consider the idea, then bent to retrieve his book. As he turned pages and Luke made comments about how good the boy's drawings were, I considered reasons Tia might be looking for Gabe.

"Do you know the man your mom went to see?" I asked Damon.

He shook his head and kept turning pages. I watched absently as he flipped through the book. Unlike a boy I once knew who drew only baseball-related pictures, Damon's drawings covered a variety of topics. Merlin. Their car. Festival

booths. Trees. Butterflies. Some people I couldn't necessarily identify. One looked like Aunt Rowe with the cannon; another resembled Winnie.

Though I made appropriate noises about Damon's talent, my mind was still on whatever might cause Tia to associate with Gabe and reasons he might give her cash.

"Heads up," Luke said. "Judges are getting ready to say something."

Aunt Rowe thumbed the mike on and the loudspeakers screeched. A few minutes later, I was holding a green third-place ribbon.

"You did one better than me." I turned and held my ribbon for Damon to see, but he had already run over to the tables.

Tia returned and thanked us for keeping an eye on her son. She interrupted the cats' playtime and took the end of Merlin's leash. "I need to get back to work, but we'll be over here for the closing ceremonies."

"When are you leaving?" I said.

"In the morning. Thanks for keeping an eye on my guys, and for the gift."

"You're welcome. We'll see you later."

Tia hurried to catch up with Damon. She had her hands full, so this wasn't the time to quiz her. If she left town before I had some answers, though, I'd continue to wonder about her and Gabe.

"Congrats on the prize," Luke said after she walked away.

I pulled my attention back to him. "Thank you, sir, but I'm sorry to disappoint. You thought I'd get the blue ribbon."

"You can always come over to my place and practice," he said. "Put that big country kitchen of mine to use."

His dark eyes pinned mine, and I felt a blush rising. Thoughts of spending time with him in his kitchen, at his home, were very pleasant.

"We'll have to plan on that," I said. "Right now I sure would like to know what Tia wanted to see Gabe about."

"You think she's involved in something shady?" he said.

I shrugged. "I don't know. She seems so innocent, so quiet."

Luke said, "They always say it's the quiet ones you have to watch."

36

LUKE WENT BACK to work. I should have opted to do the same. My book wasn't going to write itself. Realistically, though, I knew my brain wouldn't shift from the real mystery to the one on the page. At least not until this festival was over or the sheriff officially named the killer. I hoped he had more evidence to go on than the facts I knew about.

With the bake-off ended, the air filled with polka music and the chatter of tourists. My brain felt like it was spinning in circles. What had led to Calvin Fisher's murder?

Gabe had backed down from his interest in me pretty quickly when he'd learned about my relationship with Luke. That didn't seem like a guy who'd kill to keep Fisher out of my face.

Whatever Tia and Gabe had going on probably wasn't connected to murder. I remembered Tia's anxiety when she talked about what would happen to Damon if she went to

jail. I couldn't see her putting her family at risk for *any* reason.

The deal involving the jewels was obviously the most suspicious avenue to follow. I wondered if the sheriff had reached the same conclusion. Or if he'd tracked down Coco and Axle yet.

Aunt Rowe's fellow judges seemed to have disappeared as soon as the bake-off results were announced, leaving her to clean up by herself. I went to help.

"I wanted to give you first place," she said when I reached her, then looked down at the cat. "I know she's first in your book, Hitchcock."

"Mrreow," my cat said.

"This was a fair contest," I said, "and you couldn't show favoritism. I made sure you didn't spot me bringing my entry over here myself."

"You think I don't know your light, flaky piecrust?" she said with a wink. "I knew exactly what you entered."

"I'll have to do better next time."

I looped the end of Hitchcock's leash around a table leg so he'd stay put for a little while. Aunt Rowe and I gathered dirty dishes and wiped tables in silence for a few minutes.

"I don't suppose Schmidt said anything to you about what happened last night," I said.

Aunt Rowe looked up. "Not a word."

"You ever hear that he's into jewel collecting?"

She licked off a sticky finger. "Not exactly, but he's one of those who doesn't trust banks. Wouldn't be surprised if he has gold bricks hidden somewhere."

"Huh. Maybe jewels hold their value, too." Schmidt seemed like a relatively intelligent, if quirky, man. Not exactly the sort to deal with the likes of Coco and Axle. Had he been trying to make an honest investment and unwittingly involved himself with crooks?

"You sticking around for the fireworks?" Aunt Rowe said.

"Hitchcock and I will watch from a distance. Does someone need to keep an eye on you, make sure you don't blow yourself up?"

She waved a hand. "Jeb's making a nuisance of himself, watching my every move."

I glanced around and didn't see any sign of the sheriff. She was being facetious. "He's jealous of you spending time with Thorn."

"He's all talk," she said, but I noticed that her cheeks colored slightly.

"Give him a chance. I'll bet he proves you wrong."

She didn't comment, and I got the signal that she wanted to drop the subject. When we finished with the cleanup, I unhooked Hitchcock from the table and went to nose around Fisher's jewelry booth.

The girl, Amber, was still by herself. I wondered about the wisdom of leaving her with the business and whatever money she'd taken in. Was she even old enough to drive herself away from Lavender when the festival ended? Hitchcock and I strolled around the neighboring booths while I kept an eye on the girl. She was packing things up whenever there was a lull in customers.

The Mosers were packing up, too, painstakingly wrapping every little salt-and-pepper shaker individually. I stopped by their booth to say hello.

"That's a big job," I said. "You need a hand?"

Cecil looked up from wrapping a pink pig shaker. "Wouldn't turn down help."

"Oh, honey," Winnie said. "Sabrina has better things to do." She looked down at Hitchcock. "She has her sweet kitty here, and he'd be awfully bored sitting around and watching us work."

Hitchcock stretched his leash to slide under the tablecloth and reach Winnie's legs. He rubbed against her ankles.

"Isn't he such a sweetheart?" Winnie left her chore to bend down and pet the cat.

Cecil stopped working and addressed me. "If you don't mind helping, I'm going to fetch us some coffee. We have to get on the road, and it's a long drive home."

Winnie watched him go. "I'd much rather stay the night and get an early start. I'm not feeling so great."

I looked at her with concern. "Why, Winnie? What's wrong?"

"I think it's just a bout of low blood pressure. I'm feeling a bit dizzy."

"Does Cecil know?" I walked around to the other side of their table and took her arm. "Come sit down." I led her to a folding chair and she went willingly and took a seat.

"He knows, and that's part of the reason he's going for coffee. That's a home remedy for this problem, and he doesn't like me to take drugs."

"Do you have medication for it?" I said.

She nodded, then propped an elbow on the chair arm and rested her forehead on her hand. Hitchcock jumped up on the woman's lap.

"Do you need to take the medication now?" I said with alarm. "Where is it?"

She waved a hand in the direction of their car, which was backed in trunk-first as close as possible to their space. "In my tote, dear. I think I left it in the front seat."

"I'll be right back."

I quickly walked to the Buick and looked through the passenger-side window. Darkness was beginning to fall, and it was hard to see anything. The door was unlocked, so I opened it and spotted the tote with the appliqued scarecrow. I slid onto the bench seat and punched the overhead light, then opened the tote and peered inside. There was so much stuffed in there that I wondered if I'd have to dump everything out to find a prescription bottle. I felt around for a minute, then opened the glove compartment and found a flashlight. Shined the brighter light directly into the tote.

Winnie had obviously picked up a lot of things at the

festival. A stretchy bracelet, a pair of earrings, one of Maybelle's candles, like the one I'd bought. I paused for a second
and remembered how carefully Maybelle had wrapped my
candle. This one wasn't wrapped.

Maybe Winnie had unwrapped it to show someone.

I kept looking for the pill bottle. Saw a recent mystery
paperback. A painted plate that ought to have the protection
of some bubble wrap.

Wait. I recognized the plate.

I held it up, looked at the back. This was Aunt Rowe's
special hand-painted plate from the Florence cottage. A
memento of her trip to Italy. Why was it in Winnie's tote? I
sat still for a few seconds, trying to come up with a better
answer than the one that first popped into my head.

Winnie had stolen Aunt Rowe's plate.

Not a good enough reason for keeping the elderly woman
waiting while I was supposed to be retrieving medication
she needed. I found the pills and took them along with the
tote back to Winnie.

She was doting on Hitchcock and his purr was going
full-tilt. I handed the pills to her and grabbed a bottle of
water that was sitting near the shakers she'd been wrapping.
Her tote was looped over my arm, but she didn't seem to
notice. I couldn't help but wonder why the woman sent me
for the tote knowing what was inside. Did she have memory
issues?

Watching her take the medicine, I wondered if she'd purchased any of the things inside the tote. I remembered the
drawings from Damon's book, especially the one that resembled her. As I recalled the picture in greater detail, I realized that the woman depicted was dropping something into
a bag as she looked over her shoulder. Had the boy witnessed
Winnie stealing? Should I call her on it? Or should I tell Aunt
Rowe to quiz Winnie about the plate missing from the Florence cottage? She might not have time to do that if the couple
planned to leave shortly.

I glanced at Winnie, busy with the cat, and looked down at the tote. What else might Winnie have in there? I moved to a spot out of her line of vision and opened the bag wide to inspect the contents.

And spotted a glittering stone.

This one was green and much smaller than the sapphire. My thoughts flashed back to finding Hitchcock with the blue stone in between Gabe's car and the Mosers' Buick. I'd associated the misplaced gem with Gabe, but what if it was Winnie who had the jewels all along?

What possible innocent reason would she have for carrying a loose stone? I hadn't spotted anyone selling such things at the festival. I would never have suspected this sweet old woman of being a thief, but I knew of Aunt Rowe's sentimental connection to the plate. She hadn't gifted the souvenir to Winnie.

Had Calvin Fisher somehow passed valuable gems to Winnie Moser? The valuables Coco Fisher accused *me* of having? If not, how else had the green gem ended up in her possession?

Winnie's tote suddenly felt heavy in my hands as I thought about the possibility that the woman had stolen nearly everything inside. I looked up and spotted Cecil coming back with a cardboard tray holding coffee cups. I returned to Winnie and placed the tote next to her chair. She slipped her pill bottle into the bag.

"Did you take the medicine?" I said.

She nodded imperceptibly.

Cecil grew closer and hurried to the booth. He put the tray down on the table and rushed to his wife's side. "Are you okay, hon?"

Winnie managed a weak smile. "I'm fine. Just got winded for a second there."

The man's pained expression eased. "Good. Have some of this coffee. It'll perk you up." He retrieved one of the cups and handed it to Winnie. He looked at me, then Hitchcock, and his gaze slid past Winnie's tote.

Should I take him aside and ask him about the contents of her bag?

That wouldn't go over very well. I fought the urge to grab Aunt Rowe's plate from the tote and run with it, but that seemed like a childish way to handle the problem. I didn't want any harm to come to Winnie, but this discovery really needed to be reported.

I excused myself for a minute and sent a text message to the sheriff.

"You need to question Winnie Moser. Maybe involved with jewels. Check her tote."

I hit "Send," then began wrapping merchandise with Cecil to pack into cardboard boxes in preparation for their departure. After a few minutes, Winnie claimed she felt much better and got up to help. Hitchcock made himself comfortable resting on top of the tote by Winnie's chair, almost as if he were protecting evidence until the sheriff could get to us. I checked my phone every minute or so, but no response came from Sheriff Crawford.

At nearly full dark, Cecil announced that enough of the merchandise was ready to lock in the car while he and Winnie went to watch the fireworks display. Winnie looped her tote over her arm, and I collected Hitchcock. I followed the couple to the field by the pumpkin cannon, where it appeared that a team of people—not including Aunt Rowe, thank goodness—was readying the fireworks to begin the show.

I scanned the crowd looking for the sheriff. At this point, I'd even be glad to see Deputy Rosales. I spotted Tia with Damon and Merlin, and we headed over to them.

"Have you seen the sheriff or a deputy around here?" I said.

"No." Tia shook her head. "Why? Is something wrong?"

"Nothing for you to worry about," I said, then punched my speed dial to place a call to the sheriff. Got his voice mail.

Luke was a law enforcement officer, too, so I tried him. Reached another recording.

Aunt Rowe stood on the trailer with Thorn and the pumpkin cannon. She'd told me the sheriff kept an eagle eye on her so I picked Hitchcock up and went that way, scanning the area for any person in authority. Found no one. The first pumpkin flew from the cannon to the playing of the national anthem. Everyone stood at attention as the song played, including Cecil and Winnie.

I wasn't going to climb up on the trailer to make a spectacle of myself to report a stolen plate to Aunt Rowe. I should be able to handle this myself. When the song ended, I walked back toward where I'd left the Mosers. I would confront Winnie, ask her about things she'd purchased while at the festival. See what she had to say about the plate in her possession.

The pumpkin shooting from the cannon hadn't seemed to affect Hitchcock, but I worried about having the cat too close to the noise when the fireworks started. I'd have to hurry to talk with Winnie before the really loud display began. I coaxed Hitchcock into my tote and held him close so he'd feel secure as I quick-stepped through the crowd and crossed back to the spot where I'd left Winnie and Cecil.

The Mosers weren't in sight. Had they suspected I knew something they wanted to keep secret and made a run for it? That seemed slightly crazy.

While I hesitated in trying to decide what to do about them, Tia came running toward me with Damon trailing her. The boy looked like he was crying.

"Merlin is missing," Tia said. "We have to find him."

37

MY HEART WAS in my throat at the thought of a black cat lost on the festival grounds. It was far too close to Halloween for comfort, and there were a lot of strangers visiting Lavender. Hard to tell who to trust. I silently prayed Merlin was okay.

"When did you last see him?" I said.

"I was holding the leash," Damon said between sobs. "It flew out of my hand, and he disappeared. Maybe he got scared from the big boom."

"That's possible." I patted the boy's back in an attempt to console him. "Don't worry, we'll find your kitty."

I looked at Tia. "Did *you* see which way Merlin went?"

She shook her head. "I should have kept a closer eye on them."

"Let's split up," I said. "We can cover more ground. I'll go this way."

She nodded her agreement. Damon took his mother's hand, and we headed in opposite directions.

Hitchcock poked his head out of the tote. "Mrreow."

"You want to help us find Merlin?" I said.

"Mrr."

"Okay." Maybe my cat could actually help with the search, so I put him on the ground and gripped the end of his leash. It wouldn't do to have two lost cats, so I held on tight as Hitchcock took off at a trot. Could he seriously be following the other cat's trail? I didn't know, but I wasn't going to discount his instincts.

I looked every which way as we moved along, and worried because it would be hard to pick out a black cat in the dark. The orange twinkly lights in shop windows didn't give off much illumination. Hitchcock soon veered off the sidewalk and crossed the lawn near the town square.

The hubbub of the crowd around the pumpkin cannon faded into the distance. Some of the vendors were still packing things up at their booths. Other areas were stacked with boxes ready to be loaded for a move on to another town, a different festival.

I didn't stop to ask anyone whether they'd seen a cat whiz by, deciding to trust Hitchcock's instincts, as he was clearly acting like he knew what he was doing. I hoped this trek didn't turn out to be a mysterious mission that only a cat would understand.

Within a few minutes, I realized my cat was taking me to Eddie Baxter's black tent. This was at least the second time Hitchcock had come here, and I worried that there was another reason behind his interest in the tent. Merlin might not be here, and I would have wasted valuable time in following Hitchcock's lead.

The cat slipped easily under the flap door of the tent, and I followed. I pulled out my phone to turn on the flashlight app so I could see where I was going. Inside, the strands of white lights were lit, and I saw Baxter's products remained in place on the tables. Eddie wasn't here, though, and I guessed he wasn't concerned about shoplifters picking up

a rabbit's foot or some other trinket on the festival's closing night.

I heard catlike shuffling as Hitchcock pulled me farther into the tent. He went straight to a cardboard box sitting on the ground near the center pole that held up the structure.

Scratching came from inside the box. Hitchcock looked up at me. "Mrreow."

I bent and hurriedly opened the box flaps to find Merlin inside.

What the heck?

Merlin leapt from the box, and I grabbed for the end of his leash and missed.

Dang it.

I didn't want the cat to get lost again after I'd had the good fortune to find him. How'd he get inside that box anyway? He continued to race away from me and almost seemed to glance over his shoulder with fear in his expression. I didn't know why he'd be afraid of me, but cats were mysterious creatures.

At my feet, Hitchcock froze. "Mrrreeeoooowww," he howled.

The hairs on my neck stood at attention as I turned to find Cecil Moser standing behind me.

"Oh, Cecil." I put my free hand to my chest. "You scared me. I found Merlin right here in this box, but now he's run off."

"Merlin?" the man said. "I thought your cat's name was Hitchcock."

"It is," I said, trying to interpret the weird expression on Cecil's face.

Before I knew what was happening, Cecil grabbed my wrist and my phone flew from my hand. I heard a snap, then he yanked on my arm. Another snap. Handcuffs. He'd attached one of my hands to the pole that held up the tent.

Fear slithered up my spine. I released my hold on Hitchcock's leash so he could get away from us. The cat could

take better care of himself than I could in my current predicament.

"Cecil?" I stared at the old man in the dim light. "What on earth are you doing?"

He shook his head. "Oh, Sabrina, I'm so disappointed in you."

"*You're* disappointed?"

"I saw you nosing around in Winnie's things," he said, "and you know."

I shook my head. "I don't know anything, Cecil."

"You're a smart lady," he said. "You'll go to the sheriff."

"No, Cecil."

Should I admit I'd already alerted Sheriff Crawford? Not yet.

I glanced around me at the things lining the tables. A box of rabbit's-foot keychains wasn't going to be helpful unless good luck emanated into the air space surrounding it. I could possibly use the smooth stones in the next box if I could reach them with my free hand to throw at Cecil, if nothing else.

"You told me you have to see everything wrapped up, and I believe you do," Cecil said. "That's why I had to take action. I knew you'd come after your cat."

"You took the cat?"

He'd meant to get Hitchcock and grabbed Merlin by mistake. The cats looked identical, especially now that they each wore a harness. Cecil put a hand in his pants pocket and pulled something out. I squinted, trying to see what he held, but he kept it concealed in his palm.

"I really don't want to hurt you, Sabrina, but I don't have much choice."

"Sure you do," I said with more bravado than I felt. "Everybody has free will. You can turn around and march right out of here. Leave me. Drive away. Never look back."

"They'd find us," he said.

"So what? They won't have any evidence to use against you. I'll keep my mouth shut."

"Maybe you would," he said. "But I can't take chances with my precious Winnie. She can't help it, you know."

I stayed silent. If Gabe was still stalking me, he could burst into the tent and save the day. That probably wasn't going to happen. Should I shout for help? I was vaguely aware the fireworks had started. No one would hear me.

I tugged on my arm that was attached to the tent pole, but the tall wooden support wouldn't budge.

"What do you mean, she can't help it?" I said.

"She doesn't realize she's doing anything wrong," he said.

"Tell me what she did, Cecil." I leaned hard on the tent pole and tried to rock it out of place. "I'm guessing Winnie did something that caught Calvin Fisher's attention in a bad way."

Cecil's shoulders slumped. "She picked up a bag of jewels. She isn't a bad woman. She has kleptomania. It's a disease. Fisher was going to turn her in."

Uh-oh. I *had* turned her in, so telling Cecil about my text to the sheriff would only backfire. My best bet was to keep Cecil talking.

"So you had to kill Fisher?" I said.

"I had to protect Winnie," he said. "And I returned the jewels so no one else would come after her, but here you are."

He opened his hand and held up a syringe.

My stomach dropped. "What is that?"

"Nicotine," he said wryly. "You know, it's going to kill my sweet Winnie sooner or later. With this much, it only takes ten minutes."

He took a step toward me. I grabbed for the boxes on the table. Clutched a handful of keychains and threw them in Cecil's face.

"Now, now," he said. "This will be very fast."

I kicked out and connected with his shins. Rattled the cuff on the post. "Don't do it, Cecil. I'm going to scream, and they'll come get you, then they'll take Winnie."

"It doesn't have to be this hard." He dodged my kicks. "Calvin was much more cooperative."

"Calvin was sleeping off a hangover when you killed him." I kept thrashing and kicking. "I'm not going without a fight."

From the corner of my eye, I saw one of the cats jump up on the table. As I fought to keep the syringe away from my skin, a second cat appeared next to the first. Cecil glanced at the table and seemed shocked to see two black cats. Maybe he thought he'd developed double vision. One cat nudged a box of plastic four-leaf clovers over the edge of the table and it clattered to the ground. The second cat pushed over a box holding metal bells.

"Make them stop," he said, grabbing at my arm.

I couldn't let him inject me with a syringe full of nicotine. That was *not* going to happen.

C'mon, good luck charms. Help me out.

I stretched and managed to grab a handful of stones and dragged the whole box off the table in the effort. The rest of the stones crashed to the ground, and I threw what I held into Cecil's face. He ducked, and that's when Coco Fisher raced into the tent, gun drawn.

She saw me and stopped in her tracks. "There you are," she said. "Give me back my stone."

Cecil straightened and saw the woman with the gun. "What are you doing here?" he said.

"None of your business, old man." She fired a shot into the air and yelled at me again. "Give me the stone. Now."

"I'm kind of incapacitated here." I slid the cuff higher on the pole to demonstrate my situation. "If you could get the sheriff over here, we can clear up this whole mess, including what happened to the sapphire."

"I *knew* you had that stone," she said. "Where is it?"

Cecil waved a hand toward the floor. "We got plenty of stones right here."

"Not those stones, you idiot," Coco yelled. "She has the sapphire."

I kicked at the pole and wiggled it frantically while the two of them were looking at the ground.

Cecil made a move toward Coco with the syringe held at the ready. Would he use the nicotine on her instead of me? I didn't want him to give the deadly shot at all, but I didn't want to shout a warning and have her shoot Cecil, either.

One of the cats arched his back and let out a loud hiss and a howl worthy of the scariest Halloween cat ever.

Hitchcock, no doubt.

Coco lifted the gun. I screamed, "Don't hurt my cat!"

But Hitchcock wasn't going to stand still long enough for anyone to get a bead on him. He ran across the table and leapt onto the pegboard wall that held the slogan-bearing wooden signs. The wall toppled. In the commotion that followed, Cecil tackled Coco.

I screamed at the top of my lungs and gave the tent pole a mighty shove. The pole gave way. I crashed into the table, and the black tent folded down over us.

38

THE SHERIFF'S DEPARTMENT didn't have enough cells to hold everyone apprehended that night. I spent the better part of the evening in Sheriff Crawford's office, answering the same questions over and over again. Winnie Moser, charged with the least offensive crime of them all—shoplifting—was distraught because her husband was charged with murder, attempted murder, and Lord knew what else.

The sheriff collected Damon's sketchbook to use as evidence. The boy's pictures would help to tell Fisher's story as well as Winnie's. I studied the drawing that clearly showed her furtively shoplifting at the festival and wondered if the boy might grow up to be a police sketch artist.

Winnie's supposedly sweet husband refused to talk to the authorities, but he'd admitted his crime to me. I had a feeling he would break down and tell all before the sun rose.

Coco Fisher pulled her grief-stricken widow act again, but nobody was falling for it. Her cohort, Axle, was caught near the tent, where he was waiting in a getaway car. Apparently

his plan to outsmart Coco and take a bigger cut of the profits had failed. Either that or he would have gotten rid of Coco at some later point in time.

The story Axle gave the sheriff was that he and Coco had planned to take off after I returned the valuable sapphire to Coco. Why she thought I'd carry that stone around in my pocket at the festival, I'll never know. I had to admit, if only to myself, that the woman might have saved my life.

With Hitchcock's help.

Sheriff Crawford explained to me that he'd connected Coco and Axle to a raft of jewelry thefts in the Dallas area, where Coco worked as a home health aide in an exclusive neighborhood. Seemed that each home she worked in reported jewelry thefts during the time period that coincided with her tenure.

Coco pinpointed the targets, Axle handled the robberies, and Calvin was the fence. He made contact with potential buyers and sometimes met them at festivals around the state. That must have been the reason he gave Tia a hard time. He didn't want Damon around. The boy became a liability when he'd spotted Calvin's hidden stash. Calvin didn't want to risk the kid ruining his lucrative business.

Axle, Coco, and Calvin deserved to star on one of those shows about stupid criminals, especially since Coco had used children who weren't hers to solicit donations to help her fake family.

Talk about greedy.

Henry Schmidt apparently did collect gemstones—in addition to his myriad other collectibles—and he'd made contact with Fisher through a website. He'd especially wanted to add the large sapphire to his collection. Somehow the sapphire and the green stone I'd found in Winnie's tote had fallen out of the velvet pouch before Cecil Moser returned the jewels Winnie had stolen.

Schmidt claimed he had no knowledge of Fisher's criminal activities, and I tended to believe him. The guy was so

hung up on rules that I didn't see him purposely associating with criminals.

I was able to doze part of the night in the sheriff's office as I waited for permission to leave. Luke spent the whole night in the front office waiting for me. Hitchcock stayed with Laurelle, who probably plied him with more treats than a cat should eat in a week.

When I went to collect my cat, Laurelle was alone in the office. "You missed some action out here," she said. "Rosales came in and started flirting with Luke. Guess he finally reached his breaking point with her."

"What happened?" I said.

Laurelle grinned and looked toward the front door as Luke entered the office. "He read Deputy Rosales the riot act. Told her he's with you, and she'd better get used to it. Said they could be friends, but that's all it'd ever be."

"Seriously?" I cast a glance over my shoulder at Luke coming up behind me.

"Believe it." He put his hands on my waist and turned me around. Planted a kiss on my lips right there in front of the dispatcher.

Half an hour later, as we pulled up to Aunt Rowe's house, the warm glow of his kiss remained in spite of my extreme fatigue. I spotted my stepfather's car in the driveway and groaned.

I looked at Luke. "Mom and Dave are here. Maybe we should go straight to my place."

"Mrreow," Hitchcock said.

Luke laughed. "I don't know if he's agreeing or disagreeing, but your aunt instructed me to bring you here so she could see you're okay. I'm not going to cross that woman, and I don't want to get on your mother's bad side, either."

I sighed. "Okay. You make a good point."

The morning was glorious with just enough sun to warm us. Singing birds flitted into and out of the trees overhead. We found Glenda in the kitchen preparing breakfast for the

group seated on the back deck. I gave Hitchcock some food and filled his water dish, then Luke and I went out to join the others.

Mom and Dave sat at the table with Aunt Rowe. I was so grateful I'd escaped last night's scary episode that I was happy to see each and every one present.

"Grab a seat." Aunt Rowe jumped up to pull out chairs for us. She gave me a hug and looked at Mom. "Brenda, don't harp on her about what happened last night. We're just happy to see her safe and sound, right?"

Mom got up without a word and came over to give me a long hug. "That's right, Rowe."

Clearly, there had been some discussion on this point before I arrived.

Mom held me at arm's length to look me in the eye. I expected her to inquire about my health and well-being, but she said, "Where's that sapphire?"

"I turned the stone over to the sheriff. It was stolen, Mom. The thing never belonged to me."

Her mouth turned down, and I expected her to say more, but she returned to her seat and dropped the subject. I sat and gratefully accepted a cup of coffee that Luke brought to the table.

Glenda delivered serving dishes filled with bacon, eggs, and hash browns, and we all dug in. I was enjoying the peaceful surroundings and the clinking of silverware on our plates when my phone rang.

Luke looked over as I slid the phone from my pants pocket and checked the screen. My hand started to shake.

"Oh Lord, it's my agent," I said.

"Answer, answer," Aunt Rowe said.

Luke grinned at me.

I pushed my chair back and stood. This didn't mean anything had happened. She might have been calling just to say hello. Maybe she'd somehow heard about my ordeal last night.

I slid my finger across the screen to take the call and walked to the edge of the deck.

"Hi, Kree." I hoped the words sounded normal but I wouldn't have bet on it. My heart was hammering so hard it felt like it might jump out of my chest.

"Happy Monday morning, Sabrina," Kree said. "I have great news. They loved your rewrite, and we got an offer."

My knees trembled. "Are? You? Serious?"

Kree laughed, and the unique, overly loud chortle struck me as the best sound in the whole world. "Completely serious," she said. "They offered a two-book contract. Hardcover. Publication next year."

Blinking back happy tears and bouncing on my toes as she went through more of the details, I turned to the others and mouthed, "I'm getting published."

Luke's grin broadened.

Aunt Rowe jumped up and looked at Mom. "Told you she'd do it."

Glenda rushed out of the kitchen to hear the news. Then they all applauded, and I felt warm and fuzzy and oh-so-happy.

Kree said, "You have an audience to help you celebrate?"

"I sure do."

"Then I'll let you share the joy with them," she said. "We can discuss things in more detail after you take a look at the contract. I'll email you."

I thanked her profusely and disconnected.

"Yes!" I pumped my fist and jumped up and down like a kid. When I went back to the table and sat, I was far too excited to eat.

Luke gave my shoulders a squeeze. "Great news. Congrats."

Mom said, "I'm very happy for you, darling."

Wow. Did she really just say that?

"Guess you won't be coming back to the firm even if I sweeten the pot," Dave added.

I shook my head. "Not in my plans."

The advance Kree mentioned wasn't earth-shattering, but I knew a beginning author couldn't expect big money. I had my savings, so I wasn't worried. The big thing—the *really* big thing—was they were going to publish my book.

My book will be on bookstore shelves.

I couldn't quit smiling.

Mom said, "Guess I'll have to stop thinking of the writing as your little hobby."

A major concession coming from Mom. "That's right," I said.

Everyone turned their attention back to their plates. I excused myself and went inside to call Tyanne. If the book news hadn't come when it did, she would have been the first person to know.

Two minutes later, Ty was screaming and crying and saying, "I knew it, I knew it, I knew it!"

We laughed a lot and chatted for a few more minutes before she sobered and said she was relieved that I'd come through last night's tent collapse unscathed. Obviously, she didn't know the whole story. I didn't want to cast a shadow on the happy news, but I'd have to tell her everything. Preferably in person, and before she heard it elsewhere.

I ended the call and heard a car door slam outside. Looked out the window to see Tia and Damon heading for the front door. It seemed like a month had passed since I'd met my look-alike in this same spot, though it had been less than a week.

I opened the door, and Hitchcock rushed up to join us. Merlin wore his harness, and Damon had the end of the cat's leash looped over his arm. Hitchcock batted playfully at the other cat.

"Hi, Sabrina," Tia said.

"Tia. So good to see you. Come on in." I stood back to hold the door open wider.

"We can't stay long," she said, "but I wanted to come by to thank you before we left town. For finding Merlin, and everything else."

They followed me to Aunt Rowe's formal living room and sat. Tia didn't want anything to eat or drink, but Glenda collected Damon and took him to the kitchen for a treat. The cats followed.

"The lawyer contacted me," Tia said when we were alone.

"You mean Rita Colletti?" I said.

Tia nodded. "She told me you talked to her about the child-support case, and she's going to represent me."

"She is?" This came as a shock.

Tia nodded again. "We had a short meeting, and she's going to file papers this week. She said we could get my ex to pay her fees."

"That's great." I felt a new respect for my former boss. Whatever the reason for her change of heart, I was glad she'd agreed to help Tia.

"Even better news. She gave me a tip on a job in Austin. Someone she knows has an advertising firm, and they're looking for an art major. I may not qualify, but it's a good lead."

My hard attitude about my former boss softened even more. "That's wonderful. I wish you all the best."

What a great morning for good news. I thought of sharing mine with Tia, but I had something else I wanted to bring up.

"Tia, I hope you don't think I'm prying, but my curiosity is killing me. What did you have going on with Gabe Brenner the past couple of days? Mom saw you with him night before last."

Tia looked uncomfortable. "You warned me he might seek me out because we look alike, and he did. Not because of any romantic interest. He only has eyes for you in that respect."

"Luke made sure Gabe knows that I'm not available," I said.

"Good." Tia's gaze met mine. "Gabe is sweet in an odd sort of way. I guess he heard I'm having money trouble. He said the fried-bacon business was doing so well he wanted to share the wealth."

I blinked. "He was giving you money just to be nice?"

She shrugged. "That's what he said. I was so surprised when he handed me the cash that I took it, but that bothered me all night long. I don't want to accept charity. I can make my own way."

"So you were looking for Gabe to give the money back?"

"Exactly. I'm very happy with my profits from the festival, and if that job prospect pans out, things will be even better."

"I hope everything works out for you." I smiled as I studied her features. "So, do you think we should have testing done to settle the question—are we sisters or not sisters?"

Tia shook her head. "I'd rather pretend that we are."

"I like that idea," I said.

Damon and the cats returned. Tia stood and we hugged. "I'm so glad we came to Lavender and met you."

"Me, too."

"I brought you a little something." She pulled a folder from her bag.

Damon took the folder from his mother and removed a loose piece of paper. He handed it to me. "My mom drew this for you."

I took the page, a sketch of me with Tia and Damon at her side. Hitchcock and Merlin sat in the foreground of the picture. The black cat and his shadow.

Tears filled my eyes. "This is perfect. Thank you."

Tia looked at Damon. "We need to hit the road, buddy."

I gestured toward the deck. "You want to come out and say good-bye to Aunt Rowe or my mom?"

Tia shook her head. "No, but please give them my best. Damon and I need to cover a lot of miles today. There's a really big festival coming up in Amarillo, and I need to make a stop in Austin to see about that job. Don't worry, though. I'll stay in touch."

We joined hands for a moment, then she left. I stayed at the window to watch her drive away, then spent a few minutes

studying the picture. I would get it framed and treasure it always.

"Mrreow," Hitchcock said.

"Okay, okay. Let's go back outside. My goodness, Hitchcock, did you hear the news that our book is gonna be published? I'd have never gotten that manuscript written without your help, you know."

"Mrreow."

"You're absolutely right. I need to get back to work on the next book. It's a wonder Tyanne didn't remind me. Guess she was too excited to think straight, but I know that's coming. Right now, I'm feeling pretty darn hungry. Maybe my breakfast is still warm enough to eat."

Hitchcock trilled and followed me back to the deck. Luke was entertaining the others with tales of the deer poachers he'd dealt with over the weekend. Mom was trying to show interest in the topic, but I sensed she was fighting not to cringe. I sat and had some more coffee.

Luke was still talking when Herr Schmidt came up the deck stairs, taking us all by surprise. He wore his usual dress slacks with a white shirt and a plaid bow tie.

Aunt Rowe looked at him with her brows raised. "Henry? What are you doing here? I hope you're not coming with some post-festival report, or worse, the proposed budget for next year's event."

He looked from her to me. "No," he said. "We can get to that next week. I expected to hear from you or Sabrina by now, but no one contacted me."

"I don't understand," Aunt Rowe said. "Contacted you about what?"

Herr Schmidt held his arms out. "Where's my gift?"

RECIPES

Pumpkin Crunch

1 16-ounce can pumpkin
1 12-ounce can evaporated milk
3 eggs
1-½ cups sugar
4 teaspoons pumpkin pie spice
½ teaspoon salt
1 package yellow cake mix
1 cup chopped pecans
1 cup melted butter
Whipped topping

Preheat oven to 350 degrees. Grease bottom of a 9 x 13-inch pan. Combine pumpkin, evaporated milk, eggs, sugar, pumpkin pie spice, and salt in large bowl. Pour into pan. Sprinkle dry cake mix evenly over pumpkin mixture. Top with pecans. Drizzle with melted butter. Bake for 50-55 minutes or until golden. Cool completely. Serve with whipped topping.

Pumpkin Bars

4 eggs
1 cup vegetable oil

1 16-ounce can pumpkin
2 cups sugar
2 cups flour
1 teaspoon baking soda
1 teaspoon baking powder
1 teaspoon cinnamon
½ teaspoon salt
Whipped topping (optional)
Cream cheese frosting (optional)
Chopped nuts (optional)

Preheat oven to 350 degrees. Beat together eggs, oil, pumpkin, and sugar. Stir in remaining ingredients until evenly mixed. Pour into a greased and floured 9 x 13-inch pan. Bake for 30 minutes or until center springs back when touched. Options: Serve with whipped topping or a cream cheese frosting. Chopped nuts can be tossed on top of the frosting.

Paradise Pumpkin Pie

8 ounces cream cheese
¼ + ½ cup sugar
1 egg + 2 eggs, slightly beaten
½ teaspoon vanilla
1-¼ cups pumpkin
1 teaspoon cinnamon
¼ teaspoon nutmeg
Dash salt
1 cup evaporated milk

Preheat oven to 350 degrees. Combine cream cheese, ¼ cup sugar, 1 egg, and vanilla and mix well. Spread on bottom of pie shell. Combine ½ cup sugar, pumpkin, cinnamon, nutmeg, salt, evaporated milk, and beaten eggs and pour over pie. Bake at 350 degrees for 1 hour and 5 minutes.

Also From

KAY FINCH

Black Cat Crossing

A Bad Luck Cat Mystery

Sabrina has never been the superstitious type. Still, when she moves to Lavender, Texas, to write her first novel and help her aunt, Rowe, manage her vacation rental business, Sabrina can't avoid listening to the rumors that a local black cat is a jinx—especially after the stray in question leads her directly to the scene of a murder.

The deceased turns out to be none other than her aunt Rowe's awful cousin Bobby Joe Flowers, a known cheat and womanizer who had no shortage of enemies. The only problem is that Aunt Rowe and Bobby Joe had quarreled just before the cousin turned up dead, leaving Rowe at the top of the long list of suspects. Now it's up to Sabrina to clear her aunt's name. Luckily for her, she's got a new sidekick, Hitchcock the bad luck cat, to help her sniff out clues and stalk a killer before Aunt Rowe winds up the victim of even more misfortune…

kayfinch.com
penguin.com

Berkley Prime Crime titles by Kay Finch

BLACK CAT CROSSING
THE BLACK CAT KNOCKS ON WOOD
THE BLACK CAT SEES HIS SHADOW

PRAISE FOR THE BAD LUCK CAT MYSTERIES

"*Black Cat Crossing* has everything a cozy mystery could want—intrigue, memorable characters, a small-town setting, and even a few mouthwatering recipes . . . A purr-fectly cozy read."
—Ellery Adams, *New York Times* bestselling author of *Murder in the Secret Garden*

"If Charlie and Diesel ever make it to Texas, they'll be heading straight to Lavender to meet Sabrina and Hitchcock to talk about solving mysteries. I loved every page of *Black Cat Crossing*, and I can't wait for a return visit to Lavender."
—Miranda James, *New York Times* bestselling author of the Cat in the Stacks Mysteries

"*Black Cat Crossing* is an entertaining introduction to Sabrina's world, and I look forward to Hitchcock's future exploits."
—Open Book Society

"Sabrina was a fabulous sleuth, especially with the help of Hitchcock, the bad luck cat. The characters will draw you in but the mystery will keep you flipping the pages."
— Deb's Book Bag

"Don't miss out on this humorous well-written cozy! You'll be turning pages as fast as you can to find out whodunit!"
—MyShelf

"I believe Hitchcock and Sabrina make a wonderful detective team and can't wait to read about their next big case."
—TheBookReview.com